5.6/ 12.0 points

The Shield, Sword, and Crown

SWORD OF WATERS

Hilari Bell

Simon & Schuster Books For Young Readers
New York London Toronto Sydney

The Shield, Sword, and Crown:
Sheild of Stars

SIMON & SCHUSTER BOOKS FOR YOUNG READERS
An imprint of Simon & Schuster Children's Publishing Division
1230 Avenue of the Americas, New York, New York 10020

SIMON & SCHUSTER BOOKS FOR YOUNG READERS is a trademark of Simon & Schuster, Inc.
Book design by Lucy Ruth Cummins
The text for this book is set in Celestia Antigua.
Manufactured in the United States of America
2 4 6 8 10 9 7 5 3 1
Bell, Hilari.
Sword of waters / Hilari Bell.—1st ed.
p. cm.—(The shield, sword and crown; bk. 2)
Summary When fourteen-year-old Arisa, aided by Prince Edoran and Weasel, tries to find the
long-lost sword, she faces betrayal of the worst kind.
ISBN-13: 978-1-4169-0596-7 (hardcover)
ISBN-10: 1-4169-0596-0 (hardcover)
[1. Conduct of life—Fiction. 2. Courts and courtiers—Fiction. 3. Betrayal—Fiction.
4. Mothers and daughters—Fiction. 5. Kings, queens, rulers, etc.—Fiction. 6. Fantasy.]
I. Title
PZ7.B38894Swo 2008
[Fic]—dc22
2007052081

FIRST
EDITION

CHAPTER 1

THE FIVE OF STARS

The Five of Stars: the quest.
A search for something of value, or aspiration toward a significant goal.

Silken skirts floated like bubbles as the ladies swayed through the stately measures of the dance. Music swirled over the conversation. Candlelight glowed on polished wood and high-dressed hair, and glittered in the jewels.

Arisa hated it.

She hated the jewels, just one of which could have kept a struggling farm family for a year. She hated the sycophantic laughter that rippled around the bored-looking prince. But most of all, she hated the fact that *she* was wearing one of those never-to-be-sufficiently-accursed ball gowns.

She wasn't certain which aspect was worse, the corsets that kept her from bending or the big hoop and the layers of petticoats that kept her from moving. The ridiculously high heels on her shoes came in a close third.

Her mother didn't care about clothes. The Falcon danced through the set, partnering some old man who was probably politically important. Her movements were as easy and graceful as if she were teaching a new recruit to fire a pistol, or mounting a horse to flee the law. As if she belonged in this overheated ballroom as much as she did in the woods, or on the moonlit high road.

Arisa could barely walk in her gown, much less dance. And she *was* trying, whatever the dancing master said. It was just—

Another burst of laughter rose from the group around the prince. Louder now, because he was smiling too. Her friend, Weasel, laughed with them.

Hang it. She'd been here long enough to claim that she'd "attended" evening court. Arisa turned abruptly, stepped into another set of billowing skirts, and bumped the body beneath them hard enough to make Lady Danica stagger into Lady Ronelle.

Arisa also hated all the girls who swarmed around the court, hoping to catch Prince Edoran's eye. Danica and Ronelle were the worst of them. Still . . .

"I'm sorry," said Arisa. "I didn't mean—"

"I'm all right." Danica reached up and patted her hair, making sure her curls were in place—though to Arisa they looked as if they'd been glued there.

She was suddenly aware that her hair was slipping out of its pins. Again. Her hands twitched, but Arisa refused to reach up and confirm it. Her thick chestnut hair was the only thing about her that her maid approved of. In a ballroom, Arisa thought that her ordinary face made her look like a weed in a bouquet of roses, but she didn't mind. Very few court ladies qualified as pretty, and only the Falcon was beautiful. And Arisa was leaving, anyway.

"Well, if you're all right, I'll just—"

"Don't worry about it. I'm sure you'll learn to walk in heels . . . eventually."

Arisa felt heat rise to her cheeks. "I only tripped once. Anyone can trip. Besides, that was weeks ago."

4

"While making your first curtsy to the prince." Ronelle's voice oozed pseudo-sympathy. "You poor thing. I'd have died of embarrassment."

That's because you want the royal runt to notice you. But the Falcon had asked Arisa to befriend the prince, so she didn't say this aloud.

"I'm sure you would have," Arisa said instead. "But I was just leav—"

"It's not your fault, dear," Danica chimed in. "You're only fourteen, and growing up in a bandit camp, surrounded by common thieves . . . Well, we make allowances." Her smile was pure poison.

Danica and Ronelle were only a few years older, but Arisa knew she should leave. Just turn and go. Her feet seemed to stop of their own volition. "My mother was a rebel leader. And she's never been *common* in her life. You two are common." She gestured to the crowded room. "Dozens just like you. My mother is one of a kind."

Several of the people near them had broken off their own conversations to listen.

Ronelle's face flushed, and Danica glared. "Common" was a serious insult in their circles. That was why Arisa had used it.

"You don't deny she's a thief," said Ronelle. "And before that she was a whore."

Someone gasped, and Arisa smiled. "No, she was a courtesan, which is what you aspire to be. At least, you act and dress like you want to be courtesans. But I expect you'll fall short of the mark and end up whor—ah, not courtesans."

She couldn't deny that her mother had been a thief.

"Revolutions need money," Arisa continued aloud. "When you can't work within the law, you have to—"

"Your mother wasn't some kind of rebel hero." Now temper reddened Danica's cheeks. "She was a road bandit. A *common* road bandit."

Several of the bystanders winced. Whatever she'd been, the Falcon had power now. For just a second Arisa wished she'd use it to crush these stupid girls, but her mother was above that kind of pettiness.

"She had to steal, to support the cause."

The smooth, rich faces in the crowd around her were either politely blank or titillated. They didn't understand. They would never understand. She really should go.

Danica snorted. "So you say. But she turned in her *cause* for a soft appointment at court the first chance she got! If it wasn't for the shield, she'd have—"

Arisa froze. "You take that back."

"Take what back, dear?" Danica smirked. "If it wasn't for that clerk finding the shield, she would have been hanged. On a common gallows."

"That's a lie," Arisa snapped. "Running the army's not a soft appointment. She's still fighting, still working to—"

"To get rid of Pettibone?" Ronelle sneered. "But he's dead now. She's dancing in court, and taking the prince's coin, so—"

Words weren't going to work. Arisa punched Ronelle in the

stomach. Not too hard, and Ronelle's corset robbed the blow of even more strength, but she still wobbled back.

Childhood in a bandit camp was good for some things. Arisa grinned, even as Danica shrieked and leaped at her. Arisa stepped aside and tried to trip the girl, but two sets of fluffy petticoats got in the way. Arisa stumbled instead, and Danica's nails raked over her neck. There *was* a reason to grow them so long and sharp. If the manicurist had pointed that out, Arisa might have cooperated instead of—

Danica reached in again and Arisa scowled, ducked, and punched her in the stomach. This time she didn't pull the blow, and corset bones snapped like twigs. Danica doubled over, and Arisa was turning to leave when Ronelle slammed into her from behind.

If she hadn't been wearing high heels, she might have pivoted with the blow and recovered. But in heels and hoops she toppled, with the larger and heavier girl on top of her.

Impact with the floor was stunning, but a sharp pain in her scalp roused her. Ronelle was pulling her hair—a girl-fighting move, but it still hurt!

Arisa rolled over, more encumbered by her own skirts than by Ronelle's flailing limbs. The corsets were the worst, Arisa decided as she freed her right arm. Hoops kept you from moving, but corsets kept you from *breathing*.

Ignoring the fists still yanking at her hair, Arisa punched Ronelle's nose. Blood spurted in a satisfactory fashion. Ronelle shrieked and let go of Arisa's hair, hands flying to her face. When she saw the blood on her fingers, she began to scream in earnest. Arisa shoved at her.

"Get off of me, you cow! I can't brea—"

Ronelle levitated off her as if by magic. Then a strong hand under her arm hauled Arisa to her feet and steadied her.

"What's going on here?" the Falcon demanded.

"She started it!" Ronelle and Danica wailed, in perfect chorus.

Arisa shrugged. The courtiers around them rustled and chirped like a flock of birds.

"Is that true?" her mother asked.

"I did punch her," Arisa admitted.

"Why?" the Falcon asked calmly.

"It doesn't matter why!" Ronelle's father, Lord Ethgar, burst through the crowd and pulled his daughter out of the Falcon's grip. "If your daughter cannot restrain her savagery, Mistress, then I shall have to . . . to . . ."

The Falcon waited. Lord Ethgar was a handsome man, with his powdered hair and high-nosed aristocratic face. Most of the courtiers would consider him a powerful man as well, for he was the master of the royal household and essentially ran the court. But the Falcon was lord commander of the army and navy of Deorthas, and her expression said more plainly than words that she didn't care what he might do.

"Let's all calm down here, shall we?" The man who now pushed his way through the crowd looked like a clerk beside the fashionable lord. His unpowdered hair showed gray, and spectacles winked in the candlelight. But the courtiers stepped back, giving him space, and Ronelle chose that moment to burst into tears and huddle in her father's arms. Justice Holis, now Regent Holis, was unimpressed.

"It appears there's been little harm done," he began.

"My nose!" Ronelle whimpered.

"She hit me, too!" Danica exclaimed. "She started it."

The regent looked at Arisa. "I threw the first punch," Arisa admitted. "But I didn't start it. And I *finished* it."

His expression remained grave, but she thought there was a twinkle in his eyes. "I hope that's sufficient to console you," he said, "when your mother has finished with this matter."

Arisa winced.

"It won't be," said the Falcon.

Arisa sat in the chair in front of her mother's desk, scowling. That shimmering ball gown should have looked ridiculous in the office of the lord commander, but it didn't. Not when the Falcon wore it.

"They were fighting too," Arisa complained. "And Ronelle wasn't the only one who was hurt. See?"

She pressed her fingers against the scratches on her neck—they came away red, though the bleeding had almost stopped.

"That's not the point. And you know it."

"Ronelle's nose wasn't broken," Arisa went on. "And Danica was barely bruised. No one was hurt," she concluded. "Not really."

"That's not the point either," said the Falcon. "I'm not even too concerned that you started it."

"You're not?" Arisa blinked. "Lord Ethgar won't like that. Justice Holis might not like it either."

"I don't care what Ethgar likes," said the Falcon. "And neither does Holis. But you can't solve all your problems with fighting!"

It *certainly simplified things.* But that wasn't what her mother wanted to hear.

"Maybe not with fists," Arisa conceded. "But one way or another, you always have to fight."

"Fists aren't the only weapon." Her mother leaned forward over the desk. "Words can be a weapon. Even clothing can be a weapon."

Arisa looked to one side at the portrait of King Regalis, which had hung on the wall behind the desk until the shield had taken its place.

"You want to turn me into a withless peacock, like him."

The king in the portrait wore green velvet, so richly embroidered she could barely see its color through the masses of gold. Emeralds were embedded in the heels of his shoes, and his short cloak was trimmed in ermine fur.

Arisa sneered.

"Am I a withless peacock, Ris?" her mother asked.

Arisa looked back at the Falcon. Satin gleamed. Jewels flashed.

"No," Arisa admitted. "You couldn't be. It doesn't matter what you wear."

"*That's* the point," said the Falcon. "One of them, anyway. Why do you think I keep that portrait here?"

"How should I know? It's pretty?"

Her mother snorted. "No, not because it's pretty. Or maybe it is, in a way. Look at those clothes, Arisa. Look at that handsome, kingly man. He *looks* the part. But he was the most useless king in Deorthas' history. Worse even than Pettibone, and that's saying something. I keep that portrait to remind me that it's not what you wear that matters. It's what you do. Clothes are just a tool, to help you reach your goal."

"If you have a goal," said Arisa.

"I assigned you a task when we first came here," said the Falcon. "Remember?"

"To befriend the prince." And she'd been avoiding him ever since.

"We've been here almost a month," the Falcon continued. "So why is Holis' clerk standing beside the prince at court, while you watch the dancing and pick fights?"

"Weasel likes him," Arisa protested. How he could stomach the foppish little toad she had no idea, but he did.

Her mother's eyes narrowed. "So Holis' clerk has the prince's ear, and you don't."

Arisa squirmed. She knew her mother regarded Justice Holis as a political rival, but Arisa liked the man—even if he did bore her with lectures on politics and law. Besides . . .

"Justice Holis doesn't need Weasel to talk to the prince. He's Edoran's regent and guardian. If he wants to say something to

Edoran, he just says it. And you're the lord commander of Prince Edoran's army. If you want to say something to him, you can."

"Don't pretend to be stupid, Arisa. There's a huge difference between something that comes from a friend your own age and something that comes from an adult in power."

"But if you already have power," Arisa argued, "why do you need to influence Edoran? He won't become king for another seven years, when he's twenty-two."

The political rivalry between her mother and Justice Holis worried her. Her mother had saved the justice from Regent Pettibone's dungeons, and shot Pettibone herself. Then Weasel had given her the shield, and she and Justice Holis had agreed to work together. Arisa thought Justice Holis was keeping that agreement, but she wasn't entirely certain about her mother.

On the other hand, it probably made sense to try to gain some influence with Edoran before he became king. Half the shareholders in the realm seemed to think so, anyway. All of their daughters did.

Arisa sighed. "If I don't have anything to do but wear gowns and befriend that . . . prince, I'll go stark mad from boredom. Next time I'll probably kill someone. I can think of several people who'd be the better for it." More than several, actually. She could make a list, and work her way down.

Her mother laughed. "Are you telling me you started that fight because you were bored?"

Could she get away with saying yes? Arisa had been praying her mother wouldn't ask what the fight had been about.

"In part, I think it was," she said truthfully. "They made me angry, and I don't like them. But I don't think I'd have punched them if I hadn't . . . If I wasn't . . . I feel like there's a corset around my entire life! And it keeps getting tighter, too."

The cause they had fought so hard for had triumphed—she should rejoice. But who could have predicted that victory would turn out to be so wretched? Arisa rose from the chair, kicked off the clumsy heels, and began to pace.

"It's not just the clothes, and the dancing, and embroidery; it's me. I feel all out of balance, like a piece of me is missing. I hate this! I'm bad at it too," she finished glumly.

"You have to learn to be a lady." The Falcon's voice was gentle. "That's our rank now. That will be your status for the rest of your life."

Arisa grimaced.

The Falcon's chuckle held a note of sympathy. "Would you rather go back to banditry, Ris? Always in hiding, everything you own stolen from others?"

"Yes!" said Arisa.

Her mother waited.

"Oh, all right, I wouldn't. Not really. But at least I had a job then. A real job," she added, before her mother could nag her about Edoran again. "One that mattered."

She waited for her mother to tell her that influencing Edoran did matter, but the Falcon sat in silence, watching her pace.

"Then maybe I should give you another job," the Falcon murmured finally. "A real one. It will be hard. It might not be possible. Though if you could bring it off . . . It's certainly important."

"What?" Arisa asked warily.

"I'd planned to assign one of my men to this," said the Falcon. "But you might do better. You have access, if you choose to use it. And you're not stupid, even if you sometimes act that way."

Arisa blushed with shame and anger. "So, what is this job?"

"I'd like you to find the sword for me. Do you think you could handle that?"

Arisa's heart leaped, but . . . "No," she answered reluctantly. "The sword's been lost for centuries, just like the shield was."

"The shield was found." The Falcon gestured at the wall behind her.

"Every item in the storeroom where the shield was found has been examined ten times over," Arisa reminded her mother. "And every other storeroom, and passage, and cellar, and stable, and closet in the palace has been searched and searched again. When Justice Holis decreed that the five-hundred-blessing reward for the sword still stood, the servants were crazy to find it. And they know this palace better than I ever could."

"So what does that tell you?" the Falcon asked.

"That it's not in the palace," said Arisa, working it out as she spoke. "But if it's not here, it could be anywhere in Deorthas. Anywhere in the world by now!"

"I don't think it left Deorthas," said the Falcon.

Arisa didn't either. The sword and the shield were bound to Deorthas . . . unless Justice Holis was right, and they were only symbols, after all. Still . . . "Deorthas is a pretty big closet."

"So?" Mischief glinted in the Falcon's eyes. "If it wasn't harder than embroidery, it wouldn't be a real job."

"Real isn't the same as impossible," Arisa grumbled. "And nothing's harder than embroidery. Except that cursed pianoforte."

"I thought you liked your embroidery class. And you do like music," the Falcon added.

"I like listening to music," said Arisa. "Not plunking out wrong notes. And I like my embroidery teacher, but that's not the same as liking embroidery."

"How do you feel about historical research?" the Falcon asked softly.

Arisa wasn't stupid. "The prince. You think I'll have to ask the prince for help, to access old records and things to find out what happened to the sword. You think this will force me to make friends with him."

"He has access to more records than anyone else," the Falcon pointed out. "And you can't deny that finding it is important."

She couldn't. When Weasel had given the shield to the Falcon, it had granted an ex-bandit rebel leader enough legitimacy that the army had agreed to accept her as their commander. In fact, Arisa had once told Weasel that they should look for the sword themselves, promising to give it to Justice Holis since he'd given her mother the shield.

Of course, that had been before the servants turned the palace inside out, and pretty much proved that the sword wasn't there. But if it could be found . . .

"This really is important," the Falcon echoed her thoughts. "And I think you've got a better chance than any of my men. Will you try?"

"Yes," said Arisa. "Though I might not find it." A wonderful thought struck her. "And it will take time. Lots of it. So I won't have time for dancing lessons, or singing, or—"

"No." The Falcon's voice was firm, even though her lips twitched. "You have to learn to be a lady, and putting it off will only make it harder. On the other hand . . ."

Arisa waited hopefully.

"On the other hand, it might be a good idea to give your aggressive impulses some target besides the court ladies. Would you like to share the prince's fencing lessons?"

"With the *prince*? It's not enough if he helps me find the sword? Besides, ladies aren't supposed to fence with men. It would cause a scandal if I shared his lessons."

"Ladies aren't supposed to fence at all," said the Falcon. "Or shoot, or fight with knives. But that didn't keep you from begging lessons from every man in my camp. You don't care about scandal any more than I do."

Arisa had begged lessons from her mother's men, learning to use every weapon she could lay hands on. But the sword was a nobleman's weapon, and the countrymen who had joined her mother had known little about it. In fact, it was her weakest weapon, which made lessons with the foremost master in the realm a tempting bribe.

"All right," said Arisa. "Fencing lessons with the prince, and

I'll try to find the sword in my free time. Though I can't guarantee I'll succeed."

"I know you might not find it," her mother said soberly. "All I ask is that you try. And free time means afternoons, and when there's no evening court scheduled. You're not getting out of coming to court by punching a couple of girls. You'd enjoy it more if you talked with your friend, Weasel."

"Weasel is usually with the prince, and that's the most boring part of a really boring crowd," Arisa told her.

"Then why isn't Weasel bored?" the Falcon asked.

Arisa grinned. "He says he uses the time to practice picking pockets, but I think he's bluffing. Mostly."

"Then get him to teach you to pick pockets," said her mother. "Maybe he'll teach the prince as well, and you can all practice together. Do we have a deal, Ris?"

She'd gotten fencing lessons out of it. And trying to find the sword, even if it proved impossible, was more interesting than anything she was doing now.

"Deal," said Arisa.

CHAPTER 2

THE SEVEN OF FIRES

The Seven of Fires: the battle.
Conflict, whether spiritual, emotional or physical.

2

Most mornings, the sound of the chambermaid sweeping out the hearth in the room next to Arisa's barely roused her. This morning she had set herself to wake when the clattering thumps came through the wall, for she knew the prince's fencing lessons commenced soon after sunrise.

The sun wasn't up yet, but the sky in the long windows that opened onto her balcony was gray with its approach. Arisa could see the sky, because once her maid had put her to bed, drawn the brocade curtains and left the room, Arisa had gotten out of bed, opened the curtains, and braced the glass door open just an inch. Yes, it was winter, but the great city that surrounded the palace was a seaport. Even in Udan it was seldom cold enough to snow on the coast.

Arisa was accustomed to sleeping in a tent. The hot, dark cavern her maid considered "proper" stifled her.

Still, she shivered as she slid from her warm blankets and pulled on her dressing gown before she went to the wardrobe and dug into the drawer where she'd insisted on keeping some of her old clothes. The rough britches and coat were still there, and slipping into them was like slipping into the embrace of an old friend.

The first time Arisa had seen herself in one of the gowns the seamstress presented she'd been delighted with its beauty, and enjoyed the swish of its heavy skirts. Of course, at that point she hadn't worn it for more than a minute.

She hadn't realized how good it was to be . . . well, not poor—but certainly not so cursed rich!

At least this morning she could wear her britches again, for not even her maid would expect her to fence in a skirt.

She splashed some water onto her face, rinsed her mouth, and wove her hair into a thick braid that would keep it out of her way in a fight. She was ready!

The servants stared as she passed them in the corridors. Arisa nodded politely, and winked when one of the footmen grinned at her.

She knew the way to the mirrored salon where the prince's fencing lessons took place. The sun was barely over the horizon when she opened the door, so she was surprised to hear voices inside. Or rather, one voice, speaking in tones of bored disdain, "Today we will work on your guard, Your Highness. Again. Do try to—"

Light flooded through the windows and shone in the mirrors that covered the opposite wall. Weasel and Prince Edoran stared at her, and the fencing master turned, his brows rising.

"What are you doing here, Mistress . . . Arisa, isn't it?"

She had met Master Giles at evening court, a man of medium height and average looks whose compact body moved like a spring. He was a very good dancer. Now, watching his brows draw down and his mouth prim as he took in her country clothes, she realized he was also a snob.

Arisa stiffened. "My mother has given me permission to join the prince's fencing lessons."

And my mother works with the man who pays your salary. But she didn't say that aloud. She was beginning to get the hang of this wealth and power business. She gazed at him, trying for hauteur. His face tightened further, and then relaxed in a martyred sigh.

"If your mother wishes it. But I can't start today, for you have no padding. And I'd hate to see you bruised."

Arisa looked at Weasel and the prince, who were wearing stiff canvas britches and jackets that would lessen the sting of a blow. But the practice foils they held had blunted edges and wooden buttons on the tips.

The prince's thin face showed only lingering surprise, but Weasel's lips twitched.

Arisa returned her gaze to Master Giles' face. "I'll take my chances. I need to borrow a sword."

The fencing master's eyes widened, as he realized she was serious. "That I can provide. But I have no mask, to protect a lady's face."

Weasel and Edoran weren't fighting with masks. "My face isn't a lady's," Arisa told him, and his brows climbed again.

"If you say so, Mistress Arisa. First, we will all stretch."

The exercises that followed weren't completely unfamiliar. Rudy, who had taught Arisa the finer points of knife fighting, had insisted on stretching before a bout. Arisa had been skeptical— you didn't have time to warm and loosen your muscles before a real fight, so why do it in practice?

Rudy had replied that if you limbered up for practice, when a real fight surprised you, you'd be more flexible even if your muscles were cold.

Perhaps he was right; Master Giles moved far more easily than Arisa and Weasel, and the prince was stiffer than they were.

"Enough," Master Giles finally decreed. "Today, as I said, we work on guards, but first I will evaluate my new pupil. Mistress Arisa," he pulled a fencing foil from the stand and extended the hilt toward her, blade over his arm, "your sword."

The hilt was wrapped in leather to keep it from slipping in a sweaty grip. It was too big for Arisa's hand but she was used to that. It was also lighter than the other swords she'd handled, and she slashed it back and forth, getting a feel for the balance.

Master Giles frowned. "Spread your fingers. It gives more control. And raise the elbow. All your opponents will be taller than you, so your— Not the shoulder, the elbow! Now hold."

He walked around her, correcting her stance as she posed for him. She felt like an idiot.

Weasel and the prince stood aside, watching, and Arisa wondered why Master Giles didn't set them some exercises. She'd never had formal lessons before, but some of her mother's men had been masters of their various weapons. None of them would have let a class stand idle while he evaluated a new student.

But perhaps those who taught noblemen used different methods from those who taught common soldiers.

Master Giles moved in front of her, coming on guard himself, though far more gracefully than she had. "Now, Mistress, set to!"

Arisa just managed to block his blade as it swept in, and the next thrust had her skipping back.

He wasn't fighting at full speed, she realized, as he backed her down the room. He might not even be at half his speed, but he was fighting at the very top of hers. His foil seemed to come at her from all directions at once, but she remembered the training Clem and Murray had given her and managed to keep her tip forward and her blade in position as she blocked and blocked again.

"Not bad," said Master Giles thoughtfully. He wasn't even breathing hard. "Not a strong guard, to be sure, but a guard." His gaze flicked to Prince Edoran. "Note, Highness, how her point remains forward, upon me, even when she moves the blade to block. Thus, should I give her an opening, she'll be in position to thrust."

He'd just given her an opening when he'd looked aside, but Arisa had been so focused on blocking that she hadn't taken advantage of it. She gritted her teeth. Next time.

She stepped to the side as they neared the end of the salon, so Giles couldn't pin her in the corner, and he gave her an approving nod.

"Note again, Highness, that she remains aware of the room, of her surroundings, just as I've tried to teach you."

He could have forced her into a corner, Arisa realized. He could cut her to ribbons anytime he chose. He was toying with her. Or maybe he was evaluating her skills, but it felt like he was toying with her.

She was breathing in gasps now; the hilt was slippery in her grip despite its leather wrapping. Her wrist ached. Her shoulder began to tire.

Come on, you arrogant bully. Do it again!

"Also note, Your Highness, that she controls her feet better than you do, though there is still room"—his blade lashed down, faster than Arisa could possibly block, stinging her knee—"for improvement."

He drove her back up the floor, and if anything he'd picked up the pace. Sweat ran down her face into her eyes. Her shoulder ached. Her wrist was on fire.

"Her wrist, on the other hand, is almost as weak as yours." Master Giles' gaze flicked to the prince.

In that small blind moment, for the first time since the fight began, Arisa lunged. Her point slid over his blade, past his guard, into his ribs.

Master Giles stepped back, knocking her blade aside.

It wasn't a perfect strike, Arisa thought, in the startled silence that followed. Not to the heart. But if they'd been fighting for real, with sharp weapons, it would have pierced his lung.

Of course, if they'd been fighting for real, he'd have killed her in the first ten seconds.

Arisa lowered her sword, then laid it down and rubbed her wrist. Her right hand was numb. Now that she had time to notice it, every muscle in her body shook, and she was breathing like a bellows.

The shock died from Giles' face, leaving a faint frown.

Arisa scowled back. He might be the best swordsman she'd ever seen, but that didn't mean she liked him.

"You've been very ill taught," Master Giles pronounced. "But there is . . . aptitude. I will teach you."

Arisa considered. She didn't like him. On the other hand, he was the best swordsman she'd ever seen.

"All ri—"

Master Giles turned away. "You will walk for a time, while I work with the prince. William will join you. When you have cooled, I shall set you some exercises."

Weasel didn't like being called William, but he said nothing.

The prince's mousey face was blanker than usual as he picked up his foil and stepped forward.

"Your Highness." Master Giles saluted him, a hissing swipe of the blade. "Set to!"

"I wanted to talk to you," Arisa told Weasel as the swords clashed, and they started walking around the room. "My mother's given me a job."

A foil cracked on canvas. Weasel grimaced but he didn't look over at the fight, which told Arisa that he knew who'd been hit. Which meant that Edoran wasn't good enough to get past Master Giles' guard—not that many people were.

"If you think that's worth letting Giles pound on you," said Weasel, "then you're out of your mind. Of course, I already knew that. Dawn rising and all." He shuddered.

Arisa grinned. She usually woke early, but Weasel never got out of bed before he had to.

"Edoran's like you," Weasel added glumly. "No, he's worse. He wakes up at sunrise every day, even when he doesn't have to do this."

Arisa wouldn't have taken the prince for a morning person. And she was nothing like him, in any way that mattered. "You don't have to get up just because he does. Or is that part of being such a good little courtier?"

The sour note in her voice made her flinch.

But the gaze Weasel turned on her was thoughtful, and only a little wary. "I don't *have* to. I'm just providing . . . moral support. Just because I'm friends with Edoran, that doesn't mean you and I can't still be friends. Does it?"

"Of course not," said Arisa hastily. "I'm not as . . . as petty as that. I just don't like him."

"If you dislike Edoran so much, then why are you here?"

"To learn to fence," Arisa told him. "Besides, I wanted to talk—"

The crack of metal on wood drew her eyes to the bout. The prince stood, disarmed, his foil still skidding across the floor.

"Weak," said Master Giles curtly. "That's what comes of a weak grip, Your Highness. Pick it up."

Edoran did, but the moment the bout started again, Giles' sword flashed past his guard and struck the prince's wrist. Arisa wondered how much of the blow was blocked by the canvas. Not all of it, she thought.

Master Giles pushed Edoran down the room as easily as he had Arisa, making comments she couldn't hear over the crash of steel. Judging by the prince's set expression she doubted he was hearing any praise. On the other hand, there wasn't much about Edoran's fencing *to* praise.

"His grip is weak," Arisa murmured. "And his footwork's . . . Wait a minute. Edoran's left-handed, isn't he? Why's he fighting right?"

The sword was in the prince's weaker, less dexterous hand. No wonder he—

Giles' blade snapped against the prince's ribs. "Cover that side!" he ordered crisply. But he didn't tell the prince how to adjust his guard to cover it.

"Giles insists that Edoran fight right-handed," Weasel told her. "He says that all the moves, all the defenses, are designed for right-handed people."

Arisa stared at him. "That's not true with knife fighting. The man who taught me said that left-handed people have an *advantage*, because right-handed people aren't used to fighting against them. They have to modify the moves, of course. He even taught me what to watch out for if I came up against a left-handed fighter."

Weasel frowned. "That's not what Giles said."

Arisa watched the fight. Master Giles was pushing Edoran even harder than he'd pushed her. The fencing master's blade slapped the prince's down and then swept through to strike Edoran's ribs again.

"Is it always like this?" Arisa asked, troubled. "I mean, he never explains anything."

"He explains some," said Weasel. "When he gives me exercises. But not much. I think . . . I think maybe that's how noblemen are taught."

"Rot," said Arisa crudely. "No one could learn from this."

A blow to the elbow sent the prince's sword flying. He went to pick it up more slowly this time, stealing a moment to catch his breath.

"All his lessons are like this," Weasel told her. "Oh, not physically, but the same style. 'The treaty of Maranus was signed on the *fourteenth* day of Luric, in the fourth year of the reign of King Ambrose, Prince Edoran. As I told you quite clearly just last month!'"

"You're joking," said Arisa. "Or exaggerating, at least. You must be!"

"Not much," said Weasel. "But since all his tutors are like that . . ." He shrugged.

Arisa frowned. "My etiquette teacher's like that. And my dance and music masters are too, though not as bad. My embroidery teacher's not like that at all. But I never had formal lessons in anything before, so I thought . . . Maybe all teachers are like that."

"I wasn't taught that way," said Weasel. "Not in the church school, and not by Justice Holis."

"So maybe that is how nobles are taught," said Arisa. "Though, if that's true, it's a miracle they ever learn anything."

"Maybe," said Weasel. "But I don't trust anyone who knows how to hurt without leaving a mark."

"What?"

"He hit your knee." Weasel gestured to Master Giles, who was backing Edoran into the corner Arisa had avoided. "And it hurt, right? Still stings?"

Arisa nodded.

"Well, you won't have a bruise there. Nothing you could show someone, or complain about."

"It wouldn't matter if I did. You get bruised learning to fight. That's part of it."

"That's what I mean," said Weasel. "You're supposed to get *bruised*, but not in lessons with Master Giles. Hurting someone without leaving a mark takes a lot of practice."

"So maybe Giles is really good," said Arisa. "Good enough to pull his blows exactly the right amount."

Weasel's eyes narrowed. "Maybe."

Arisa returned to her room, sweaty and depressed. Sweaty because when the prince had neared collapse, Master Giles had abandoned him and set Weasel and Arisa to practice simple thrust patterns. While they exercised together, Master Giles "worked" with the prince. Worked the prince over was more like it, Arisa thought grimly. If this was how nobles were taught, she'd have to show them some sympathy in the future. Or did you owe someone sympathy when they did something crazy on purpose?

Though "crazy" was the same word Weasel had applied to her desire to find the lost sword, and he was right; in two hundred years it probably had been thrown into a lake, or buried in someone's grave, or broken and melted for scrap.

But she'd promised to try.

And Weasel had agreed to ask Prince Edoran about the historical records, which meant that she didn't have to.

Arisa pulled open the door to her room and walked right into the full force of her maid's glare.

"Mistress Arisa, what *are* you wearing?"

Arisa looked down at herself with exaggerated care. "Let's see. Boots, stockings, britches, a shirt and a jacket. What do you think I'm wearing?"

Katrin's eyes flashed. "What you wear, Mistress, reflects not only on you but on your lady mother. You do realize that, don't you?"

It also reflected on her maid, and the servants' rivalry about whose mistresses' clothes were the best was even more passionate than the ladies' rivalry. Katrin lost face when Arisa wore britches, so Arisa swallowed her first sharp answer. And the second.

"My mother has given me permission to share the prince's fencing lessons," she said. "I have to wear britches for that."

"If your lady mother says you must learn to fence, then I shall be pleased to find you clothing for the sport that is also suitable to your station," said Katrin, not looking at all pleased. "My family has been connected to the palace for six generations, and I know what's proper far better than you can. Which is why your lady mother put me in charge of dressing you! You simply must allow me to select . . ."

Arisa washed herself, ignoring Katrin's scolding. Why did servants think that if they politely called you "Mistress" they could go on to insult your intelligence in every possible way? Arisa didn't understand why anyone would be proud of six generations of helping useless peacocks become even more useless, but Katrin was. She wasn't alone in that attitude either—palace servants had roughly the same social status as master craftsmen. And Katrin did know more about gowns and fripperies than Arisa ever would or wanted to, so Arisa resolved to let the maid have her way . . .

. . . a resolve that lasted no longer than Katrin's third tug on her corset strings.

"That's too tight!" Arisa yelped. She clung to the bedpost, because if she hadn't, Katrin's tugging would have pulled her off the tottery heels.

"It's not tight enough," said Katrin. "A lady needs a slim waist."

"No, she doesn't," said Arisa. "Half of them are fat! It wasn't this tight yesterday."

"I've been leaving you a bit loose," Katrin told her, "because you're new to lacing. But now it's time . . ."

The corset cinched down and Arisa gasped.

". . . to dress as a lady should!"

The bones cut into Arisa's flesh, and she couldn't squeeze a speck of air into the lower half of her lungs. Her corsets had never been this tight and she'd fit into her gowns just fine. Maybe her britches had embarrassed Katrin, but this was too much!

"Loosen them," Arisa ordered. "Now."

Instead Katrin tied the laces, finishing the job. Arisa already knew she couldn't reach the knot—she'd tried several times in the past.

"There you go, Mistress," Katrin chirped. "I'll get your petticoats."

Perhaps this was how nobles were taught. Arisa thanked the Lady that she wasn't a noblewoman.

"Katrin, loosen these laces. I'm not joking."

Katrin turned from the wardrobe, her arms full of frothy underskirts. "Perhaps the green gown today? Or would you prefer the pink with rose ribbons?"

Katrin was ignoring her. Katrin thought she couldn't get out of her corsets by herself, and that she was too modest to go into the corridor in her chemise and demand the nearest footman's aid. She might have been right about that. At least Arisa would have thought twice. Fortunately, there was a better way.

Arisa stalked to the bureau, dug into the top drawer, and pulled out the knife she'd taken from one of Weasel's enemies a few months ago.

She turned toward Katrin, and the maid backed up a step.

Arisa smiled, inserted the knife into her corset—blade side out—and pushed it down. The taut fabric screamed as it gave way. Air flooded Arisa's lungs. The sharp point cut the underlying chemise in several places, but Arisa didn't care. Even though she'd worn them only a few seconds, the corset bones had printed red stripes on her skin. That corset had been much too tight, and her maid had known it.

Arisa turned the knife thoughtfully, making the blade flash, and Katrin gasped.

It was tempting, but fighting an unarmed maidservant with a knife was hardly fair. Arisa grinned tightly and stuck the knife into the top of the bureau, ignoring the damage to the polished wood.

She walked over to the long windows, threw them open, and stepped onto the balcony. She'd wanted a room that overlooked the sea, but those were reserved for important people, and her view of the park was pleasant enough. A lady might have objected to looking over the stable yard, but Arisa didn't mind—particularly today.

The bright winter day made her skin tingle beneath her thin chemise. Or perhaps it was returning circulation. Or perhaps it was fury. Arisa was so angry she didn't even care when the stable boys, who were exercising their charges in the muddy yard, began to whistle and clap.

Arisa spun her corset over her head and hurled it as far as she could. It wouldn't have reached the horse pen if the obliging breeze hadn't caught it, whisking it over the graveled drive and the fence, and laying it neatly in a big puddle of mud and manure.

The stable boys cheered.

Arisa almost responded with a rude gesture, but then she had a better idea. "If you can get a horse to trample that," she shouted down to them, "I'll come back out tomorrow!"

She turned and went inside. She wasn't sure if she'd have the nerve to keep her promise, but Katrin's scarlet face and bulging eyes made it all worthwhile.

"There," said Arisa. "That settles that."

"Well," Katrin huffed. "Well, I never . . . I never . . . Your mother will hear about this!"

CHAPTER 3

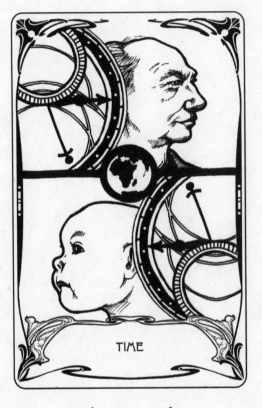

TIME

Time: the past creating the present.

3

Arisa chose a gown that laced in front, and managed to dress herself perfectly well, though she had to tie her hair into a ponytail instead of piling it up with hairpins.

Despite her success she was late for her embroidery lesson, rushing breathlessly into Yallin's snug parlor.

The gray-haired seamstress eyed her shrewdly. "It's not being late that's got you so flustered. Plain stitching today, my girl. It'll soothe you."

Arisa didn't like plain stitching either, but it was better than fancy embroidery, and when you mended the hem of a kitchen maid's petticoat, no one cared if your stitches were crooked.

This morning Yallin passed her a worn sheet, while the seamstress herself settled in to mend cuffs and collars and things that would show . . . at about three times the speed with which Arisa stitched.

"You're so good at that," Arisa said ruefully. Yallin's small stitches were perfectly even, too. And though Yallin was usually mending, Arisa had seen Yallin produce embroidery that passed from decoration into art.

"It's my job." The creases around Yallin's eyes deepened, though her mouth stayed quiet. She was the only person Arisa knew who could smile with just her eyes. "When you've had a lifetime of practice, you'll be good at it too."

Arisa shuddered at the very thought, and Yallin laughed.

"Don't let it worry you. The future comes as it will, despite any plans we puny humans make. What's got you so rattled, this early in the day?"

"I had a fight with Katrin," Arisa admitted.

"What, she didn't take to those britches of yours?"

Arisa stared at her, startled. "How do you know about that?"

Yallin gave her a use-your-brain-girl look, and Arisa sighed. "The servants are gossiping about it."

"Of course they are, and by luncheon they'll have passed it on to their masters. The palace is like a small village—everyone knows everything, soon enough. I'm told you looked quite fetching, if a bit raggedy."

"Who cares what you wear for a fight?" Arisa asked. "It's just going to get torn up. . . . Yallin, you're a tutor in the royal palace."

Yallin's brows rose. "I'm the head seamstress, who got tapped to give a lesson where it was needed. But I've heard rumors that Master Giles is . . . strict with the prince."

"I suppose you could say that. Is that really how nobles are taught?"

Yallin's gaze was on her busy hands. "It's what Regent Pettibone commanded. And most folk here were hired by the old regent."

"Then I'm sorry for Edoran," said Arisa. "Even if he is a spineless little—um."

Yallin glanced up from her stitching, her old eyes sober. "Do you know that Prince Edoran once ran away?"

Arisa blinked. "From the palace, you mean?"

"When he was seven," Yallin confirmed. "He evaded the guards for more than two weeks before they found him. He'd been living in an alley, down by the docks, running errands for tin nothings and eating scraps from the market dump."

Arisa stopped sewing, which was small loss to the sheet. "Edoran did that?"

"He did. I'm told he was so dirty when they brought him back, it took four tubs of hot water to get him clean. And his valet had to shave his head to get rid of the lice."

"But . . . Hmm. I wonder if that's when he started thinking that Regent Pettibone killed his father."

Watching Yallin's face, Arisa saw that the prince's obsession was known to the servants. Though she had yet to see Yallin surprised by anything.

"Maybe it was," the old woman agreed. "Or maybe it was something else. The servants speculated at the time, but no one knows. They watched him like hawks after that, for the old regent made it clear that if he vanished again, every one of us would be hunting a new job."

Arisa frowned. "But he could have run away again. There's always a chance, sooner or later. If I thought someone had killed my father, I wouldn't run. I'd find evidence against him and see him hang! Or make up evidence, or find some other way to destroy him!"

Yallin's brows rose. "As I understand it, Regent Pettibone did kill your father."

"And I helped my mother avenge him," said Arisa. "If I'd tried on my own, I'd just have gotten in her way. Besides, the one thing Pettibone didn't do was kill the king. There were a dozen people watching when his horse went down, and the investigation found no evidence of tampering. But if I was Edoran, I'd still have found a way to fight."

"There are times," said Yallin softly, "when a body can't fight. Or at least, you can't win."

"I'd have tried," said Arisa stubbornly.

The skin around Yallin's eyes crinkled. "I'll wager you would. But that's your nature, girl. Some folks are wiser than that."

Dancing was the usual disaster. The dancing master explained more than Master Giles, but he never gave Arisa enough time to practice a move. She turned right when she should have turned left, tripped in the quicker steps, and never once got through a set without messing it up.

A kitchen maid brought luncheon to her room instead of Katrin, and Arisa was bored, despite the excellence of the food. She could have eaten with Weasel, but Weasel ate with the prince and she saw more than enough of the crowd that surrounded Edoran during evening court.

Watching her teachers as the day went on, Arisa realized that the music master had tried in the beginning, and then given up hope when he'd seen she had no talent at all. Her slaughter of the simple tune pleased neither of them, but at least he didn't harass her about it.

The mistress of etiquette had clearly heard about the britches and taken Katrin's side. Arisa spent the whole hour walking around with a book balanced on her head, repeating after the mistress all the reasons why ladies must dress as ladies. That an ox might mistake her for a man and charge at her was the most ridiculous of the lot.

By the time she was free to join Weasel, the fair morning had become a cloudy afternoon with thunder grumbling in the distance. Afternoon rain was more common in the winter than clear skies were, but in Arisa's present mood it seemed to be the final straw. If the weather had been good, she could have asked a groom to saddle up a horse and she could have ridden off her temper. As it was, she had nothing to do except go to meet Weasel and the prince when they emerged from their final lesson.

Weasel came out of the classroom rubbing one ink-stained hand. "I hate this," he grumbled under his breath. "I'm *good* at math and I hate it."

Prince Edoran offered her a brief nod, and said nothing.

Was she supposed to curtsy? That was the kind of thing the etiquette mistress went on and on about, and Arisa couldn't remember half of it. She didn't want to curtsy, so she simply returned his nod as Weasel went on.

"I told Edoran that you want to find the sword, and *he* thinks you're crazy too. With a reward that large, if it still existed, someone would have brought it in long ago. And they didn't, so—"

"I don't think you're crazy," Prince Edoran interrupted quietly.

"But you're not the first to think of studying the old records to find it. I believe my father looked for it for a while, and he was the king."

"So if he couldn't find it, nobody could?" The sarcasm leaked into her voice before she could stop it, and Edoran flushed.

"He wasn't a fool, and he had the same access I do. More than you'll ever get, without me."

Here was the arrogance Arisa had expected. She opened her mouth to snap back at him, but Weasel got in first.

"Edoran thinks you're going to despise him because he can't fence."

Arisa's mouth hung open, but no words came out. The red in the prince's cheeks deepened. If she'd been treated as he had, it would have embarrassed her to have someone watching.

"No one could learn to fence from Master Giles," said Arisa. "Especially not fighting with your off hand."

Edoran eyed her warily. Arisa couldn't read enough of his expression to know whether he realized that she did despise him for other things, but after a moment he nodded.

"Very well. If you believe you can succeed where every scholar in the realm has failed, I'll assist you."

"I don't believe I can succeed," said Arisa, nettled. "But I promised my mother I'd try. I keep my promises."

"Then you're going to need an ungodly amount of luck," Weasel told her.

The idea struck Arisa like a thunderclap. "Or some guidance! I can lay out the cards. Maybe they'll show me where to start."

"Arcanara cards?" Edoran stiffened. "I don't approve of arcanara cards. In fact, I've forbidden their use in the palace."

"Then don't watch," Arisa told him. "I'm going to go get my deck."

"She really believes in them," Weasel told the prince. "It's no use arguing. She thinks she's got withe."

Arisa walked away. To her annoyance, Weasel and Edoran followed.

"Withe is some sort of mystical ability," Weasel went on, "to be one with the universe, or nature, or something. It—"

"I know what withe is," Edoran said.

"Well, she's got it," Weasel continued. "And when she lays arcanara cards, it makes them reveal the future."

"They don't reveal the future," Arisa intervened. She knew better than to try to shut him up. "They show the forces that are working in your life."

"You don't believe in arcanara cards?" Edoran asked Weasel.

Weasel snorted. "I believe that I've seen a lot of con men make money with them."

"They told us the truth when I laid them out for you," Arisa pointed out. "The fish and the craftsman saved you from Pettibone."

"There are opportunities in any heist," Weasel told her. "And man-made objects are everywhere. That card could have meant your mother's pistol as easily as the shield."

"You know it was the shield," Arisa said. "Come on in."

There weren't enough chairs for three to sit around the small round table, so Arisa pulled the table over to the bed, and then went to the bureau to get her deck.

Edoran took a chair and Weasel sat on the bed, so she took the second chair and shuffled the cards.

"I don't approve of this," Edoran repeated stiffly.

"Then go away," Arisa told him.

"If he goes," said Weasel in a soft singsong voice, "you'll have trouble getting what you want from the records."

"Um. You could wait outside. Your Highness."

Weasel snickered. Edoran's slight shoulders were so tense that Arisa thought he was going to rise and stalk out of the room.

"This is my significator," she said hastily. "The card that represents me." She cut the deck and turned over the top card.

The ancient goddess was walking on clouds, and lightning shot from the places where she stepped.

"The storm," said Weasel. "That's about right, for you."

"The storm is almost always my significator," Arisa admitted. "If it doesn't show up, I can't be sure if my withe is working or not."

"Well, you're a stormy sort of girl," said Edoran.

He sounded far more relaxed, and Arisa wondered why.

"It doesn't really mean storms," she told the prince. "The storm represents something that brings both good and bad in the same package. Like water for crops, but also floods and sinking ships."

"Like courage and loyalty," said Weasel, "combined with violence and temper."

Arisa scowled at him. "This supports me." She drew a card to lay beneath the storm. "This is what I'm relying on. . . . Oh."

"The lost messenger," said Weasel. "That means missing information, doesn't it?"

"Yes, and I'm not sure I like that," said Arisa. The card that supported you was supposed to be something you could count on. Relying on important information that was missing or unknown was like stepping onto a grassy hummock in a swamp and hoping it wouldn't sink.

"But it fits," Edoran pointed out. "You are relying on missing information, to lead you to the sword."

"So I am," said Arisa. "This is what inspires—Now that's ridiculous!"

"The traitor?" Weasel asked, eyeing the cloaked figure stealing out of a quiet camp. "What does it mean?"

"It means a traitor," Arisa snapped. "Lies, and betrayal of trust. But that certainly doesn't inspire me!"

"Even if they lied and betrayed for a cause?" Weasel asked. He was cynical about causes, which worried Arisa. Without a cause, without something he cared enough to fight for, a person was . . . smaller.

"Even if they're doing it for a cause," Arisa confirmed. "You should fight an enemy honestly, not gain his trust and then betray it."

"Then I'd say your quest for the sword is off to a rocky start," the prince told her. "What next?"

"This to mislead me," said Arisa, laying a card to the storm's far left. The six of stars met her curious gaze. "Trust? Trust *misleads* me? That doesn't make sense."

Was her withe not working, after all? But she'd drawn her usual significator, and that could hardly be random.

"It might make sense," said Weasel, "if there's a traitor around. What guides you true?"

Arisa laid the five of fires between the storm and trust.

"The thief," said Weasel. "So you'd better listen to me."

"But your significator is the hanged man," Arisa murmured, puzzled. The thief indicated sudden loss of wealth, from any cause.

"What threatens you?" Edoran asked.

He might not approve of the cards, but he knew what came next in the layout. Somewhat apprehensive, Arisa laid a card to the storm's far right.

"Vacillation," she said, relieved. "I'm not usually wishy-washy, but I can see how it might be a problem."

"No, you're not," Weasel murmured, not quite under his breath.

Arisa glared. "Vacillation is not a good trait! Anyway, this will protect . . . The weaver? How can the creation of beauty protect me from anything?"

She stared at the scattered cards. If there was guidance here, she couldn't see it.

"Baffling," said Weasel, shaking his head. "Very baffling. We must contemplate this for a long, long time, trying to discern its deep, hidden meaning. Or we could go and find out where the sword was last seen, and who had access to it."

"All right." Arisa sighed. "I admit, it doesn't seem to have worked this time."

She gathered up the deck and put it away.

"No one really knows when the sword was last seen."

Edoran led Weasel and Arisa toward the public rooms in the older wing of the palace. Arisa hadn't gone there since she and her mother had first toured the place, shortly after they'd moved in.

"The official version of the story is that the sword and shield were stolen by a burglar," the prince continued. "But my father didn't think much of the investigation. You know I've been reading his journals? He says no one ever asked why would a burglar steal only two items, that couldn't be melted down or recut. They could only be held for ransom, and no one ever demanded any. Or if they did, my father couldn't find a record of it."

"According to Justice Holis," said Weasel, "to prosecute any crime you need to know who, what, when, where, why, and how. And no burglar would steal something he couldn't fence."

"The sword and shield were important," Arisa protested. "Even back then. They couldn't just vanish without anyone noticing."

"They didn't," said Edoran. "There were all kinds of rumors about their disappearance, most of which made even less sense than burglary."

"I like the one where King Regalis lost them gambling in a

low tavern," Weasel put in. "But since we found the shield in the palace, we know that isn't true."

"Maybe the burglar started out of the palace with both of them," said Arisa. "But the shield was too heavy and awkward, so he hid it with those old theater props. He intended to come back for it, but then he died or something. That's why there was no demand for ransom."

"Demanding ransom for something like that would be really stupid," Weasel told her. "All they'd have to do is grab you when you show up to get the money, and then what? You can't threaten to have your partner kill a sword if they don't let you go."

"You could threaten to break it," said Arisa. "King Regalis wouldn't have liked that at all. He probably would have paid to get it back, if the burglar hadn't died!"

"There's no real evidence that there was a burglar," Weasel retorted. "Much less that he died. And no burglar would take—"

"Excuse me," Edoran interrupted firmly. "Since there's no way to know what really happened, or where the sword is, I thought we'd start with what it was, and who lost it. That's why we're here," he finished, opening the doors to the royal portrait gallery.

Arisa looked curiously into the long stone-floored room. When she and her mother had been here, all the portraits had been swathed in sheets. Today they were visible, and the wall sconces between them augmented the dim light that came through the rain-splattered windows. Clearly, the servants had prepared the room for them. Having the prince on her side might be worth putting up with him after all.

Their steps echoed in the empty gallery, but Edoran stopped before Arisa could become self-conscious about it. The first portrait showed a burly dark-haired man wearing a long red robe in the ancient style.

"Is that King Deor?" Weasel asked. "Really?"

"No," Edoran admitted. "This is what some later painter thought he might have looked like. Deor, and the sword and shield themselves, came into the world so long ago that there are no portraits from that time. Only legends."

"Let's skip the legends, shall we?" said Arisa.

Edoran scowled. "The sword and the shield come from the legends. It all starts with him." He gestured to the stocky black-browed man on the canvas. Outside the thick walls, thunder grumbled.

Arisa shivered. Despite the glowing sconces, the gallery was cold.

"King Deor united the warring tribes," said Edoran firmly. "He was the first king of Deorthas, which clearly took its name—"

"From him," said Weasel. "We can see that."

Edoran scowled. "Do you want to hear this, or—"

"No," said Arisa.

"Yes," said Weasel. "Go on. We might come across a clue sometime—that we'll miss if we don't know the background."

He was right about that. Arisa sighed. "All right. Go on."

Edoran eyed them a moment, then shrugged. "Anyway, toward the end of Deor's reign something terrible happened. Scholars think it might have been a drought, but there were droughts before, so I'm not sure if that was it."

"It's happened since then too," Arisa put in.

"And it's happened since," Edoran agreed. "But the tribes were too newly united, the chieftains too rebellious, for the new realm to endure a famine. King Deor went to the high priest of the old gods and asked for help. The priest prayed, and then he told Deor that the gods were willing to help him and all his descendants, but in return they required a sacrifice."

The last word was so weighted that a chill ran down Arisa's spine. "You're not talking about a goat or a pig, are you?"

"No." Edoran's face was sober, but his voice held a gruesome relish as he went on. "Deor said yes—the sacrifice was voluntary, all the legends agree on that—so the old pagan priests hung him upside down and cut his throat."

"Voluntary," Weasel murmured. "Voluntary like a jail sent . . . Wait a minute. He's the one on the card, isn't he? The hanged man. Voluntary sacrifice."

"My father thought so," said Edoran. "Though arcanara cards are supposed to predate even Deor. My father speculated that the card originally represented one of the old gods, but was changed to reflect Deor's sacrifice."

"So where do the sword and shield come in?" Weasel asked. "And why does this next king have them and old Deor doesn't?"

The next portrait in line showed a man with lighter hair than Deor and the same stocky build. But then, Arisa reminded herself, this was all some long-ago artist's guess. And this king wasn't alone in his portrait either. Another man stood to his left, holding the sword, and the man who held the shield stood at his right. The sword bearer looked enough like the king to be his brother, but the other man had red-blond hair, graying with the approach of age.

"The old priests gave the sword, the shield, and the crown of earth to Deor's heir, after his death," Edoran told them. "That's him. King Brend."

"He's not very happy," said Arisa, looking at the painted man's eyes. "Why doesn't he hold the sword and shield? And if he was given a crown, why isn't he wearing it?"

"I don't know, and I don't know," Edoran told her. "But my father wondered about that too. All the legends agree that Brend was given the crown of earth, in exchange for his father's sacrifice, but my father thought it must have been lost long ago, because there's no mention anywhere of what it looked like. The sword and shield are the real ones, since they were still around when these portraits were painted."

"But why does someone else always hold them?" Weasel asked. "The statues are the same way."

Edoran shrugged. "All I know is that that's the way the sword and shield were 'supposed to be' portrayed. You won't see any picture of a king holding them until Regalis, who probably got tired of the old form. It's this way," Edoran added.

He led them past what seemed like hundreds of kings, all shown with two companions, one of them holding the battered shield Weasel had found. Arisa could tell when painting portraits had come into fashion, for both the kings and their companions suddenly became much less handsome and kingly.

"He's quite . . . portly, isn't he?" said Arisa, stopping before the picture of a very plump balding man. A woman held the shield for him. A good-looking woman, Arisa noted.

"That's Marfus," said Edoran. "And according to the stories, he enjoyed life a lot. But he was a good ruler, too."

"He's got a different crown from the one behind him," Weasel observed. "And the one after him isn't wearing a crown at all. But the sword and shield are always the same."

This was the sword she was looking for. Arisa stepped close to study it, for surely the artist who had made Marfus so fat hadn't misrepresented the sword, either.

It was plain, the blade broad and double edged, not at all like the slim rapiers men fenced with now. In fact, it looked just like all the other old swords she'd seen. There were half a dozen in the hall of armor that could have replaced it.

"How do you know that the real sword isn't sitting in a sheath in the hall of armor right now?" she asked Edoran.

The prince glanced aside. "There are . . . marks on the true sword and shield. They're subtle, to make it unlikely that a forger would reproduce them, but if you know what you're looking for . . . After the sword and shield vanished, the kings of Deorthas taught their heirs how to identify those marks in case they were found again. And"—he smiled suddenly at Weasel—"to keep us from paying out the reward to some rogue, who turned up with an old shield he found in a pile of theater props."

Weasel, who had been more astonished than anyone when

the shield he'd thought was fake proved true, grinned back at the prince.

"At least I wasn't—" He peered suddenly at the portrait. "What's the king holding? Like a little twig with leaves on it."

Arisa looked closer and whooped with laughter. "I like this king! Either that or this painter had a lot of nerve. That's a sprig of aramanthus, also known as cock-in-the-meadow."

"Why is that funny?" Edoran asked, and Weasel looked just as puzzled.

"City boys." Arisa grinned. "All the goodwives know that if you carry a sprig of cock-in-the-meadow on your person for three days . . . Ah, how to phrase this. Romance will bloom for you? Except it's not romance, exactly."

Weasel laughed aloud.

"But a k-king . . . ," Edoran spluttered. "I mean, even in that day and age, surely no one believed . . . I mean . . . It doesn't work, does it?"

Arisa took pity on him. "No, it doesn't. Or so I've overheard my mother's men saying. And sooner or later most of them tried it."

"I'll bet he believed it," said Weasel, looking at Marfus' hopeful face. "Even in *this* day and age, every priest I've talked to thinks those three comets a couple of months ago were a portent. Of course, they were all remarkably vague about what it was a portent of."

"I know what you mean," said Edoran. "There an earthquake when I was born—I'm told my mother was quite alarmed. Anyway, half the priests and all the old wives in the palace claimed it was a portent that I'd do great things. Either that or die horribly. They couldn't make up their minds."

Weasel's face sobered suddenly. "Do you remember your mother?" he asked the prince. "At all?"

"A little, I think," said Edoran. "But I might be imagining that. My father used to tell me about her."

And he clearly remembered his father well, though he'd been only six when the king's horse had fallen and then rolled on its rider.

"Anyway," said Edoran, moving down the line to another picture, "this is the man during whose reign the sword and shield were lost."

Arisa gazed up at Regalis' clever, familiar face. "Why is he the only king who holds them himself?"

"No one knows," said Edoran. "But this is the last portrait in which the sword and shield appear, so I thought you'd want to see it. There are other portraits of Regalis too. The palace practically crawls with them."

"There's one on the main landing," said Weasel. "And another over the fireplace in the ballroom."

"He probably wanted to show off his clothes to posterity," said Arisa contemptuously. The shoes in this portrait had rubies in the heels.

"He must not have loved his clothes too much," said Weasel, eyeing the portrait critically. "In the story where he loses the sword and shield gambling, he lost everything else first, even his smallclothes, and walked home from the tavern nak—"

"That can't be true," said Arisa. "If nothing else, he could have sent someone for a coach and clothing."

"The story said it was the middle of the night," Weasel told her. "But I agree, it doesn't sound likely. And he wouldn't have taken the sword and shield to a tavern in the first place, so it's probably all rot."

"Not all of it," said Edoran. "He is the king who lost the sword and shield, however it happened."

"That wasn't all he lost," said Arisa, gazing up at the king who had also lost the country folk's respect. "If the sword and shield aren't in any other portraits, he probably lost them soon after this was painted. If we can find out when that was, it might give us a date!"

"The approximate date is well known," Edoran told her. "The sword and shield vanished sometime in the third week of Rish, in the second year of Regalis' reign. Some of the kings in later portraits are holding swords, but it's never *the* sword."

Weasel stepped back a few paces, gazing at the portrait to Regalis' left. "Regalis doesn't look much like his father. In fact, he doesn't look like any of the previous kings."

"Not all men look like their fathers," Arisa said. "I don't look like my mother. I bet Regalis takes after his mother."

"I'm afraid not," said Edoran. "There's a portrait of her in the blue salon, and she's small and plump and very fair."

"So maybe he resembles her father," said Arisa. "Or one of her other ancestors."

"You could be right," Edoran admitted. "But I'm afraid my father agreed with Weasel; he thought that the line of Deor's descendents was broken here."

"Why?" Arisa asked. "Just because he doesn't look like his parents is no reason to assume—"

"It was more than that," Edoran told her. "The old king's advisers detested the queen. She was . . . She evidently wasn't a responsible person. Regalis took after her that way, at least. He was a terrible king."

He didn't seem upset about it, and Weasel eyed him curiously. "So you think you're descended from Regalis, and not Deor at all? That doesn't bother you?"

"I'm descended from my father," Edoran said proudly. "And he was a fine king. He'd have been one of the great ones, if he hadn't died." He looked wistfully toward the last portrait in the line.

Weasel took advantage of a rumble of thunder to lean close to Arisa's ear and murmur, "That's easy to say, since it can't be proved."

If Arisa's father had kept journals, she'd have read them. And he'd been a good naval officer too.

"I've heard nothing but good about the king," she replied to both Weasel and Edoran. "So you may very well be right."

Edoran smiled at her. "He wasn't perfect. He could get lost in his studies and forget things—both cabinet meetings and promises to his son. But he'd have been a good king, no matter who his ancestors were. And I'm descended from Deor, anyway."

Weasel glanced up at Regalis' portrait. "How could you be, if the line of descent was broken with him?"

"I had two parents," Edoran reminded them. "One of the things my father did before he came to the throne was track down King Deor's other descendants, to ask them about their family history and stories."

"His other descendants?" Arisa asked. "Who besides them . . . ?" She gestured at the line of paintings.

"Don't be silly," said Weasel. "I'll bet old Marfus alone produced dozens of kids." He turned to the prince. "So how are you related to Deor?"

"Through my mother," said Edoran. "My father met her when he was tracking down the other descendants. My mother's family weren't even shareholders any longer, since her line came through a couple of younger sons. The whole court was scandalized when my father married the second daughter of a minor baron, but he told the court that King Deor's blood should be good enough for anyone. Of course he also said, in his journal, that at this point half the realm probably carries some of Deor's blood. I think he'd have married her no matter who her ancestors were."

Weasel was looking cynical again, so Arisa said swiftly, "That's very romantic. But it doesn't get us closer to the sword. What's the next step, research-wise?"

Edoran visibly shook off the past. "I thought that since it's going— That is, if the weather's decent, we could ride out to the university and look at the records of the official investigation. My father didn't think much of it, but it might give us some ideas."

"That sounds good," said Arisa. "There might be other documents from that time too."

"Probably more than you want," said Edoran. "My father took me there sometimes when I was little. I don't remember much, but there were lots and lots of papers."

To a six-year-old, "lots and lots" could be a stack two inches high, but Arisa didn't say this. Separated from his courtiers, alone in this cold, quiet gallery, she was finding Prince Edoran less ... obnoxious than she'd expected.

His gaze had gone back to Regalis. "He was a bad king," the prince said softly. "But I always felt sorry for him. I wondered if maybe he didn't want to be king ..."

He stopped speaking, but the silent "either" at the end of the sentence was as clear as if he'd shouted it.

Arisa woke well before dawn the next morning. Her bedroom was hot, and under the thick blankets she was roasting. Hadn't she cracked the door open?

Pulling on her slippers, Arisa went over to the balcony door. Shut tight. She must have forgotten to brace it open, for she'd been both troubled and puzzled when evening court finally drew to a close.

The stares and whispers that had followed her were uncomfortable—though she hadn't minded being snubbed by Danica and Ronelle's friends.

But watching Edoran, surrounded by the usual crowd of courtiers, she had finally seen past the glowing jewels and smiling faces. Edoran had mostly looked bored.

Arisa flung the door wide and stepped out onto the balcony. Soon she would be cold, and glad to return to her bed, but for now the cool air felt wonderful.

The moon shone through the scattered clouds, frosting the long lawns, the barren flower beds, and the slates of the stable roof. It was lovely, though much tamer than the forest and country fields she'd grown up with. If she'd been raised here, as Edoran had, it would probably seem perfect.

Did he mean what he said, about not wanting to be king?

Arisa frowned. He'd been wrong about Regalis—that overdressed popinjay had adored being king. At least the flattery that came with it, if not the work. Once she'd been certain that Edoran was the same, but now she wasn't sure.

When she'd first seen him he'd been dressed as richly as Regalis, though in a modern style, and cringing with fear as her mother held him at pistol point.

Of course, Weasel had brought the shield into a state dinner, which she now knew you had to dress up for. And while Arisa had known that her mother wasn't going to shoot the prince unless she had to, *he* might not have known that.

But if he did have some spine, why hadn't he fought Pettibone himself? Why hadn't he pardoned Justice Holis, as Weasel had begged him to? And supported the conspirators who'd plotted Pettibone's overthrow?

There are times when a body can't *fight,* Yallin's voice echoed in her memory.

Arisa leaned on the balcony rail, scowling at the moon-silvered park. If the cause was important, you had to fight! Even if you couldn't win. Even if . . .

Something cold and clammy was sticking to her arm. Mud. There was mud on her balcony railing. How had it gotten there?

Now that she was looking for it, Arisa saw more mud between the posts to one side, right where someone would step off the vines that clung to the wall, and then swing their feet over the rail to where Arisa stood. Reaching down, she found fresh mud on some of the vines as well.

Those vines were one of the reasons she'd approved of this room—she'd liked knowing that if she ever wanted to sneak out, she could.

But she didn't like the idea of someone sneaking in! Had someone gone through her room while she was asleep?

Arisa wrapped her arms around herself, and her sudden chill had nothing to do with the honest night air.

She hadn't been harmed. And the more she thought about it, the less likely it seemed that someone could have gone through her bedroom without waking her.

If you climbed onto her balcony railing, you could step up onto the wide sill of Katrin's window, and if you inched along that, you could step off onto the next balcony, and then the next, all down that side of the building. There were several places where the vines were sturdy enough to climb.

Arisa's lips twitched. This was probably the nighttime version of the servants' stair. Most of the servants lived in the city and came into work in the morning, but the upper servants were supposed to live in the palace, ready for a summons to duty at anytime—the palace's doors and the gates into the grounds were locked at night.

If someone had found her balcony door open, they might well have shut it to keep her from hearing the vines rattle as they climbed down.

Still, Arisa went inside and closed the door behind her. Later in the morning she'd have to find the key, or some other way to secure it. And then convince Katrin not to build up the fire in the evening. If, of course, Katrin was still her maid.

CHAPTER 4

THE BOOK

The Book: the creations of man's intellect, both good and ill.
Knowledge, scholarship, and the affairs of men.

Unfortunately, Katrin was still her maid. She showed up just before dawn, carrying a pair of britches and a jacket that looked like a footman's uniform, though none of the footmen were as small as Arisa. Had they shrunk in the wash? There hadn't been time to have anything made.

Arisa decided that as long as she could fence in them she didn't care, and she thanked Katrin politely.

Katrin, who hadn't said one word all morning, sniffed frostily.

Arisa sighed.

Fencing was the same as the day before, except that instead of fencing with her, Master Giles simply corrected her and Weasel's exercises—and she felt even sorrier for the prince.

Yallin had her work on fancy stitches, and Arisa spent most of the lesson staring out the window at the hovering clouds. If their expedition to the university depended on clear weather, they weren't likely to go today, whatever the prince had thought.

But shortly after luncheon the overcast began to break up. By the time her etiquette teacher finished, patches of sun were breaking through.

Arisa returned to her room. Slipping her arms out of her

sleeves and sucking in her stomach, she managed to pull her dress around so she could unfasten it—no need to summon Katrin. She could get into her riding habit by herself!

But holding the heavy skirt in her arms, she hesitated. It was even more voluminous than most of her gowns, in order to conceal the slit skirt, and it was cut longer to keep from showing too much of her legs when she sat in the saddle. It was almost as bad as hoops for restricting her movement.

Hang it! Arisa decided. Katrin had taken her fencing shirt to be washed, but the britches and jacket still hung in her wardrobe.

Arisa chose a more feminine blouse to go with them, and thought she looked . . . well, not proper, but quite fetching.

Besides, countrywomen often wore britches for rough work, and she *was* going to work, after a fashion.

She strode down the corridors to the stable, ignoring the shocked or amused looks sent her way. There were fewer such looks than there had been that first morning. If she wore nothing but britches for a week, no one would think twice about them, but that was . . . not a bad idea, actually.

Arisa walked into the muddy stable yard, with plots for a clothing rebellion blooming in her mind.

The prince had evidently remembered their plan; three horses waited in the yard, saddled and ready. The neat mare Edoran favored wore the prince's gold-embroidered saddlecloth, and at the mare's side stood the sluggish gelding Weasel rode and a fiery chestnut mare that was Arisa's favorite mount—with a regular saddle, not the sidesaddle she'd refused to ever use again after the first time she'd tried it.

She went up to the mare, taking the reins from the groom, who stood on the horse's other side. "Hello, Honey-girl. Did you miss me yesterday?"

In fact, Honey hated to get wet, but she pranced and snorted warm breath into Arisa's face—and if that wasn't horse-language saying she'd missed their ride, it was plenty close enough.

Arisa laughed, gathering the reins and inserting one foot into the high stirrup, but a pair of firm hands on her rump boosted her into the saddle before she could pull herself up.

A groom was supposed to cup his hands for a lady to step into, or at worst discreetly grip her waist to hoist her up. Arisa turned and then gasped at the familiar craggy face beaming up at her.

"Lady's supposed to wait for a groom t' help her. Don't you know that?"

"Sammel!" Arisa exclaimed. "What are you doing here? I thought . . . Did Justice Holis change his mind?"

One of the first disagreements between Justice Holis and her mother had been about the fate of the bandit-rebels her mother had led. The Falcon had wanted them to replace the palace guardsmen who'd been loyal to the old regent—and thus found themselves out of work after his death.

Arisa felt sorry for the old guardsmen, though her mother pointed out that most men in Holis' position would have had them executed. Summarily firing them was an act of mercy on his part.

That had made it even more shocking when Holis had fired her mother's men, refusing to allow them to take the palace guardsmen's place, or even go into the army or the city guard. In fact, Justice Holis had told her mother that according to the law her men were more deserving of prison or hanging than Pettibone's! Her mother had pointed out that Holis owed his life and freedom to her men, as much as he owed it to her!

They'd argued about it for days, but in the end the men Arisa had grown up with had been dismissed to make their own way in the world—though they had been given full legal pardons for any crimes they'd committed under the Falcon's command. That much her mother had insisted on.

But all that made it unlikely . . .

Arisa dropped her voice to a murmur. "Does Justice Holis know you're here?"

Sammel considered. "There's a 'yes' and a 'no' to that, young mistress. He might know a new groom's been hired, if he cares about such things. As to the rest . . . Every lock has a key, doesn't it now?"

Suddenly he straightened, stepping back from her horse, his expression blankly polite. Before she even turned to look, Arisa knew that Weasel and Edoran had come out to join her.

Half a dozen grooms flooded out of the stable to see the prince safely onto his horse, and one of them deigned to assist Weasel, who needed it.

"Henley, go fetch a cloth," the head groom snapped. "One of the prince's boots is besmirched."

Sammel turned obediently, offering Arisa a flickering wink. *Henley?*

If that was the only way her mother could get jobs for her loyal men, then more power to both of them! Arisa would have to be careful not to call him Sammel. Or to publicly recognize any more of her mother's men if she saw them working around the palace.

Were there others?

"My boots are fine," Edoran told the head groom. "Don't bother with a cloth. Just open the gate so we can go."

"But Highness, you can't go out in public—"

Edoran's mouth thinned. "Open those gates. I comm— Open them now."

His exasperated tone was as effective as a command. The gates flew open and Edoran kicked his mare out into the quiet residential street that abutted that side of the palace. Arisa sent Honey cantering after him, and they both had to stop at the corner to wait for Weasel, who never urged his horse even to a trot if he could avoid it.

"They're only doing their jobs," Weasel told the prince as the old gelding ambled up to them.

"I know, but . . . Never mind." Edoran cast Arisa a wary glance. "Have you been to the university before? It's this way."

Soon the quiet mansions gave way to shops and craft yards, and the chaotic bustle made Arisa think more kindly of Weasel's placid mount. Edoran's mare didn't give him quite the ride Honey gave her, but no one was trampled—and surprisingly few people recognized the prince, despite his fancy saddle blanket. He'd dressed plainly, Arisa realized. Or at least, plainly for him. Her britches attracted more attention than the prince did.

As they neared the edge of the city, the traffic thinned enough to let them ride together.

Arisa had passed the road that led to the university complex several times, but she'd never gone in. It was bigger than she'd thought, almost half a dozen buildings, each reflecting the age in which it was constructed, scattered over the flanks of a low hill. A squat tower perched on the hilltop.

"That's the astronomical observatory," Weasel told her. "Where they study the stars and planets. Justice Holis dragged me up there several times."

The drone of lecturing voices came from the barely cracked windows of the building on their right, and billows of evil-smelling smoke surged through the fully open windows of the building on their left. Someone inside that building was shouting, but none of the people walking along the paths seemed concerned.

"That's where they do chemical experiments," Edoran told them. "I've found it's best not to ask what goes on in there."

Weasel frowned. "Won't they tell you about it? That would worry me."

"On the contrary." Edoran shuddered. "If you so much

as look interested, they'll tell you *all* about it. In detail. For hours!"

Arisa laughed. "I trust we're not going there."

"No, we're going to the records room in the library," said Edoran, gesturing to a large stone keep. Judging by its architecture, it was the oldest of the buildings.

The servants must have sent word ahead, for a small man, with mousey hair pulled back into a queue, waited on the steps to greet them.

"It's been too long since we've seen Your Highness here!" He sounded as if Edoran were his favorite grandson instead of his prince. "How may we assist you?" He waved a hand, and a couple of students came forward to take their horses.

"Master Horace." Dismounting, Edoran assumed the look of bored politeness with which he responded to similar smiles in evening court. "We want to take a look at the archives. The records of King Regalis' reign."

"At once, Your Highness!"

Arisa thought Edoran suppressed a sigh, but he did it so smoothly she couldn't be sure. When she first met him, Arisa had taken that smooth blankness for arrogance, but now . . . He was different around other people than he was with her and Weasel, and she wondered why.

"The archives are this way," said their host, leading them up the main stairs. "And may I say, Your Highness, how pleased I am that you share your father's interest in history."

Edoran and Master Horace exchanged polite comments

as they turned down a long hall, lined with small statues and display cases. Arisa glanced at one of them and stopped to gape at the mushroom-mound of gold, jewels, and velvet. "Isn't that the crown Marfus was wearing?"

"This is the hall of crowns," Master Horace told them. "That particular crown was in use from"—he peered at the label—"the reign of King Adan through the reign of King Gerand, so it might well have been—"

"You're correct," said a woman's cool voice. "Marfus favored that crown, and had two more made in the same style. Those two," she added dryly, "were in even worse taste than this one."

"Your Highness," said Master Horace. "Allow me to present Mistress Margood, the head librarian."

Edoran nodded. The thin dark-haired woman in the drab gown sketched a curtsy, then looked at Weasel and Arisa. "And these are . . . ?"

"Ah," said Master Horace. "Prince Edoran's companions."

Arisa bristled, and amusement glinted in Edoran's eyes.

"Mistress Arisa Benison," he told the librarian. "And Weasel."

Mistress Margood nodded. "You want to look at some of the old records?"

"Legal records," Edoran confirmed. "From King Regalis' reign."

"Humph. Looking for the sword, are you? Well, it's a better idea than thrashing around at random."

"The Prince," said Master Horace repressively, "will inform us of his intentions when he wishes to do so. We are here to serve, not to quest—"

"Yes, it's the sword," Edoran told her.

"Then you'll want to start with the official investigation," Mistress Margood said crisply. "This way."

She strode rapidly down the corridor, not so much as if she wanted to be rid of them, Arisa thought, but as if she preferred to waste as little time on them as possible.

Something caught Weasel's eye, and he stopped beside another display case. "Is that the first crown? The one they say is the crown of earth?"

Arisa looked through the glass at a plain gold circlet resting on a bed of black velvet. The sunlight that came through the high windows couldn't reach it, but its rounded curves glowed. Nicks and scratches marred the smooth surface.

"Yes," said Master Horace proudly. "This is the crown of earth, worn by King Deor himself."

"Actually," said the librarian, "this crown's origins are ambiguous. There are no records from Deor's time, and while one legend from that era says that the gods themselves gave King Brend the crown of earth, in return for his father's sacrifice, there is also a story in which King Deor passed the crown to his son *before* he was killed. In any case," she finished dryly, "this appears to have been made by men instead of gods."

"So does the shield," Weasel told her, smiling in response to the humor in her face.

"Was this really Deor's crown?" Arisa asked. Manmade or not, its sheer age was awesome.

Edoran frowned. "I thought Deor's crown was lost, a long time ago."

"That's yet another theory," said Mistress Margood. "And there is a jeweler's bill, presented to King Peremin, for a crown in the old style, a simple circlet of gold. There's no way to be certain if this crown was Deor's, or was made later for King Peremin, or came from some other, unknown source."

"Can we touch it?" Arisa asked.

"No!" Mistress Margood yelped.

"Well," said Master Horace. "Ah. Technically, it belongs to Prince Edoran."

"It was donated to the university," Mistress Margood said firmly.

"On loan," said Edoran softly. "I could command it . . ."

He met Weasel's scowl with a mischievous grin.

"There's no need for that," said Master Horace. "Mistress Margood, open the case for His Highness."

The librarian sniffed, pulled a thick ring of keys from her pocket, and opened the lock. She stepped back with a scowl that clearly indicated that if they broke anything she'd break them—prince or no prince!

Arisa hardly cared. She reached slowly into the case and removed the crown. She didn't know what she'd expected, but it was only a hoop of gold, smooth and cool.

"What does it feel like?" Weasel asked.

"Heavy." She held it out to him, and he braced himself before he touched it. Then his shoulders sagged with relief and he took it from her, weighing it in his hands.

"It is heavy. And judging by the nicks, it's soft enough to be pure gold. I might be able to mark it with my fingernail."

He cast Mistress Margood a wicked glance, but she refused to rise to such obvious bait. Weasel turned to Edoran. "Put it on."

Edoran took the crown and lowered it onto his head. His head was too small, so he tipped the crown back to keep it from falling over his nose. He looked . . .

"You look silly," Arisa told him.

"That's why I don't wear crowns." He passed it to the librarian, with an apologetic smile, and she put it back into the case and locked it.

"Shall we go to the archives *now*, Your Highness?"

It seemed they had forfeited the librarian's goodwill. She hustled them down the corridor—probably to keep them from playing with other priceless artifacts along the way—and herded them into a small room. It held two long tables and a handful of uncomfortable-looking chairs, but the shelves lining all four walls were packed with books and papers.

Master Horace excused himself, leaving them in "Mistress Margood's capable hands." The librarian went straight to a shelf and pulled out a sheaf of papers, bound with a thin leather tie, and laid them down on one of the tables.

"This is the official report of the investigation into the

disappearance of the sword and shield," she said. "It is the original document, so handle it with care, first making certain that your hands are clean and dry."

For a moment Arisa thought they'd have to hold up their hands for inspection, but Mistress Margood went on.

"No food or drink of any kind is allowed in this room, and no documents leave this room. If you need additional records, come to my office and I will find them for you. Is that clear?"

In other words, keep your hands off my documents.

"Yes, Mistress Margood," said Weasel, in a schoolboy singsong.

The librarian glared at him. "Don't get the pages out of order. Leave it on the table when you're finished; don't try to put it back yourselves. My office is two doors down this hall." She swept out, closing the door behind her.

"Witch," Weasel muttered.

"She's only doing her job." Irony dripped from Edoran's voice.

Weasel's glare faded to a slightly shamed grin. "Let's get to it, shall we?"

They started with all three of them trying to read at the same time, and soon found that Weasel, the law clerk, read far faster than Arisa did, and that she read faster than Edoran. Soon they worked out a system where Weasel read a page and then passed it to Arisa, who passed it to Edoran when she'd finished. The pile of unread pages between her and Weasel grew at about the same rate as the pile between her and Edoran, which silenced any comments she might have made about slow readers. Besides, if Edoran had been taught to read in the same way he'd been taught to fence, it was a miracle he could read at all.

Time dragged past, but even through the tedium of the long-dead justice's formal prose . . .

"There's something wrong here," said Arisa. "It's like . . . It's like the justice is going through the proper moves, but he doesn't care if the sword and shield are found or not."

"It's worse than that," said Weasel, who was nearing the bottom of the stack. "He's doing things that are useless, and skipping things that would have made sense."

"What do you mean?" Arisa asked.

"One of the first things the city guard does after a robbery," said Weasel, "is send men out to try to find a witness. But no one looked for witnesses around the palace."

"Or asked the palace servants who cleaned that room when someone first noticed the sword and shield were missing," said Edoran. "According to this they were mounted on the throne room wall, and while that room is used only for formal events, the servants keep it clean. If the sword and shield suddenly weren't there to be dusted, they'd have noticed."

"And why question people at the docks, when he says just a page later that he thinks the sword and shield were stolen for ransom?" Weasel asked. "You wouldn't have to take them out of the city for that."

"So what does it mean?" Arisa asked.

"No one could be this incompetent by accident," said Weasel. "This investigation is fake."

"And no one could have ordered a fake investigation," Edoran added, "except Regalis himself. At least, that's what my father said. No one but the king would have dared."

"But why?" said Arisa, frustrated. "I mean, Regalis was *king*."

"That was the problem," said Edoran. "What do you think the country folk of Regalis' day would have thought of a king who lost the sword and shield? Or sold them. Or whatever he did."

"The country folk already hated him," Arisa replied. "If they knew he'd been careless with the sword and shield ... rebellion. Not like the one the Hidden priests led, a real rebellion with every farmer and goodwife in the realm. . . . No, surely it wouldn't have gone that far. The shield and sword mattered to the country folk, but to rise against the king for that alone ..."

But it wouldn't have been for that alone. It would have been for the years of drought that impoverished the whole kingdom. Impoverished it to the point where Regalis had sent the city guard to raid the countryside to feed the city's starving poor. If he really had done something stupid with the sword and shield, it could have proved the final straw.

"And we know Regalis did something to lose them," said Arisa slowly, "because they disappeared. But why was the shield still in the palace?"

"At a guess," said Weasel, "someone under Regalis' orders hid it there."

"Why?" Arisa demanded. "Losing the sword was bad enough. Losing both of them—"

"Was actually better," said Weasel. "How about this: Regalis gambles away the sword—or loses it some other stupid way. Then one of his brighter advisers points out how the already-angry country folk are going to feel about that. But if he can convince them that the sword was stolen for ransom, by a burglar who for some reason never contacted him, they'd have to see that it wasn't his fault. He investigated, he offered a reward. What more could he do?"

"But if a burglar took the sword," said Edoran, "why would he leave the shield behind?"

"Exactly," said Weasel. "Regalis himself had the shield hidden away, for the same reason he ordered the fake investigation—to support the story of a burglar, and to get himself off the hook. He probably intended to get the sword back. Then he could dig out the shield and claim he'd recovered them both from that nasty thief. But he never found the sword, so the shield stayed where it was."

There was a long, thoughtful silence.

"It fits," said Arisa.

"It fits," Edoran agreed. "And that was further than my father reasoned, though he didn't know that the shield was hidden in the palace."

"But where does that leave us? All these records"—Arisa gestured to the crowded shelves—"are useless. Any official record will be useless."

"Then we check the unofficial records," said Edoran promptly. "That was something my father thought of, though he never had time to pursue it. You may not know this," he added, "but lots of the court ladies, and some of the men, keep diaries."

"And giggle over them," said Arisa glumly. "And tell you they've written something nasty about you, that people will be able to read for centuries. As if anyone would bother."

"I know," said Edoran cheerfully. "But they're right about one thing—those diaries last. When someone's great-aunt or grandmother dies, their relatives often donate their diaries to the university archives."

"Given what most courtiers write about, why would the archives want them?" Weasel asked. "Who cares who flirted with someone else's fellow sixty years ago?"

"No one," said Edoran. "Though the relatives go through them pretty carefully before they turn them over, just in case. But the archives take them, hoping they'll also mention things that are important."

"Such as gossip about the disappearance of the sword and shield," said Arisa slowly. "They would have gossiped, wouldn't they?"

"They gossip about everything," said Edoran. "And if you think reading this report was boring . . ."

His gaze met Arisa's. Moving as one, they turned to stare at Weasel.

"Oh, no you don't," said Weasel. "Justice Holis gives me more than enough boring reading."

"But you're so fast," said Arisa. "Much faster than either of us. And smart, too. Really smart about documents and things."

"I'm smart enough to keep the two of you from dumping this job on me," Weasel told her.

"But you have legal training," Edoran said. "You could sort out anything important much quicker than . . ." He paused, frowning. "Much quicker . . ."

He rose to his feet and stared toward the south.

"Is it the weather?" Weasel asked.

"No. No, it's not."

"What do you mean?" Arisa asked. "It's still clearing up, I think."

"It is," said Edoran. "This is something else." His frown deepened. His expression was that of someone groping through a dark closet, but his hands were still.

"What are you talking about?" Arisa demanded.

"Edoran can sense the weather," Weasel told her. He watched the prince with curiosity but no alarm.

Arisa snorted. "So can dogs and horses. And every goodwife whose big toe aches when a storm's coming in."

"Maybe," said Weasel. "But I've never seen a goodwife who can tell you it'll start raining at midnight, rain hardest between two and four, and stop three quarters of an hour before dawn."

"That's ridiculous," said Arisa. "No one can do that."

"Edoran can," said Weasel. "And I've never seen him get it wrong."

"Then it's creepy," said Arisa. "If it's true, which I don't—"

"We should go," said Edoran abruptly. "We should go now."

"But we haven't even looked at the diaries," Arisa protested. "Whoever's going to read them."

"We're leaving," said Edoran. "I command it."

The old arrogance rang in his voice, and Arisa scowled.

Weasel kicked the prince's ankle, and he yelped and hopped a few steps. He glared at his friend.

Arisa was relieved that he no longer stared toward the south.

"Justice Holis and I are trying to break him of his habit of snapping out commands," Weasel told Arisa. "It annoys people."

"All right," Edoran grumbled. "But we're still leaving. We can come back another day. Or send for the diaries. Or get some clerk to waste his time over them, instead of ours."

Arisa snorted. "Well, I certainly wouldn't want to waste Your Highness' precious time. You have so much to do."

Weasel glared at her. Arisa had a feeling that if her ankle had been in range, she'd have been kicked too.

Edoran turned and walked out of the room. Weasel shrugged. "I guess we're leaving."

Their sudden departure took Master Horace by surprise, but he came out to the steps where they waited for their horses, and bade the prince a fulsome farewell.

Now that she had time to look around, Arisa noticed a set of small statues in niches beside the great double doors. One of the old kings, with his sword and shield bearers beside him.

"No wonder Regalis lied," Arisa murmured. "In those days

the sword and shield were almost as important as the king."

"This is the king who paid for this building," said Weasel, reading the worn inscription. "Founded the university, I suppose. Another lefty."

"How can you tell?" Arisa asked. "He's not holding anything."

"His purse is hanging on his left side," said Weasel. "Only left-handed people put their purses in their left coat pockets."

As an ex-pickpocket, he would know.

"Most of the old kings were left-handed," Weasel added.

Arisa might have questioned that, but Weasel was more observant about such things than anyone she knew.

"What about Regalis?" she asked.

"Right-handed," Weasel told her. "But according to their portraits, some of the kings before him were right-handed as well. In the early paintings where the kings are all handsome, they made them left-handed all the way back to old Deor. But they were just guessing then."

"You can hardly call Deor old." Arisa wrapped her arms around herself; the breeze was brisk despite the sunlight. "He didn't live long enough to get old. Why would he do that? I know kings are supposed to care for the realm above all else, and so on, and so on, but that's rot. They're men, just like anyone else. Do you think he really, deliberately, laid down his life?"

"Yes," said Weasel. "At least, I think it's possible."

It was the last answer she'd expected from Weasel-the-cynic.

"But why?" Arisa asked.

"Not having been there, I can't say for sure." Weasel stuck his hands into his pockets. "But I'd guess it was for the future."

Arisa frowned. "I don't understand."

"The One God willing," said Weasel softly, "you never will."

Edoran spent most of the long ride home looking to the south, and ignoring his companions. Arisa was happy to ignore him in return. She wasn't sure if this was arrogance, or creepiness, or both.

Probably both, she decided. The wind had grown colder, and she was glad when they reached the stable yard . . . until Sammel told her, in a groom's respectful murmur, that her lady mother wanted to see her when she returned.

Arisa knocked on the office door, and the Falcon's voice told her to come in. Her mother was alone, wearing a plain trim gown and frowning at one of the many papers that flooded the desk. Arisa was sorry—she'd hoped for a crowd of officers and officials, so she could come back later.

Her mother put down the paper she'd been studying, and looked Arisa up and down.

"Britches for all occasions? Katrin told me you've sworn off corsets, but she didn't say you'd abandoned skirts as well."

Arisa scowled.

"I'm glad to hear you've been with the prince," the Falcon added.

Arisa's scowl deepened. "He's an arrogant twerp. A *creepy* arrogant—"

"Don't talk about him like that," the Falcon said. "Whatever you think of him, he *will be* the next king. And you have to become a lady, whether you like it or not. This is important, Ris."

"But I can't breathe or move!" Arisa burst out. "I'm trying, mother, I really am, but I can't stand this!"

She dropped into the chair in front of the Falcon's desk, blinking back tears. Her mother never cried.

The Falcon sighed, then smiled. "I suppose it's foolish to pin a peacock's tail on a kestrel."

Arisa grimaced. "You're the hawk in the family. I'm a sparrow. At best. Is there any bird drabber than a sparrow?"

"I wasn't talking about your face," the Falcon told her.

"I just don't fit here," said Arisa.

"Not in court, perhaps," said the Falcon. "I'll make you another deal. I'll tell Katrin no more corsets if you keep trying with the rest of it. Especially with the prince. All right?"

Arisa's whoop of joy wasn't at all ladylike.

CHAPTER 5

THE TWO OF WATERS

The Two of Waters: discovery.
The appearance of something unexpected, or sometimes, recovery of
something that was lost.

5

Having lost the great corset battle, Katrin avenged herself by laying out the stiffest, heaviest gown Arisa owned, and lacing it very tightly. But even the dark-brown velvet, with its stiff brocaded front panel, was better without corsets than the lightest gown was with them. Arisa spun, nimble in her stocking feet, making the heavy skirt bell and sway. Perhaps she would dance tonight—one of the simple dances.

"Stop that," said Katrin sharply. "The prince will arrive at court soon; you've no time to prance about."

Arisa didn't care who engaged the prince's attention, but she knew her mother would care, so she stopped twirling and allowed Katrin to dress her hair, fasten a necklace, and slip high-heeled shoes onto her feet. When she looked in the mirror, she forgave her maid for battles past. The rich brown brought out red lights in her hair, and the wide stripe of gold brocade that ran down the front of the bodice and skirt brightened the somber color.

"I look very fine, Katrin," said Arisa. "Thank you."

Katrin sniffed. "Even the scullery maid goes laced."

"Then the scullery maid can neither move nor breathe," Arisa retorted. If Katrin wanted to be miffed because the gown looked wonderful without corsets, then that was her problem.

Arisa's uncorseted state didn't draw a glance from anyone,

even when she reached the gold salon, where the prince was "taking his ease" this evening.

Though her mother could move in her corset, Arisa noted. The Falcon was dancing with a man in the blue coat and white britches of a naval officer, his feet light in his polished boots. Only army and naval officers wore their uniform boots to court. Low-heeled boots. Arisa wondered if she was the only one who envied them.

The Falcon, always alert, saw Arisa watching and flashed her an approving smile. Because she was there? Because the gown looked so nice?

Arisa sighed. She'd have to approach the prince tonight, to keep her part of the bargain, and the Falcon would doubtless prefer to have it happen sooner. So why didn't *she* cozy up to the brat, Arisa wondered crossly, instead of flirting with sailors?

But the officer didn't look like he was flirting, his expression far too serious for someone dancing with the most beautiful woman in the room. Of course, Arisa reflected, she was also the deadliest.

Arisa wove through the crowd, which would grow denser as she neared the end of the room where Edoran sat on one of the few chairs. At least she had no fear that her mother would suddenly introduce her to a stepfather; she'd loved Arisa's father too much for that. He had been hanged, when the old regent purged the navy of all the officers who'd been loyal to the admiral who had challenged him. The Falcon had watched the hanging, one of her mother's men had told Arisa, her hand gripping the locket he'd given her and her face as hard as stone . . . except for the tears pouring down and down. She'd never cried since, they said, and Arisa couldn't prove otherwise.

The Falcon had worn that locket when she'd stolen a load of gunpowder from a naval depot, or guns being shipped to the army troops who patrolled Deorthas' borders, or especially when she'd relieved one of the king's tax collectors of his strongbox.

She hadn't worn it for the "ordinary" jobs, when the tax money was gone and the Falcon's men robbed coaches to feed themselves and their families. Only when she struck an important blow against her enemy did the locket come out.

Arisa would probably never see that locket again, and she wasn't sure whether she felt relief or regret. With the old regent finally dead, her mother was free to build a real life for herself—and her daughter, too, Arisa supposed.

But why did she have to do it at court?

No, Arisa told herself firmly, this was better—court and all. Perhaps one day her mother would introduce her to a stepfather. That would be another good, healing thing, though it would certainly feel odd.

"Why are you standing there, staring into space?" Weasel asked. "People are walking around you, like a statue in a town square."

"I'm putting it off," Arisa admitted. Weasel knew her well enough to understand what "it" was without being told. "Remember what happened last time?"

Weasel's grin held as much sympathy as amusement. "Well,

you can't put it off any longer. Edoran sent me to fetch you."

"Is he in arrogant mode, or weird mode?" Arisa asked.

Weasel frowned. "That's not fair."

Arisa waited.

"Weird mode," Weasel sighed. "He's still looking off to the south and he won't tell me why. The last time I saw him like this, we heard later that a heavy snow had come down on a couple of mountain villages. Collapsed several buildings. But he says it's not the weather."

"Definitely weird," said Arisa.

"Coming from Mistress I-Have-Withe," said Weasel, "that's a bit much. Don't tease him about it. I think the servants used to, or someone did." He turned and led her through the crowd.

"Withe isn't like that," said Arisa, following. "Lots of people have withe, some much stronger than mine. But I won't tease him if he's sensitive about it."

Weasel smiled.

"No matter how weird he is."

Weasel choked down a laugh, and Arisa grinned. But she'd keep her promise. It would be hard to have a . . . a gift of weather sensing that no one else believed in, especially as a child. She could all but hear some nurse saying, "Now, you stop making things up, Prince Edoran." Or even worse, "Stop telling lies."

No, she wouldn't tease him. No matter how weird he was.

In fact, now that she was accustomed to reading that blank expression of his, Edoran looked more bored than weird. No wonder, that; most of the men and women around him were old enough to be his parents. In some cases, his grandparents.

The most important, most powerful shareholders paid their respects to the prince early in the evening, Arisa's etiquette teacher had told her. These people must be them. And Edoran wanted *her* to interrupt them? He must be bored to madness.

But she was there—too late to run.

Weasel stepped up, right in front of Edoran's chair, and bowed. "May I present Mistress Arisa Benison to Your Highness' attention?" He could do an excellent noble imitation when he wanted to.

All eyes turned to her—impatient, critical, powerful eyes. Arisa stiffened her spine and stepped forward, careful in the awkward shoes. This time she wouldn't fall. This time she would make her mother proud, instead of being scraped, scarlet with embarrassment, off the polished floor.

She took the final step and sank into a deep, graceful curtsy. And as she sank, she felt the stitches at the top left side of her bodice break—snap, snap, snap.

The sound was so soft no one else could have heard it. Arisa might not have heard it, if the sudden loosening of her dress hadn't given it away.

She clamped her arm tight to her side, spoiling what her etiquette mistress called the "line" of her curtsy. Even so, two more stitches popped as she rose to her feet. The stiff front panel of her bodice started to gape, and she swept her forearm up to hold it in place, striving to look graceful, or flirtatious, or like she was going to scratch her chin—anything to hide the fact that her clothes were falling off. She stood perfectly still, afraid even to breathe. Her only chemise that was sufficiently low to accommodate this low-cut gown was far too sheer for modesty. Arisa had complained about transparent underwear the first time she'd worn it—but it was the fashion and no one was ever going to see it anyway.

The whole court would be seeing it, if any more stitches gave way.

Weasel's eyes were wide with alarm, but he was as frozen as she. Arisa offered a heartfelt prayer to the god of the affairs of men to get her out of this.

Edoran made a soft choking sound and stood. His eyes weren't wide, but narrowed in amusement—curse him. When he spoke, his regal voice gave nothing away. "I'm pleased to see you here, Mistress Benison. I wanted to thank you for . . . for your assistance with my research this afternoon. But alas . . ."

No one said "alas" in real life, not even in court. Arisa scowled. What was he up to?

". . . I have no token suitable to repay a lady."

The prince's gaze roved over the crowd and settled on an elderly dowager.

"Lady Varent, may I beg the gift of your pin? I need a favor to bestow, but I have nothing to hand. You'll be repaid for it from the royal vaults, severalfold."

The dowager managed to look puzzled and simper at the same time. "Of course, Your Highness. Anything to assist your"—she glanced at Arisa, clearly not seeing her as courtship material—"your need."

She pulled on the oval of rubies and gold that sprang from the middle of her bodice, and it proved to be attached to a pin. A beautifully, blessedly *long* pin.

Arisa closed her eyes and expanded her prayer to include the Lady, the Lord, and any other of the old gods that might care to take a hand.

She heard a light footstep, and opened her eyes. The prince stood a bit to one side, his body shielding the rent in her dress from the rest of the crowd.

"Accept a royal favor, with royal thanks."

"Sure," said Arisa faintly. "Whatever you say."

His light hands pinched the top of the seam together. He inserted the pin and began to weave the point though the layers of cloth, neat as a tailor. His lips were only inches from her ear.

"Walk out with your head up," Edoran murmured. "And if those catty girls try to delay you, say you're on an errand for your mother and can't stop."

"Why are you doing this?" Arisa whispered. "Everyone will think you're flirting with me, and those catty girls will tear me to shreds before I reach the door!"

"So tell them you are flirting," said Edoran. "And that if they don't get out of your way, when you're queen, you'll set them to scrubbing the privies."

"I'd rather marry a toad," said Arisa. Then she realized that might not be the brightest thing to say to someone who could still take back his pin.

"I couldn't agree more." Edoran drove the point through the

final fold of fabric and stepped back. "There. It looks well on you."

The rubies probably did look good, glinting between dark velvet and pale skin, but all Arisa cared about was that it felt secure.

"Thank you," she said, with such sincerity that several courtiers' brows rose.

"You're welcome," said Edoran. "You may go."

He turned back to his chair, drawing the crowd's attention with him, and Arisa fled.

She made it out of the salon without any of the girls trying to stop her, which was a sure sign that they didn't know what had happened.

What almost happened, Arisa thought, hurrying down the corridors to her room. She owed Edoran for this, no question.

There was also someone to whom she owed a different sort of debt, and she wanted to pay it right now—but when she reached her room, Katrin wasn't there.

Arisa strode to the door that connected her room with her maid's, and threw it open so hard that it banged against the wall. Katrin had been sitting in a chair, reading, the very image of a loyal maid waiting for her mistress to return.

"You set this up!" said Arisa furiously. "You sabotaged my dress. Deliberately!"

Katrin laid down her book, rose, and walked calmly toward the door. Arisa stepped into her own room, and Katrin closed the door behind her.

"I don't know what you're talking about, Mistress Arisa. Was something wrong with your gown?" Her voice was innocent, but malice gleamed in her eyes.

"Rot!" Arisa was so angry her hands shook. She balled them into fists and began to pace, fighting down the temptation to pound them into Katrin's trim stomach. Not because she was averse to punching Katrin, but because she was so angry now that if she started, she might not be able to stop. The part of her that liked that idea, that wanted Katrin bloody and moaning on the floor, scared Arisa more than anything Katrin could do.

"You know exactly what I'm talking about," Arisa told her. "So stop pretending. Coward. Witch!"

Katrin's eyes rested on the pin. "Why Mistress, did that seam rip? How embarrassing. If only you'd worn your corsets."

Fury boiled in Arisa's gut. She pulled the pin from her bodice, holding it like a dagger. "Get out. Get out of my room. I never want to see you again, not in here, not in the palace, not anywhere in the realm! You're fired!"

"We'll see about that," said Katrin coolly. But when Arisa stalked toward her, she backed to the corridor door and then through it, closing it behind her.

Arisa looked down at her sagging bodice and knew she couldn't follow the maid, even if she wanted to. Her whole body was shaking now. She sat down on the floor and burst into tears of rage and humiliation. Then she wept because the whole last month had been so horrible, and her life was horrible, and she felt horrible too.

When her sobs finally eased, Arisa discarded her soaked handkerchief and poured cold water into a basin to soothe her burning cheeks. Her eyes and nose were red and swollen. Her heart felt raw, empty of everything except determination—Katrin would pay for this. But if she was going to convince her mother to fire the woman, she needed proof.

With the bodice half-open, it was easy to slide her arms from the sleeves and turn the dress so she could unfasten and then examine it. Most of the stitches on the left side had already ripped, but near the bottom of the seam a section of thread was still intact . . . almost intact. Every other stitch had been severed about two thirds of the way through, with only a wisp of fiber left to hold it.

Arisa scowled. It would have taken a very sharp knife, a very fine touch, and several hours' work to so carefully sabotage such a long seam. Evidently, Katrin had all those things. It was expert craftsmanship, she had to admit, for the seam was just strong enough to hold if she did nothing to stress it, nothing but stand and walk about. But the moment she bent or moved swiftly . . . It could have happened on the dance floor, Arisa realized. In the midst of exertion and concentration, she wouldn't have noticed until her bodice flopped like a dead goose, right in front of all her enemies. Embarrassing her, shaming her mother.

Hmm. Katrin might have done it for spite—she probably had—but she'd put in a lot of work just to embarrass Arisa. And it would have, at least it should have, embarrassed Katrin as well. If her bodice had come undone in such a spectacular, public fashion, no one would have blamed Arisa for firing the maid who looked after her clothes.

Was spite over losing a fairly minor argument worth getting fired for?

It might be, if you were sufficiently stupid, but . . .

Was Katrin trying to accomplish something more than leaving Arisa half-naked in front of her enemies? Had she been trying to humiliate Arisa in front of her *mother's* enemies?

What Arisa did reflected on the Falcon. Her mother had repeated that time and again, and Arisa knew it was true. That was why she kept trying with all this lady stuff.

But as far as she knew, the closest thing her mother had to an enemy was Justice Holis, and Arisa didn't believe the justice would do anything like this. He might be ruthless, if he had no other choice. In his long career as a judge, he had doubtless sentenced men to hang. But he would never come up with such a petty scheme.

Petty and malicious; that's what this was. And if Weasel's mentor wasn't either of those things, about half the courtiers in the palace qualified just fine.

The Falcon had been given the position of lord commander of the army and the navy, all of Deorthas' military. The real commander of the army, the man who held their loyalty, was General Diccon, and Arisa thought he was content with his position. But Regent Pettibone had put men loyal to him in charge of the navy, and the Falcon and Justice Holis had fired most of them. Along with the palace guard, all its officers, and quite a few other government officials as well.

How many of those men had relatives at court? Relatives who might hate Justice Holis and the Falcon for their families' loss of power.

For the first time Arisa understood what Justice Holis meant when he said his government was "precarious."

But if someone had bribed Katrin to embarrass the Falcon through Arisa, there might be evidence. If Arisa could find it.

Arisa put on her robe, went to Katrin's door, and pressed her ear against it. She heard nothing. Was Katrin reporting to her true master or mistress right now? Or was she in the servants' hall, complaining? Or having a good laugh at Arisa's expense? Her cheeks grew warm.

When she'd first moved into the palace, Arisa had envied the close friendships that formed in the servants' hall. Friendships the nobles, intent on their rivalries, almost never managed. The servants had their own quarrels, but they would close ranks against an outsider. Arisa would have to prove any accusation she made, or she'd be accused of making the whole thing up to get back at her maid. And all the servants would turn on her.

She knocked softly. If Katrin was there, she might think Arisa was about to apologize—and she'd never do that! Not for anything! She could say that she wanted to be sure Katrin was packing.

No sound. No answer. Arisa knocked again, then tried the doorknob. Locked.

Arisa frowned. She didn't remember Katrin locking the door

when she came into Arisa's room, but she'd been so angry she might have missed it. And it would have been easy for Katrin to return to her room through the corridor and lock the door, unheard, while Arisa was bawling. But why would she?

If this door was locked, the door in the corridor probably was too. Arisa didn't have Weasel's skill with a lock pick, but she didn't need it—the keys to all the doors that led into her room were in her jewelry box. She'd never used them before, but she had cause enough now!

The second key she tried opened the door.

"Katrin?" she called softly. "I just wanted . . ."

No need for a lie; the room was empty.

Arisa stepped in and looked around. She had never been in her maid's room before today—even when they weren't fighting, she and Katrin hadn't been friends.

It was smaller than Arisa's room, though not as small as she'd expected. It held a bed, with a chest at the foot, a wardrobe, a stand and washbasin, and the upholstered chair with footstool where Katrin had been reading. The chair looked a bit lumpy, and the upholstery was patched.

Arisa went first to the chest. If Katrin had any papers, they would probably be there. Her heart pounded as she lifted the lid. She could explain her presence in her maid's room, but Arisa had no excuse for going through her things. A hat, broad-brimmed straw to protect a white complexion from the sun. Come summer, no doubt, Katrin would be nagging Arisa to wear one. Beneath it Arisa found several more books, blank paper and ink, and a purse that jingled when she lifted it. A spool of half-finished lace and a well-stocked sewing kit that contained, among other things, a small sharp knife. Although her lips tightened, Arisa replaced it in the tidy kit. By itself, the knife proved nothing.

There was also a doll, some inexpensive jewelry, and a number of personal items, things you'd expect to find in any female servant's room. No contract offering Katrin a hundred gold blessings for making the Falcon's daughter look like a clumsy, ignorant fool. A contract signed, of course, by both parties.

Arisa sighed. Had she really expected to find such a thing? Katrin was petty and malicious—or a highly competent traitor—but she wasn't an idiot.

Arisa replaced everything carefully in the chest and went to the wardrobe. Probably nothing there but clothing, and Katrin might return at any time, but she knew she should look.

Smaller hats on the top shelf, dresses, skirts, blouses, petticoats. Arisa's eyes slipped over the shoes so quickly she almost missed it. Mud. A pair of worn sturdy shoes, thrust toward the rear, crusted with dried mud.

Arisa picked one up and examined it, the dirt gritty against her palms.

Weasel would tell her that there were dozens of reasons for Katrin to have muddy shoes. She might have gone for a walk in the garden after a rain. Or had to run an errand in bad weather. Or, or, or . . .

Arisa knew that Katrin was the one who'd climbed up over her balcony after the last big storm. Katrin, who was sneaking out of the palace, not because she was meeting a young man but because she was up to something.

Perhaps she shouldn't ask her mother to fire the maid after all. Because if she didn't, the next time Katrin went out, Arisa could follow her.

CHAPTER 6

THE SIX OF STARS

The Six of Stars: trust.
Faith in a person or principle.

6

The next morning Arisa slid into her britches and jacket and went down to Prince Edoran's fencing lesson without catching a glimpse of Katrin. She did hear a few soft sounds in the room next to hers, but that only made her hurry more. Another confrontation with Katrin was the last thing she wanted.

After they'd warmed up, Master Giles set her and Weasel to somewhat more difficult exercises, thrusting and blocking each other's blades in a set pattern, while he chased Edoran around the room. He claimed that the prince's fencing was sufficiently advanced that he didn't need exercises, but even Weasel could see that wasn't true. And if that was how nobles were trained, then why was he teaching Arisa and Weasel so differently?

She watched Master Giles and the prince surreptitiously, as she and Weasel practiced, but she evidently wasn't sneaky enough—as they fenced past, Master Giles' foil flew out and smacked her thigh. "Attend your own work, Mistress, not that of others!"

Edoran didn't even try to take advantage of his opponent's distraction. Was he afraid of the stinging blow that would answer such an attempt? But he was getting those blows anyway. In fact, as far as Arisa could see, the only thing the "noble" method of instruction accomplished was to teach someone how to take a mild beating in silence.

That seemed to work on a lot of levels, for Edoran took all kinds of things in silence. Not only from his teachers, either, but being stuck in evening court, and herded about by his servants as if he were a prize cow. It was almost as if he didn't know how to stand up for himself, to fight back. To fight at all, she thought, wincing at the slap of a foil on canvas.

Then inspiration struck, so suddenly that she stopped midform and Weasel's blade whacked her ribs.

There was a moment of confusion while he apologized to her at the same time she apologized to him, and Master Giles left off beating on Edoran to scold both of them for "all this sorry-ing."

"You're *supposed* to be trying to hit each other! If she gives you an opening, inside the bounds of the form, then take it and look for another! You're not on the dance floor! Though I couldn't swear to it, as badly as you fence. Again. One, guard, low, guard..."

As she went through the rest of the set Arisa thought about it, and the more she thought, the better she liked the idea.

When Master Giles finally gathered up their swords and departed, instead of letting Edoran slink away with Weasel, she followed them.

"I want to thank you again for last night," she told Edoran.

"It was nothing," he said coldly.

Once Arisa might have taken that for arrogance, but now she sensed the burning humiliation that lay behind his stiff expression.

Last night he had spared her even worse, so she made her voice as casual and friendly as she could when she went on,

"Anyway, I'd like to repay you, so I was thinking that if you like, I could teach you to fight with your left hand."

Color flooded Edoran's cheeks and she continued hastily, "It wouldn't interfere with your lessons with Master Giles. And I'm not a master or anything. But one of my teachers taught me how to counter a left-handed fighter, and I think I could teach you some of his moves."

"You couldn't do worse than old Giles," Weasel told her. "Not if you tried. Would you teach him knife fighting?"

"If he wants," said Arisa. "I'm better at that than I am with a sword. On the other hand, I don't see him getting into many knife fights."

"Odds are good I'll never fight a duel, either," said Edoran. "But I'm supposed to be prepared for it. Just in case." A sneer slipped into the last words, and Arisa grinned at the hint of rebellion.

"If you learn to fence left-handed, maybe you can surprise your opponent enough to get in a thrust before he . . . um."

But the set look was fading from Edoran's face, despite her lack of tact.

"Not in public," he said. "I don't want an audience. And I doubt that kind of privacy is possible, Mistress Benison."

"You never know unless you try," Arisa told him. "If I can find a place where no one but Weasel could watch us, would you show up?"

Edoran thought about it. "If you could perform such a miracle . . . Very well."

"Very well what? Is that a 'yes'?"

"Yes," said Edoran. "If you find us some privacy, I accept your offer."

"Good," said Weasel. "You need someone who'll actually teach you something."

In more ways than one, Arisa thought. If the prince could learn how to fight with a weapon, perhaps he could learn to fight in other ways as well.

One of the footmen caught her before she reached her room, but this time Arisa was delighted to hear that her lady mother wanted to see her. She strode off to her mother's office and knocked firmly on the door.

"Come in." The Falcon waited until Arisa had dropped into her usual chair before continuing mildly, "Your maid has complained to me. In fact she says you threatened to gut her with a dagger, which I have to admit seems like a legitimate cause for complaint."

Arisa snorted. "It was a pin. And she deserved—"

"You threatened to gut her with a pin?" The Falcon's lips twitched.

"I didn't threaten to gut her at all," said Arisa. "I only told her to get out. And I fired her."

The Falcon rubbed her chin, her expression thoughtful. "That's hard for you to do, since I'm the one who employs her."

"Well, she earned it! Did you hear what she did?"

"No," said the Falcon. "Should I have heard about it?"

Arisa opened her mouth, then paused, considering. If her

mother hadn't heard about it . . . If none of those self-absorbed courtiers had noticed . . . If Katrin hadn't spread the story all over the servants' hall . . .

The Falcon frowned. "In truth, I don't really want to know. What with pirates raiding a coastal village, I don't need to be bothered by squabbles with your maid."

"Pirates raided a village?" Arisa asked. "But they never raid ashore. They only take ships."

"It seems that's no longer true," the Falcon told her. "Pirates, or someone the survivors describe as looking and acting like a pirate crew, raided Helverton yesterday afternoon. We didn't hear about it till late last night, and Holis sent someone to investigate—and offer aid—first thing this morning. But as lord commander of the navy, the task of finding and stopping them falls to me."

"The survivors." Sick sorrow churned in the pit of Arisa's stomach. "That means there were deaths."

"Too many," said the Falcon. "And half the village burned into the bargain, but I'll get them. If I can do that, surely you can settle things with Katrin by yourself. Without violence, or threatening violence, even with pins. I don't think that's asking too much. Though I'm pleased to see you getting on better with the prince."

Arisa considered telling her mother about the fencing lessons, but she'd promised Edoran privacy—after what he'd done for her, she couldn't betray him by telling someone else . . . even if he'd never know about it.

Should she tell her mother her suspicions about Katrin? If her maid was trying to undermine the Falcon, wouldn't she have spread the story herself? Suspicion was all Arisa had—a pair of muddy shoes proved nothing.

"I'd rather you fired her," said Arisa slowly. "It would be simpler." And probably safer. Cast out of the palace, Katrin could do no further harm . . . and Arisa would never have a chance to learn who her true master was.

The Falcon sat back in her chair. "I know you're angry. And I know you well enough to accept that you have good reason to feel that way. But is your quarrel, whatever it is, worth ruining the woman's life? And perhaps impoverishing her family as well?"

"I said fired," Arisa protested, "not ruined. And what does her family have to do with it?"

"Who do you think will hire her, once it becomes known she was fired from the palace?" the Falcon asked. "No noblewoman will have her, that's for sure. Some rich merchant's wife in a distant town might take her on, but how could she find an employer in another town? And most of the servants are supporting families, even if they only get to go into the city to see them one day a week. You could do a lot of harm here, Ris."

Arisa sighed. "All right. You don't have to fire her."

"That's good," said the Falcon. "Because the servants don't forgive that kind of thing, and they have power too, in their own way. Look what happened to Prince Edoran."

"What happened to him?" Arisa asked.

"Well, maybe that isn't the right way to say it, because nothing happened *to* him, and it sounds like he deserved it. He evidently has a dislike for arcanara cards—I have no idea what that's about, but you probably shouldn't tell him you use them. Anyway, one of the maids was laying them out and he fired her for it. She had three children, and the family depended on her salary. The other servants never forgave him, not to this day, and that was almost five years ago."

"But . . . but he'd only have been ten years old then!" Arisa exclaimed. "How could the old regent let a ten-year-old fire anyone?"

"He was a ten-year-old prince," said the Falcon. "He's still a prince. Watch your step with him, Ris. I asked you to get close to him, but that's a real job. It's not going to be easy."

Katrin was waiting in Arisa's room when she returned, and helped her into a gown in icily correct silence. Her eyes glowed with triumph, but Arisa told herself that that was good. It would make her careless.

Arisa was late to her embroidery lesson. Anyone else would have scolded her, but Yallin just set her to stitching.

Arisa thought about the events of the night and morning. The hour was almost over before she realized she'd hardly spoken a word the entire time—and Yallin had given her the quiet she needed.

"Thank you," she said. She would have explained what she was thanking her teacher for, but Yallin smiled.

"It's good to have something to occupy your hands, when

your mind is busy." And she didn't ask what Arisa had been thinking about, the Lady bless her.

"Yallin, my . . . I was told that the prince had a maid fired, some years ago. But he was only a child then! Did Regent Pettibone really fire that girl, just because a ten-year-old asked him to?"

Yallin sighed. "Yes, he fired her. But young Edoran didn't just ask—he threw a screaming fit! You could hear him all over the palace, and him usually so quiet. A mouse of a boy, creeping here and there. But not that day."

"But why? Just because she was laying out arcanara cards? Why would he care?"

He hadn't cared when Arisa laid out her cards. He'd objected at first, but soon he'd gotten involved in it.

"In fairness to the prince," said Yallin, "he'd forbidden anyone to lay out the cards, first in his presence, then anywhere in the palace, many times. But the fool girl refused to take him seriously and kept on with it. They say that he was so hysterical the regent feared he'd make himself ill. And they also say Edoran calmed right down once he got his way." Her lips primmed disapprovingly. "It was a hardship for the lass, no mistake."

Arisa frowned. "I also heard that the servants never forgave him for it. If he did it deliberately I can see why, and he was wrong. But if he was only ten . . ."

"Just turned ten," said Yallin. "His birthday ball had been held a week before." Her needle flashed in and out.

A formal ball wasn't something most boys wanted for their tenth birthday, but that was beside the point.

"Why did he do it?" Arisa asked. "Why would he care so much about her laying out the cards? About anyone laying out cards?"

"I don't know," said Yallin. "Not for certain, though I've a guess or two. But I can tell you that that temper fit was an extreme action for the young prince. And when people take extreme actions, it's usually because they're very angry, or very frightened. Or both."

It lent more weight to the Falcon's admonition for Arisa to watch her step with the prince. But Arisa owed him, and he'd agreed to come, so later that afternoon she tracked down Sammel, whom she found brushing horses in the stable.

When he asked why she needed a room for fencing, when the prince already had a whole salon and the best master in the realm, she told him. Only the occasional stamp of hooves disrupted the stillness, and it felt natural to tell Sammel her troubles. If she'd closed her eyes, they might have been back in one of the bandit camps where she'd spent her childhood. She had no hesitation about exposing the prince's ineptitude, for she knew Sammel would never reveal or exploit it. Not that her mother would, of course, but Sammel was . . . Sammel.

"Seems to me," he said calmly, "that if that's how royalty's supposed to be taught, then you've no call to interfere." The brush in his hand moved smoothly over the mare's brown rump.

"I don't care about supposed," said Arisa. "It's not working. And I think it would do him good to know he could defend himself—even if he never needs to do it."

"It does most good to be able to," said Sammel, "whether they use it or not. I'm just surprised, given what I've heard of the lad, that he wants t' learn."

"What you've heard from the servants," said Arisa slowly. "They don't think much of the prince, do they?"

Sammel snorted. "That's putting it mild. And servants know their masters better than any, or so they say."

"*They* don't always tell the truth," said Arisa. "What do you think of the prince, Sammel?"

"Of my own knowledge, you mean? I don't know much," the groom admitted. "He's a good rider, and handles a horse well. Gentle hands, and never needs the spur. He's a light weight in the saddle too, which horses like."

The soft swish of horses' tails filled the silence for a time.

"It seems odd," said Sammel slowly, "that a lad that rides a horse so light would ride his servants hard."

"It does, doesn't it."

Sammel sighed. "All right, I'll find you a place. I'll have to check 'em out—and likely clean it as well!—but I can think of a couple of places that might do."

Three days later Arisa received a message from "the groom Henley" that the bridle she'd asked for would be ready the next time she and the prince went for a ride.

Arisa passed the word to Weasel and Edoran in court that evening. It worked out well, for the next day was Mansday, when they had no lessons, although Edoran was supposed to attend the speaking of the court's priest.

Arisa, who'd been raised in the countryside where the worship of the One God was a casual affair at best, preferred to avoid the cold stone chapel. Weasel, who'd been raised in the city, usually went—though Arisa thought that was more to "support" Edoran than from faith. Weasel had once told her that the One God hadn't treated him so well that he owed him any prayers.

Arisa would have spent a fair morning walking or riding in the palace park, but the cold rain discouraged walking, and might discourage the prince from riding out as well.

Still, Arisa ignored Katrin's scowl and changed into her britches when the time arrived. She also refused her good jacket and pulled her shabby, but much warmer coat from the wardrobe. If the rain stopped Edoran and Weasel, she was restless enough to ride without them.

But when she reached the stable yard, they were already mounted and waiting for her.

"I thought the rain might keep you in," she said, walking around the puddles to join them.

"He rides in almost any weather," said Weasel, jerking his head to indicate the prince. "Idiot that he is."

Edoran smiled slightly. "It will let up in less than an hour."

Arisa looked at the sky. It didn't look like it was letting up, but Sammel was leading Honey out of the stable.

"So, Master Henley," said Arisa, in her best lady-voice. "Where can we ride in this muddy stuff?"

Sammel's lips twitched. "You might head round the old wing

of the palace. The ground's a bit higher there. Not so much mud. Of course, you'd have to avoid the old stable. Not that it's not sound. In fact, the gardeners keep a couple of mules there, but there's not much gardening this time of year so you'd likely not meet them."

Several other grooms frowned at this—the palace gardeners would keep out of the prince's way wherever he rode. And if they didn't, Arisa was sure Sammel would arrange something to keep them away.

"Thank you," she said. "We'll give it a try."

Edoran took the lead, for there was no bridle path through the rocky ground around the old wing, only a few tracks—probably made by the gardeners' mules.

"I already knew where the old stable is," Edoran told them as they drew near the shabby-looking building. "Though I haven't been inside for years. I used to play around the old wing when I was young, exploring and such."

Had he gone on those youthful expeditions alone? If he'd had any friends before Weasel, Arisa hadn't heard of them. And even Weasel, like Arisa herself, had been ordered to befriend the prince. Of course Justice Holis had probably guessed that Weasel, who had a much softer heart than he'd ever admit, would soon befriend the prince in earnest. Either that, Arisa had thought, or murder him.

When she first met Edoran, Arisa had believed that hanging for regicide was probably the better choice of the two. Sometimes Weasel was wiser than she was.

She pulled Honey to a stop at the stable door. "Let's check it out."

There were no walls inside the building, just one big room with stalls lining the far end, and open space in front of the doors.

"We can put our horses in the empty stalls," said Edoran, leading his mare forward. One of the three mules already stabled there brayed a greeting, and Honey pranced.

"This roof is *thatched*," city-bred Weasel complained. "And it's leaking."

"Not badly," said Arisa. "There's nothing wrong with thatch, if it's maintained. Well, it attracts mice, but they won't bother us."

"Look at that hearth." Weasel examined the huge fireplace that occupied most of the end wall. "This was a kitchen once, wasn't it?"

"It was turned into a secondary stable when the kitchens were moved inside," Edoran confirmed. He finished loosening his saddle girth—something Arisa was surprised he knew how to do—and then led Weasel's gelding into another stall. "It was mostly abandoned when the new stables were built."

The new stables had been built centuries ago, but this place, like the old castle, had been constructed to last. The thatch might leak—there was a puddle several inches deep in one corner—but the floor was solid. It would do, Arisa decided. She lifted the blanket that covered something in one of the drier corners and discovered half a dozen crudely carved practice swords.

It would definitely do.

"This is heavy," Edoran protested, lifting one of the swords. "It's heavier than a metal foil."

Arisa grimaced. "At our level of skill"—*or lack thereof*—"that doesn't matter. In fact, it's better that it's heavy and unbalanced, because controlling it will strengthen our arms and wrists. And with wood there's less chance we'll hurt each other."

Weasel snorted. "There's not much chance of that, anyway. What next, Sword Mistress Benison?"

"Now," said Arisa, "we work on drills, just like the ones Master Giles has Weasel and me doing. Except you, Edoran, are going to do them with your left hand, which means Weasel will have to modify his parries. Do you remember the exercises you did when you first started learning?"

Edoran's face was closing down. "I never did drills."

Arisa felt her jaw sag. "Never? Not even in the beginning?"

Edoran stiffened. "I don't lie."

The full arrogance of the royal house infused those words, but . . . had someone accused him of lying in the past?

"No matter," said Arisa. "You're going to do them now. Take a stance and extend your blade, leading with the left foot, since the sword's in your left hand. Good. Now, when Weasel thrusts high, you parry like this."

The few left-handed moves she knew soon came back to her—simple ripostes to the most basic right-handed thrusts. She wouldn't need anything more complex for some time, Arisa realized as the lesson continued, for Weasel was a rank beginner, and fighting left-handed, Edoran was too. He not only had no practice with the hand he should have been fighting with from the start, but . . .

"This isn't working," Edoran panted. He put down his sword and rubbed his wrist and forearm—again. "This is worse than fighting right-handed!"

"That's because you don't have much strength in that arm," Arisa told him. "You haven't been using it, so your right arm is actually stronger and more practiced than the left. It takes time to build up. Time for the moves to become automatic, to become part of you."

"How would you know?" Edoran grumbled.

Was she going to lose him? If he wouldn't do the work she'd lose him anyway, and the sooner the better.

"I know," said Arisa, "because—"

"'Cause she's a better fighter than you'll ever be." Sammel's voice came from the open door. "That's no shame to you, lad," he added, as Edoran flushed. "She's one of the best fighters any of us . . . Ah, Your Highness, I mean. My apologies for interrupting, but you've been gone almost two hours and the head groom's beginning to wonder. He'll be sending someone to look for you soon."

"Has it been that long?" Arisa's gaze flew to the doors. The overcast sky gave little clue to the time, but the rain had stopped. Stopped some time ago, she realized. No wonder Edoran's arm was tired. "We'd better go! But you did well, Edoran. Really well, for the first day."

She meant to encourage him, but it was also true. He wasn't a natural fighter, as her mother's men had claimed she was, but he wasn't a disaster. What had Master Giles been thinking, making him train right-handed all these years?

Arisa and Edoran tightened up the horses' girths, and Sammel checked on Edoran's—but he kept it from being obvious by checking hers as well.

Edoran watched him in frowning silence. Arisa thought he might take offense, for no one likes to see someone checking their work, but then the prince spoke. "This is far beyond your duty, Henley. I thank you for it."

Sammel shrugged. "My duty is t' do what Your Highness wants done."

"Will you answer a question then?" Edoran asked. "A question for a man who knows horses?"

Sammel glanced at him warily. "I know horses."

Edoran drew a breath. "How could someone make a horse fall?"

Sammel looked down, making a quite unnecessary adjustment to Weasel's stirrup. "There's a couple of ways. A rope across the path, at about knee height, is the most common. But even if no one sees the rope at the time, it would mark the horse's legs. There's no way I know of that leaves no marks at all."

The prince's obsession with his father's death was clearly known to the servants, too. Arisa couldn't suppress a flash of pity. But his father's death was a proven accident, and even if it wasn't, the man Edoran thought had arranged it was dead!

He was the one who needed a real job, Arisa thought, as she mounted Honey and rode out through the tall doors. Something to get his mind off his fantasies, something important to do ... In short, he needed a cause!

She grinned as Honey plodded onto the muddy track. At least the rain had obeyed Edoran's prediction—and that was downright creepy!

However, he had also sensed something to the south, and as far as Arisa knew there had been no storm in that area, no building-breaking snow, no ship-sinking winds. So he wasn't always—

Helverton was to the south.

Edoran had sensed the pirate raid.

Arisa lay awake in the darkness, staring at the ceiling above her bed. It might have been because the rain had kept her from walking, and she hadn't expended much energy leading Weasel and Edoran through the forms. It might have been the tea the maid had served at the dinner they'd shared, just Arisa and her mother, since there was no evening court on Mansday.

It might even have been guilt at the number of things she hadn't told her mother, that kept Arisa lying wakeful long past the time she usually slept.

But mostly, it was because Edoran had sensed the pirate raid. A few questions had confirmed that the raid had begun at exactly the same time Edoran's head had swiveled toward the south and stayed there. Or at least, his attention had stayed there.

If he'd known what was happening, or even that something was very badly wrong, why hadn't he spoken up? If he'd raced his horse back to the palace, ordered out troops and aid . . . no one would have believed a word of it.

Arisa shivered. How horrible, to sense something terrible happening and not be able to help. But if he'd tried, if he'd insisted, if he'd issued commands as the prince who in seven years would be king, might some of those lost lives have been saved?

He should have tried!

Arisa turned onto her side, giving her pillow an irritable thump.

He should have tried, no matter what it cost, no matter how crazy people would think him.

So why hadn't she revealed his gift to her mother?

He would have denied it, and she would have looked like an idiot, but shouldn't *she* have tried? It seemed unfair to blame him for cowardice when she . . .

A dark form flitted across Arisa's balcony, swung a leg over the railing, and vanished.

For a moment she lay still, unable to believe what she'd seen, then she flung off the covers and raced to the balcony doors. Her eyes searched the moon-drenched lawns. Nothing stirred, but Katrin might still be climbing down the vines. Or wearing too-tight corsets might have turned Arisa's brain and she was hallucinating the whole thing, including Edoran's gift for sensing pirate raids, her maid's treachery, and that nagging feeling that the old king's death might not have been an accident after all.

She pressed down the door handle to step out onto the balcony and make sure, but even as the latch clicked, a dark cloaked figure hurried across the lawn toward the trees of the park.

Arisa smiled grimly and went to get her clothes.

CHAPTER 7

THE SIX OF WATERS

The Six of Waters: the stranger.
Someone arrives, welcome or not.

7

By the time she came out onto the balcony, the dark figure had vanished into the trees. Arisa would have been frantic, if she hadn't had a pretty good idea where she could catch up with her maid. She swung her leg over the balcony rail and groped for hand- and footholds among the vines.

It was harder climbing down than she'd expected, and she was wearing britches and boots! She couldn't imagine doing it in skirts, as Katrin had. Finally she was able to release the rough, tangled vines and jump down.

She raced across the lawn and into the trees. If she didn't catch up with Katrin at the wall, where Weasel had once showed her the easiest place to climb over, she'd never be able to find her.

And if Katrin used some other route to escape the palace grounds, the chase was over already.

It was hard, alone in the dark, to find the place where the ancient stones had crumbled enough to give a determined climber a couple of good holds. It was even harder to climb it without Weasel's helping hands, but when Arisa pulled her head over the top, the cloaked figure was just turning into a side street, two blocks away.

Arisa scrambled up to the top of the wall and dropped to the other side, stumbling on the rough cobbles. Then she ran.

When she reached the street where Katrin had turned, Arisa slowed to a walk before skidding around the corner. Her maid was walking swiftly, about a block and a half ahead of Arisa. In this quiet neighborhood there was no one else on the street. If she stayed back far enough to keep Katrin from recognizing her face, she'd probably be taken for a shop boy coming home from a late delivery. Still, Katrin would be suspicious if the same person followed her for too long.

But the maid never looked back, and as they traveled into the commercial streets more people appeared. The shops were closed, but some of the craft yards still echoed with voices, thuds, and clangs as men worked to complete an urgent order. The taverns were open, doing a thriving business.

As the streets became more crowded, Arisa picked up her pace, narrowing the distance between her and her maid. On this cool night almost a third of the people on the street were wearing long cloaks, and she almost lost sight of Katrin several times. At least it wasn't raining, and wasn't likely to start, Arisa thought, although the moon winked in and out of the scudding clouds.

Soon the neighborhood grew rougher, and the streets even busier. Judging by the scent of brine, Arisa thought they must be nearing the docks. Fewer people wore cloaks here, and some of the men who swaggered past smelled of brandy or gin. Arisa pulled her knife to the front of her belt, and walked with her hand resting on the hilt. She wished she'd taken the time to grab a hat instead of just tying her hair back, but she wasn't so pretty that a single glance on a darkish night would reveal her gender.

A rotund man who reeked of fish wandered into her path. Arisa whisked around him and found that Katrin had stopped, and was looking back over the street. Her heart thudded into her throat, but it was too late to do anything but keep walking. Still half a block back, she managed to drift back behind the fishmonger as she strolled, much more slowly now.

If Katrin had recognized her she gave no sign of it. If, of course, it was Katrin she followed. Arisa had yet to see her quarry's face in the shadow of the hood—she'd feel pretty silly if she was following some other maid, off to a romantic tryst or a visit to her home.

The cloaked figure—whoever it was—turned and walked briskly onward, but Arisa maintained her slow pace, allowing the distance between them to increase. Now she kept one eye open for cover, as well as watching her quarry. When Katrin stopped again, Arisa leaped into a nearby doorway—where, she immediately realized, she had no way to see when Katrin stopped looking and started walking! The seconds dragged past. Surely it was too dark for Katrin to see much at this distance. Arisa peeked out, just in time to see Katrin turn down yet another side street. Arisa raced to the end of the block, ignoring the stares and startled curses. When she reached the street where Katrin had vanished, she stopped and peered carefully around the corner.

The maid was walking more quickly now. There were fewer people on this narrow lane, but it was darker as well and there was no help for it. Arisa followed, trying to keep behind a tipsy sailor and his lady friend. But they moved too slowly, and she was about to pass them when Katrin stopped in front of a busy tavern. Arisa darted behind a stack of barrels and crouched there, while her maid studied the dark street for several minutes.

Then she went up to the tavern door and knocked. Peering between the barrels, Arisa had a perfect view as the door opened. Light streamed out, along with a burst of conversation and laughter. Katrin stepped forward and hugged the large craggy-faced man who held the door.

At least it *was* Katrin. The cloak's hood had fallen back, and Katrin smiled up at the man as he passed her inside. But that warm greeting looked more like a friend's welcome than the prelude to a meeting with a sinister employer. Had Katrin just gone home to visit her family? The door closed, leaving the street dark and still. If she was just going home, why climb down from the balcony in the middle of the night? Even if it wasn't her off day, surely she could have made up an errand to take her into the city while Arisa was at her lessons.

A pair of men came down the street and knocked on the door, greeting the doorman cheerfully, though without hugs. Arisa watched as they were admitted. In country villages most taverns left their doors open for customers to come and go, but she knew that in larger towns, especially in rough neighborhoods, they sometimes had a man who minded the door and kept out those who appeared too quarrelsome.

Which probably meant this was the kind of tavern her mother wouldn't want her going into, but that wouldn't have stopped her. The doorman was another matter, for in the tavern's spill of light he'd certainly see that she was a girl. He would comment, and that would attract Katrin's attention, and then . . . No, she couldn't go in.

The cold cobbles dug into Arisa's knees, so she worked her way in behind the barrels until she found a place she could sit and watch the tavern door. Perhaps Katrin was meeting her employer here, and if it was one of the courtiers, Arisa might recognize him. Or her. Or them.

More than a dozen people went in or out of the tavern in the next hour or so, and Arisa didn't recognize one of them. Judging by their clothes, they belonged to the neighborhood and were probably regular customers. She learned that the doorman's name was Stu. She learned that about one in four of the people who entered or left looked around the street first, just as Katrin had. Which might mean they were fellow conspirators. Or that they were smart enough to be wary in a tough part of the city after dark. Or it might mean nothing whatsoever.

Her rump was numb from the cold stones, and her toes were freezing. Still, it seemed a shame to leave without learning anything. The fact that Katrin had sneaked out at night to visit a tavern wouldn't impress her mother, or anyone else.

Footsteps rang on the stones, and Arisa leaned forward to observe yet another tavern customer. This one was a shortish man, his clothes rough and dark like everyone else's, and he didn't look around before he knocked. But Arisa gasped when the light from the opening door flooded his face. *Master Darian?*

"Hello, Stu. Quiet night?"

The tavern was far from quiet, for several men were belting out a drinking song, but Stu nodded as he drew the man inside and closed the door.

Arisa realized she was holding her breath and let it go. She no longer felt the cold.

Master Darian had been banished from Deorthas on pain of death! Banished for complicity in Regent Pettibone's crimes, and spared only because he'd testified against his master, offering proof after proof that the old regent's summary execution had been justified.

What was he doing here? Pettibone was dead. What kind of plot could he be involved in? A plot involving Arisa's maid? It was ludicrous! Of course, he would have known all of the old regent's allies and supporters. Most of whom were probably Holis' and the Falcon's enemies at court!

But what could be worth risking a death sentence? Whatever it was, it had to be bigger than embarrassing the Falcon by making Arisa look bad. So much bigger that Arisa began to doubt her eyes. After all, she'd only seen the man once, and he'd been cowering in the corner, begging for his life. Perhaps this was just someone who looked like him.

The next visitor to the tavern appeared to be a local, but the one after that wore tall polished boots under his cloak. When he was admitted, Arisa glimpsed the white britches of a naval officer.

It was possible for a naval officer to visit a rough tavern in all innocence, but Arisa was sure now. Something was going on here. Someone was working against her mother, against Justice Holis' regency. Perhaps against Edoran himself.

She watched for another hour as people came and went—but more and more were leaving. Soon Katrin would come out, and Arisa knew she'd better be back in her own bed before her maid crossed the balcony. She'd been lucky that Katrin hadn't spotted her on the way here—she shouldn't push that luck any further.

But there was one more thing she had to do, and the moon was out now, the street quiet. Rising slowly from her hiding place, stiff with cold, Arisa crept to the tavern door and gazed up at the sign, struggling to read in the dim light.

She'd tried before, when the door had opened, but the sign hung too high for the light to reach it. She had to be certain she could find this place again, in the daylight.

Squinting upward, she brought the faded letters into focus: King's Folly. What an odd—

Lightning flashed over the sky, blinding her, and thunder crashed like the gods' own cannon.

Arisa jumped, and a handful of fat drops splattered down. So much for her ability to predict the weather. Lightning was rare in winter storms, but it flashed again, and the rain fell harder.

Arisa turned and hurried into the darkness.

CHAPTER 8

THE THREE OF STARS

The Three of Stars: the trial.
Judgment of a person or situation—make it wisely.

8

The next morning Arisa slept right through Master Giles' fencing lesson, and she might have slept through her embroidery lesson as well if Katrin hadn't brought in her breakfast tray.

Arisa, watching surreptitiously, couldn't see any difference in the maid's behavior. But why should Katrin behave differently? It was Arisa whose knowledge had changed.

With Katrin's cool assistance, Arisa reached Yallin's quiet parlor on time, but she was so distracted she had to redo half her stitches.

She still had no evidence to present to her mother. She was certain she'd seen Master Darian meet with a naval officer. Or she was almost certain it was Master Darian, and she thought it was a naval officer. A fleeting glimpse in a tavern doorway, of a man she'd seen briefly several months ago. At a time when she'd been so preoccupied with her own survival that she'd paid scant attention to Master Darian.

In the prosaic light of morning—and a dreary, drizzly morning it was—she wasn't sure. If Justice Holis sent out investigators, and they found nothing but an innocent tavern and a man who looked like Master Darian (who was a very ordinary man, curse him), Arisa would look like a total fool. Without any help from Katrin at all. But if she didn't tell her mother and something horrible happened, it would be her fault.

Arisa glared down at the uneven stitches straggling over the pillow slip, swore, and slipped her needle free of the thread to pull them out.

"At this rate, that pillow slip will end up more hole than cloth," Yallin commented.

"I'm sorry," said Arisa. "I can't seem to concentrate today."

"Having trouble making a decision?"

"What are you, some kind of witch?" Arisa demanded. "How do you keep reading my mind?"

Yallin laughed. "You've got one of the most open faces I've ever seen, girl. I hope you find yourself some position beyond courtier; you'd make a terrible liar, and being a courtier is all about lies."

"I don't want to be a courtier at all," Arisa told her. "And I can lie just fine, if I have to."

Yallin smiled. "Maybe. When you're thinking about it. But if you're having trouble making a decision, don't just spin on it—get yourself some help."

"You mean ask someone about it?" Arisa frowned. She couldn't talk to her mother, because whether or not to tell her mother was the problem. And while Sammel was fine for most things, he would never keep a secret from the Falcon.

Weasel would listen, and keep her confidence too, but . . . He hadn't been there. He hadn't seen Master Darian, silhouetted in the lamplight. He wouldn't believe that Regent Pettibone's terrified clerk would ever return to Deorthas. Arisa wasn't certain she believed it.

"There's no one I can tell," she said slowly. "No one would believe me."

She expected that Yallin would promise to believe her, but that was like someone promising not to laugh. They always laughed, and belief wasn't something you could guarantee in advance.

"Then seek the gods' guidance," Yallin told her. "They'd not have to believe you because they already know the truth."

"You mean lay out the cards?" Arisa asked.

"I'll even lend you my deck," said Yallin, "since it's plain I won't get any work out of you till this is settled."

She dug into her sewing kit and pulled out a deck that looked even older than Arisa's.

"I didn't know you had those," Arisa said. "Edoran won't like it. You could be fired for it."

"He won't know, unless you tell him." Yallin held out the deck, and suddenly the need to lay them out, to get some guidance she could rely on, was irresistible.

Arisa swept her sewing off the table and began to shuffle, thinking about her dilemma as she did. Then she cut the deck and leaned forward to lay the top card.

"The storm," Yallin murmured. "Is that often your significator?"

"Almost always," said Arisa. Her withe was working, she could feel it. Today the cards would tell her true. "This supports me. Oh, not again!"

The traitor lay beneath the storm.

"I'd not think that would support anyone," Yallin said.

"Last time he was inspiring me," Arisa told her. "But . . . this makes some sense."

Darian hadn't betrayed his master till after the old regent was dead, but he was traitor enough for Arisa. She didn't exactly rely on him, but her current dilemma did.

"This inspires me," she went on, and laid the four of waters above the storm. "Choice. That's perfectly clear, because I have to make one."

"Hmm." Yallin's lips pressed together, deepening the wrinkles around her mouth.

"This misleads me," said Arisa, laying a card to the storm's far left. "Solitude?"

"Solitude can mislead you," Yallin told her. "Few people are as alone as they think they are."

"Well, this will guide me true. Jealousy?"

Arisa stared at the card, where a dark-haired girl peered out of a cottage window at her fairer sister, who sat in a garden surrounded by laughing suitors.

"That's . . . unexpected," said Yallin.

"No," said Arisa. "Not entirely." She had felt alone in the palace, and been jealous of Katrin's close ties, her friendships with so many of the servants. The cards were telling Arisa that she wasn't as alone as she'd been feeling, and that her mistrust of Katrin was justified.

"This threatens me." Arisa held her breath as the wheel of fortune fell to the storm's far right. "Which does make sense, since acts of random chance can always threaten you."

Yallin frowned at the card. "The wheel is major arcana. It's warning you about a specific act of chance, something you need to watch out for."

"But if it's an act of chance," said Arisa, "then all I can do is try to be ready when it happens. And this"—she laid the final card between the wheel and the storm—"will protect me. Growth will protect me?"

"It's not just growth," said Yallin. "It's the increase of anything through work. That's why it shows a farmer in his field, instead of plants growing wild."

"So to protect myself I need to work. To get more information before I take action."

Yallin eyed her thoughtfully. "That helps with your decision? It looks a little ambiguous to me."

"That settles it," said Arisa. "It's just the answer I was looking for. I need real evi—information, before I can act. The cards almost always tell me true. I have a bit of withe."

"So it seems," Yallin said. "I always wondered if Edoran didn't have some withe. If that's why the cards frightened him so."

Arisa remembered the prince sensing the pirate raid, and his accurate weather predictions. "I think you're right. But if that's true, he should be glad of it! He should use it, instead of fighting it."

"That depends," said Yallin, "on what it's made of him, as well as what he makes of it."

Yallin took the deck from Arisa, shuffled once, and cut the cards.

"Astray," Arisa murmured. "The true path lost, the wrong decision." She stared at the image of a road vanishing into inky darkness, and shivered.

The storm that had started when she'd stood looking at the tavern sign was still drizzling down that afternoon, when Arisa went out to join Weasel and the prince for their "horseback ride."

"I suppose it's going to rain like this all day?" Arisa asked Edoran as she swung into the saddle.

"I have no idea!" Edoran snapped.

"You don't have to be so touchy about it." She wondered if he really didn't know, or if he did and didn't want to admit it. Part of her despised his refusal to face up to his gift, but another part remembered how she'd felt at the prospect of telling her mother that she thought there was a desperate plot going on, but she didn't know what it was, or who it was aimed at, or have any solid evidence that it even existed. No, she couldn't despise Edoran.

Her coat was wet by the time they reached the old stable and led their horses into the stalls.

"Working will warm us up," Arisa told them firmly, and Weasel grimaced.

They hung their clammy coats on an old harness rack and began their exercises, though today Arisa fenced with Weasel and Edoran in turn. It gave them a chance to watch someone who was doing it wrong, and someone who was doing it . . . if not right, at least better.

Then they went through the forms together and she corrected them.

"You're doing better today," she told Edoran, and his whole face brightened—as if he'd never been praised before.

"What about me?" Weasel protested.

Arisa pursed her lips. "You're not trying as hard. That's why you're not improving as fast. If you'd focus more . . ."

Edoran looked even more pleased, and Weasel groaned.

Arisa worked both boys till they were sweating, then decreed a rest. "Though not long. I don't want you to cool down too much."

"You'd think she was talking about horses," Edoran told Weasel. His voice was mournful, but Arisa saw the laughter in his eyes.

"That's a compliment," Weasel told him. "She likes horses more than either rich nobles or city-bred scum."

"Horses," Arisa told them primly, "are useful, friendly, and courageous." She left the rest of the comparison unsaid, but Weasel laughed and Edoran actually grinned.

Maybe now, when he was relaxed. "I'd like to ask you a few questions," Arisa told the prince. "About the pirate raid."

Edoran's expression closed. "I don't know any more than you do."

"You may not know more," Arisa persisted. "But you sensed it when it happened. It was obvious—"

"I have no idea what you're talking about," Edoran said firmly.

Weasel snorted. "If you're going to lie, you need to learn to do it convincingly. First, you have to come up with another explanation for what the witness saw. Like, 'I wasn't trying to pick his pocket! He'd just put his pipe in there, and I was checking to make sure it was out. You wouldn't want the man to catch fire, would you, Master Guardsman, sir?'"

Edoran laughed aloud, and Arisa let the subject change. But later, fencing with Edoran while Weasel observed them, she tried again.

"Since Weasel and I both know, why can't you talk about it? It's not like you have to convince us. We already believe you."

Edoran's guard faltered and Arisa swung the wooden blade and tapped his ribs. Not hard, not yet. There was a place for bruises in training, but that didn't come until the student was good enough to defend himself. Besides, she had a feeling Edoran had taken enough blows for a lifetime.

The prince brought his sword back up, but his eyes were wary. "I don't know what you're talking about. But if I did, I'd ask why you care. It's not as if you could use it for anything."

She'd gotten through to him! "It might have been used." Arisa carefully banished triumph from her voice. "It might have been used to get troops and assistance on the road that afternoon, instead of the next morning. They might have been able to save lives, or capture someone, or find a clue, or ..."

Edoran's gaze was very dark, the expression under his contained blankness so hopelessly despairing that Arisa's voice faltered. She lowered her sword.

"I'm sorry. I don't know that anything could have been changed. It probably couldn't, but sooner is better than later. And someday it might make a diff—"

Edoran's blade flashed in and struck her sword arm, not quite hard enough to hurt, but the warning was there.

"You'd call a man with a sword in his hand a liar? That's quite a challenge, Mistress Benison."

Arisa raised her blade. "You're not a man yet. And as for the sword . . ."

She broke from the form, fencing in earnest, though not as fast as she could have. Teaching him to fight back was her real goal and that was what he was doing now, no matter how awkwardly he went about it.

They danced back and forth through the old stable, with Edoran pushing her as often as she pushed him—she refused to chase him around the room as Master Giles had. And slowly, his eyes grew brighter.

He knew that she could have taken him, and his scrambling attacks became more elaborate, almost playful. But soon his laughter faded into thick panting and Arisa ended it, tangling his blade in hers and sweeping it out of his grip.

Edoran folded his arms and sneered. "You have me at your mercy, villain, but I defy you! You'll never learn the secret path to the treasure of Abadabadan from me!"

"So I'm the villain, am I?" Arisa drawled. "Then I might as well take villainous retribution!"

The prince was standing with his back to a pile of straw. It would have been irresistible even if she hadn't been the villain. She cast her sword aside and tackled Edoran into the haystack.

He yelped in astonishment as he went down, and then yelped louder as Arisa set about learning all the places he was ticklish.

She was much better at wrestling than she was with a sword, and though she hadn't had a good tickle match since she'd turned twelve, it wasn't something you forgot.

With Weasel's snickers echoing in her ears, she soon learned that Edoran's ribs were vulnerable but the soles of his feet less so—hardly worth the trouble of pulling off his boots.

And since one of the rules of a tickle match was to give your opponent a fair chance, she too had lost a boot, and Edoran had discovered just how sensitive her toes were. She had pinned one of his wrists in her bent knee and was trying to catch his other hand to finish the game, when a pair of strong hands grabbed her shoulder and belt and pulled her from the straw.

"What's going on here?" a furious voice demanded.

"I think that's obvious." Master Giles' voice came from just above her ear.

There were half a dozen shareholders present, including Ethgar. Arisa thought about what Ronelle and Danica would make of this, and winced. She wiped her tumbled hair out of her face. Edoran had pulled off the leather tie sometime during their struggle, and her hair was full of snarls and straw.

Lord Ethgar restrained Weasel, with one hand clamped over his mouth and the other pinning his arms. He was half again

Weasel's height and twice his weight—but unfortunately for him, he didn't have Weasel's brains.

Arisa watched in considerable satisfaction as Weasel's heel smashed down on Ethgar's foot, and he swore and let him go.

Too late for any warning.

The courtiers who extracted Edoran from the straw pile were more respectful than Master Giles, but not by much. Most of them, like Ethgar, were the older, more powerful shareholders, and if their fingers weren't digging into Edoran's arms, their expressions were sternly disapproving.

Arisa considered Master Giles' grip on her, then broke it with a single deft twist and stepped away. He started to reach for her again, met her eyes, and changed his mind. Or thought of something worse, for the nastiest smile Arisa had ever seen curved up the corners of his mouth.

"Sorry to interrupt your . . . sport, Mistress Benison. But as one of the prince's tutors, his conduct is my responsibility."

Sport? Yes, he meant exactly what she thought he meant. "You're disgusting," Arisa told him coldly.

"You're stupid, too," Weasel added. "Do you really think they'd be rutting in the straw, with me sitting here watching them?"

A couple of the courtiers looked doubtful, and Master Giles' face darkened. "I know nothing of the prince's taste in these matters, for I, the One God be thanked, am his sword master not his guardian! Gentlemen, shall we put this matter into the hands of the regent and the lord commander?"

Agreement rumbled around the room. It would do no good

to argue or explain, Arisa realized. These men were her mother's and Justice Holis' enemies. She made careful note of their faces as they bustled her and the two boys outside, taking their horses' reins to lead them back as if they were infants. Or prisoners.

Edoran's expression was so arrogantly bored that Arisa began to wonder how much trouble they were in. And how had they known where the prince was? And what he was doing? Was Katrin spying on them? Giles? Some courtier? Whoever their enemy was, he'd gained ground today.

During the short ride back, Arisa tried to pull the straw from her hair, but she knew she hadn't gotten all of it by the time they reached the stable yard and Master Giles dragged her from the saddle.

Edoran was allowed to dismount and walk without a heavy hand on his shoulder, but two shareholders gripped Weasel's arms—and kept their toes well out of his reach, Arisa noted. She had seen Weasel terrified, grieving, and furious, but she'd never seen him look so helplessly angry and frustrated as he did now.

Her own expression probably mirrored his—she knew how to fight, but how could you defend yourself against an enemy who used gossip and innuendo as his weapons?

With truth! she thought hotly. You fought by revealing them for the treacherous lying toads they were.

With no evidence to prove it?

After today, anything she said about these men, any accusation she made would be taken for spite, unless she had hard evidence to back it up.

Did they know that? Were they deliberately discrediting her?

Arisa was feeling much more somber when they finally reached the regent's office.

There were voices speaking behind the door, and Master Giles hesitated. Then his hand tightened on Arisa's shoulder and he stepped forward and knocked.

Justice Holis' clerk, Kenton, opened it. "The regent is occupied now. Can I assist you?"

"No," said Master Giles, shoving Arisa into the room. "This is a matter the regent must attend to himself."

The room was full of well-dressed men, seated around a long table. A few of them had risen to their feet, their faces flushed as if they'd been arguing.

Her mother was there, the Lady be thanked, looking sardonic. When she saw Arisa her brows rose sharply, and an expression Arisa couldn't interpret dawned in her eyes.

Justice Holis—Regent Holis, she supposed—rose to his feet as Weasel and the prince were pulled into the room. His worried frown deepened.

"Gentlemen, forgive me, but it appears something has come up. I know this matter is important, but we can resume shortly . . . ?"

So much for putting it off. The men departed, casting curious glances at all of them, though they mostly looked at the prince and the straw in Arisa's hair. She could feel the rumor growing, without even hearing the first word.

The Falcon hadn't stirred from her chair, and when the last

of the meeting vanished she turned her gaze to Master Giles. "Might I ask, sir, why your hand is on my daughter?"

Her voice was mild, and Master Giles was the best swordsman in the realm, but he let go of Arisa's shoulder as if it had suddenly become hot.

Ethgar cleared his throat. "Forgive the interruption, lord commander, but we're here to inform you and the regent of a serious problem—before it becomes a disaster! A disaster for the prince—perhaps for all of Deorthas. A—"

Arisa had had enough. "This is rot," she said clearly. "All I was doing was teaching Edoran to fence. When I knocked his sword away we ended up wrestling. But even if we'd been coupling, so what? Half the kings of Deorthas have produced illegits. Even if he wanted to marry me, which he doesn't and I wouldn't, *so what*? He can marry anyone he wants. His father proved that."

The Falcon's lips twitched. "I'd care if you produced a child, love. I'd prefer to see you do that under . . . favorable conditions."

"But we weren't doing anything!" Arisa protested. "We were wrestling. Which he needs to work on even more than his fencing, by the way." She glared at Master Giles.

"The prince's skill at . . . wrestling, I'm happy to say, is none of my concern. I—"

"But it is my concern," Justice Holis said calmly. "And I thank you for bringing this matter to my attention. You gentlemen may release my clerk and go."

His voice was mild, but there was a note in it that made the shareholders let go of Weasel almost as fast as Giles had released Arisa.

Weasel scowled at them. "Nothing happened," he told Justice Holis and the Falcon loudly. "I was with them the whole time, and all they did was practice fighting."

At a glance from Holis, Kenton followed the courtiers out of the room and closed the door behind them.

"I fear you're wrong, lad," Justice Holis sighed, sinking back into his chair. "Oh, I accept your word that nothing happened between Arisa and the prince. But His Highness has imperiled a young lady's reputation, which could cause serious problems for her!" He turned to Edoran. "Your Highness, you *must* learn to think about the consequences for others before you act."

Edoran hunched his shoulders and said nothing.

"It wasn't his fault!" Weasel snapped. "It wasn't Arisa's, either. None of us did anything wrong!"

"I differ with you about it not being Arisa's fault," said the Falcon coolly. "If she'd behaved like a lady, this would never have happened."

If you hadn't ordered me to get close to the prince, this wouldn't have happened. But she couldn't say that in front of Edoran.

"Weasel's right," she told them instead. "None of us did anything wrong."

Edoran said nothing. Spineless twerp. Why didn't he defend himself? He might not be able to fence, but anyone could talk!

Justice Holis sighed. "As I said, I accept that you're telling the truth. But you've both been in court long enough to realize that most of the shareholders won't believe it. Not because they care about the truth, but because they might be able to use the rumor for their own ends. We can't, any of us, treat this like the trivial matter it should be. My regency will need years to become secure. If shareholders who say I can't control the prince join up with the country folk who complain that I can't protect them from pirate raids, this could cause trouble all out of proportion to—"

"Now that's ridiculous," said Weasel. "No one could compare a tumble in the straw, which didn't even happen, to a pirate raid. And that raid wasn't your fault—Wait a minute. Did you say 'raids'? Plural? More than one?"

"We got news of the second raid yesterday," Justice Holis confirmed. "We're still waiting for details, but the loss of life seems to have been lower this time. Though the property damage is worse."

Weasel frowned. "That's still bad. Any loss of life is bad, but it's not your fault."

"So I shall argue," said Justice Holis wryly. "But my opponents will ask why these raids ashore never happened when Pettibone was regent. And I have no answer."

There was a moment of silence.

"So why are they happening now?" Weasel asked.

"That, my boy, is the question," Justice Holis told him. "And we need to find an answer before everyone in the realm starts looking for a 'stronger' regent to replace me."

If he was replaced, the Falcon would be "replaced" along with him. Arisa shivered.

Weasel's worried frown deepened. "You should have told me about the second raid."

"What could you have done?" Holis asked. "Except worry? No, you're right, I should have told you. There's nothing more foolish than leaving your allies uninformed." He laid a hand on Weasel's shoulder and smiled.

Even Arisa, who had her mother's love, didn't have her confidence to that degree. She felt a twinge of jealousy and looked over at Edoran. His face was blank, but under that shield there had to be pain.

"I'm sorry," Arisa said. "But I still can't believe that anything serious could go wrong because I'm teaching Edoran to fence. It's . . . It's silly!"

Justice Holis frowned suddenly. "Why were you teaching him to fence? Doesn't he have a fencing master already?"

Edoran stirred. "I commanded it. It wasn't her fault or Weasel's."

Oh, *now* he was trying to defend them. If he was going to command things, why hadn't he commanded Master Giles and that jackal pack of courtiers to go away? And keep their mouths shut? They wouldn't have, of course, but he could have tried.

"I was teaching him to fence," said Arisa, "because his so-called fencing master wasn't. Not only was he making Edoran fence right-handed, he was . . ."

She went on to describe the lessons in detail, and Holis' expression grew more and more shocked as she went on.

"Someone had to teach him to fight," she finished defiantly. "So I did."

Holis turned to Weasel. "Why didn't you tell me about this?"

Weasel shifted uneasily. "All his tutors are like that. I thought . . . I wasn't sure, but I thought maybe that was how nobles are taught. And Edoran didn't want to complain, and you're busy with important things, and . . ." He shrugged.

"Your Highness," Justice Holis asked. "Is this true?"

Edoran's gaze rested on the floor. His face was scarlet. "I'm not very bright. And it got better after Weasel joined my lessons. I thought I might be able to . . . I hoped I could handle it myself."

If his fencing lessons had gotten better when Weasel joined him, what had they been like before?

Holis was staring at the prince in appalled silence.

"Your Highness," the Falcon said gently. "It's not that you're stupid; it's that Regent Pettibone didn't want you to learn." Her voice slowed, and Arisa realized that she was working it out as she spoke. "The more you learned, the more likely you'd threaten his power. He kept you ignorant. Deliberately."

Edoran's expression hadn't changed. He knew all this, Arisa realized. He wasn't stupid—he must have figured out a long time ago that the regent had commanded his tutors to keep him from learning anything. But why hadn't he exposed them? Why hadn't he fought back?

Holis drew a deep, shuddering breath. "I may not be to blame for the pirate raids, but this is my fault. I should have checked . . . have made myself aware—"

"I should have told you," said Weasel.

There was a grimness beneath Justice Holis' smile.

"Yes, we'll all have to be more candid with one another in the future. But meanwhile . . . Kenton! Get in here."

Arisa wondered if she should tell them about Master Darian now, but the door popped open and the clerk looked in.

"Sir?"

"Kenton, I want you to fire every one of the prince's tutors. There will be no recommendations, no severance pay, and they have three hours to pack their things and vacate the palace, or the guards will do it for them. Indeed, you might hint that leaving the city would be a wise decision."

"But . . . All of . . . Well, if you say so, sir."

"I do," said the Justice. "That will be all."

"Yes, sir!" Kenton closed the door.

Edoran's face was alight with joy, an expression Arisa had never seen on him before.

Weasel looked almost as pleased. "No lessons? At all?"

"Why does that sound like a bad idea?" said Justice Holis dryly. "You can share Mistress Arisa's dancing and etiquette lessons—you need them, even if His Highness doesn't. As for the rest, you'll resume those lessons as soon as I find new tutors. Whom I shall select *personally*."

Weasel's pleasure faded, but Edoran, if possible, looked even happier.

"That's all very well," said the Falcon. "But it won't silence the rumors that I'm sure are spreading right now. Arisa may not care about her reputation, but I do."

The justice sighed. "I understand, but I'm afraid I can't think of anything to do about that except wait for it to fade away. It will, in time. And in the meantime, my friends, it would be unwise for Arisa to be alone with either of you—or even alone with both of you! No more afternoon rides or walks. No time together at all, except for lessons or evening court."

"That's not fair to Arisa," Weasel protested.

"It's not about fairness," said Justice Holis. "It's about not adding fuel to a fire, in the hope that it will go out instead of raging out of control."

If she told them about Master Darian, if she started making accusations she couldn't prove, Arisa would be throwing lamp oil on the blaze.

"I'll still be able to talk to you in court," she told Weasel and Edoran. "And we'll see each other in lessons as well. I'll be all right."

And with her afternoons free, she could go back to that tavern and find the proof she needed!

CHAPTER 9

THE FOUR OF STONES

The Four of Stones: growth.
You must make an effort to achieve your goal.

9

Several days passed before Arisa could go back to the tavern, because Weasel and Edoran rode in the afternoon despite the rain. And Katrin, whom the Falcon had appointed Arisa's chief jailor, wouldn't even let her out to walk when there was a chance she would encounter the prince unsupervised.

Arisa knew that the Falcon and Holis, and even Katrin, were right—but they evidently didn't realize that in saving her reputation they were taking serious risks with her sanity! Because if she didn't get some exercise soon, she was going to go stark raving mad.

When she snarled at Weasel during their dance lesson, he gave her a sympathetic smile and missed the next turn, wrecking the pattern of the set.

But he must have understood, for that afternoon he and Edoran rode to the university, and Katrin grudgingly permitted her the freedom of the park, to walk or ride as she chose.

Arisa put on her old britches and coat—if Katrin assumed that was from spite, so much the better! Moments after her release she was through the woods, scrambling over the old wall as if she'd been doing it for years.

This time of day the shops were open, and as she neared the rougher neighborhood where the tavern was, several used-clothing shops appeared.

Arisa went into one and purchased a skirt and blouse, which

were so well worn that the clerk's brows rose in astonishment. She explained that she needed some clothes for a bit of hard, dirty work—the truth, after a fashion.

The drizzle cut down on traffic, and Arisa soon found a place, in a small alley between two stacks of crates, where she could change into her "new" clothes. The skirt was too short and the blouse too big—as if she'd both grown taller and lost weight, which would make the story she was about to tell even more convincing. Her rough coat wasn't so fine as to look out of place over the rest, so she tied her britches and shirt into a bundle and carried them with her.

On a rainy afternoon the neighborhood appeared less threatening, more poor than criminal, although Arisa knew that the two often went hand in hand.

It wasn't difficult to find the main street down which she'd followed Katrin—Dock Street, as it happened—but she'd also gone through four small side streets, and the entrance to the lane that housed the tavern was so narrow she almost missed it.

She'd only traveled down it for a dozen yards when she saw the sign, as gray and drab as the street around it: King's Folly. The letters were almost too faded to read in the daylight, but the sign, like the tavern, had seen better days. The edges were cut into decorative curves, with flecks of gilt paint still clinging there. And instead of the usual iron rod attaching the sign to the beam above it, an old sword had been thrust through the iron rings. It had probably been intended to continue the kingly theme, but the peeling paint that covered the blade seemed far more symbolic of the tavern's current decrepit state. If Arisa wanted to learn anything more, she had to get inside.

She drew a deep breath and knocked. Several moments dragged past before the door opened and Arisa found herself staring, not at the formidable Stu, but at a girl not much older than she was.

"We aren't rightly open," the girl told her. "Not till the end-of-shift bell rings. But we might hustle up a sandwich if you're . . ." Her voice trailed off as she took in the patches on the knees of Arisa's skirt. "You're not looking to pay for lunch, are you?"

"No," said Arisa, in a soft country accent. She knew she couldn't reproduce the accent of the city's poor, but she could easily have come from the country, seeking a more exciting life, and fallen into trouble. According to Weasel, there were many who did.

"I'm looking for a bit of extra work," she went on. "Washing dishes, scrubbing floors, whatever you need. Problem is, I can't come t' you regular. I work mornings for a laundress." She held up her bundled clothes, in illustration. "She sometimes needs me afternoons and evenings for deliveries, but there's times I'm off, and I thought . . . A tavern's not like a mill, where you got t' have someone on their shift every day. Thought maybe a tavern could use a hand, just now and then."

Looking cold and hopeful wasn't hard, for she was cold, and she was praying to any god who cared to listen.

The girl looked doubtful. "You'll probably have to talk to Pa about that, and he's out, bargaining for kegs. But . . . Here, come out of the wet, at least. Mama! Can you come out for a bit?"

The taproom was dark on this gloomy day, but the big hearth pumped out heat and the air smelled not only of beer and brandy but also of soap and wax. The long tables that filled most of the room were clean.

A door behind the bar opened and a woman emerged. Mama, no doubt; her body was plumper than the girl's and her face rounder, but they had the same mouse brown hair and the same soft mouth.

Her brows rose in astonishment at the sight of Arisa. "What's this? You picking up rags for Farley, girl? It's not our usual day."

"No, Goodwife," said Arisa humbly. "I'm looking for work."

She repeated the story she'd told the girl, and the woman frowned. "The One God knows we could use a hand. Most evenings we've enough work to keep three of you busy! It's paying you that's the problem."

"Always is," said Arisa. "But I wouldn't expect as much, since I can't come regular. I just need t' make a bit on the side, when the laundress has a light wash day and lets us off."

"Hmm. I think we could stretch to five brass droplets an hour, whenever you show up. Though there may be days we don't need you."

"I'd expect that," said Arisa. She didn't care what she was paid, but the girl she was pretending to be would. "But five droplets is too low. I'd work hard for you, truly I would. I was hoping for a flame an hour."

"Pa won't like us hiring on a stranger," the girl murmured. "Not now." But she cast Arisa a sympathetic glance.

Arisa felt a prickle of excitement—of course they wouldn't want to hire strangers, with conspirators meeting here!

"Your pa's not the one who's trying to keep mud off the floors, or washing dishes and providing food for several score of cold, hungry men! But there's no way he'll spring for a flame an hour," the tavern mistress added, turning to Arisa. "I wouldn't myself, and it's me you'll be helping out. I'll go to six droplets, for you look like you need it and the One God teaches charity to those in need."

They settled on seven droplets, with Arisa free to show up when she was available, and the tavern mistress, Mistress Mimms, free to send her away if they had no work that day. But Arisa didn't think that would happen often. Seven droplets wasn't much, and the work of keeping the tavern running must be considerable. The floors and the bar were also clean, despite their age and wear.

Arisa hurried back to the palace, not stopping to change into her britches till after she'd climbed the wall. It might be tricky to get away—soon she'd have to tell Sammel something to explain why she wasn't riding anymore. But by the time the conspirators met again, Arisa would be a familiar part of the tavern, as invisible as the long benches and the chairs by the hearth. She had taken the first step!

That evening in court Weasel told her that she'd probably be free to walk or ride on most afternoons for some time to come.

"Justice Holis isn't finding tutors as easily as he'd hoped," he confided to Arisa.

Edoran was being badgered by a woman who wanted her daughter's husband to inherit their estate, instead of the cousin to whom the law said it should go. She was currently explaining, in detail, why it wasn't her fault that she'd borne no sons, or that her oldest daughter had yet to bear children at all. Edoran's face was soberly polite, but his ears had begun to turn pink when Weasel pulled Arisa away.

"The justice is being fussy about who he hires," Weasel went on. "Which is good. But most of the men he wants are already employed, and it will take them a while to get out of their jobs."

"Why does that leave me free to walk?" Arisa asked. "Doesn't that mean you and Edoran have even more time to ride out?"

"No," Weasel told her. "Because I talked Edoran into continuing our search of the archives. That's better than riding at the best of times, much less in this filthy weather. It hasn't stopped raining for three days."

"It's winter," Arisa told him impatiently. "It always rains in winter. Edoran can probably tell you when it will stop. By the way, did he sense that second pirate raid?"

"No," said Weasel. "I asked about that. He did his usual I-don't-know-what-you're-talking-about dance, but he finally admitted that he didn't sense the second raid. He says his ability, or whatever it is, works erratically. Which is another reason he's still not admitting it exists!"

"I can understand that," Arisa said slowly. "Though it frustrates me too. It would be harder to make people believe you if it didn't work all the time."

Impossible, in fact, because the first thing anyone would do if you claimed such a gift was demand that you prove it. And if you failed . . .

"Anyway," Weasel went on, "Justice Holis thought research was a fair substitute for lessons. And seeing the records of the investigation of that so-called burglary gave Edoran an idea. He's been looking at the records—"

"Of the investigation into his father's death," Arisa finished. If you knew Edoran, that conclusion was obvious—as inevitable as the tides.

"That's probably a good thing," she added. "Maybe the written record will convince him it was an accident."

"It's hard to convince someone who doesn't want to be convinced," said Weasel. "He'll probably spend the rest of his life in those archives. And he'll probably drag me with him!"

"Better than riding," Arisa reminded him. "And while he's doing that, you can look for the sword."

Weasel moaned, and several courtiers stared.

"Stop that," Arisa told him sharply. "You enjoy that kind of thing, freak that you are. And you really are good at it. If we could find the sword, it might help my mother and your justice. And then they might loosen up on us."

"If *we* find it?" Weasel asked. "You just dumped the whole thing on me!"

But Arisa knew he'd look. He was good with detailed paperwork, no matter how much he complained. And he loved Justice Holis enough to do anything to help him—even work.

Arisa showed up at the tavern the next afternoon, and although Master Mimms grumbled, he agreed to let her stay. He was a burly man, with whiskers growing down onto his cheeks and an apron his wife struggled to keep clean. But as Arisa soon learned, "struggled to keep clean" applied to everything in the tavern. She scrubbed the floors. She scrubbed the bar, and the tables, and the front step, and the hearth, and in between she scrubbed the dishes. It was the hardest work she'd ever done, harder than any training her mother's men had given her—but she couldn't complain since the girl, and her mother, and her aunt and cousin Stu, all worked right beside her.

"It's always hard the first few days," the girl, whose name was Baylee, murmured sympathetically as Arisa rubbed her aching back. "Any job is. But you'll soon get used to it."

As the next few days passed it did grow easier, but Arisa found she'd miscalculated on one thing—in the afternoon the tavern had no customers, and thus no conspirators would meet then. She would never learn anything, working afternoons.

So the next day Arisa told Katrin that she was sick of going out in the rain, and would nap that afternoon instead. Everyone in the city was tired of the rain, which whether light or heavy hadn't let up for the last week, so Katrin didn't find that odd. In fact, napping in the afternoon was a ladylike thing to do, and lulled by the patter of drops against the window, Arisa even managed to get some sleep.

Court that evening was horribly dull, and lasted far longer than Arisa thought it should. Then she had to allow Katrin to undress her and put her to bed, to lie in the darkness, waiting till the light under the door that connected her room to Katrin's vanished. Wait till she was certain her maid was asleep.

Then she leaped out of bed. Rearranging a few pillows and fluffing up the blankets where her legs would be produced a reasonable facsimile of Arisa asleep. One close look would give it away, but glancing through rain-splattered windows into a dark room, Katrin would see nothing odd. And if for some reason Katrin did come into her room, well, who said Edoran was her only lover!

Fortunately, given the Falcon's likely reaction to that tale, Arisa didn't think Katrin ever checked on her after she went to sleep. Her maid, she had slowly realized, thought of Arisa as a temperamental, undisciplined child—a lady, in short. She didn't see Arisa as a person who could work and fight and plan, so she'd never suspect anything.

Arisa scrambled down the vines and made her way to the old tree where she'd found a hollow place to hide her tavern clothes. The rain was colder, and the streets darker and emptier than they'd been the night Arisa had first found the tavern. But when she drew near she saw firelight in the windows, and heard a dull roar of conversation.

"Laundress kept us late today," she told Stu when he opened the door. "She's getting lots of wash with all this mud. But I still need the extra coin. Is there work for me this evening?"

Stu, whose broad shoulders and fierce face concealed a butter-soft heart, smiled as he ushered her in. "I'm sure there is. Folks are getting restless in this weather, but they don't want to be out in the wet, so they're coming here."

Indeed, the benches were crowded with bodies, and the air was thick with pipe smoke and brandy fumes. Arcanara games were in play at several of the tables.

Mistress Mimms was less inclined to question Arisa's presence than to thank the One God for it. She set Arisa to cleaning the mud in front of the door, then to picking up empty crockery from the tables, and then washing the dishes she'd just picked up. And then it was all to do over again. Baylee was busy carrying bowls of stew from the kitchen and beer from the bar, but she flashed Arisa a delighted grin.

As the night wore on, Arisa grew both tired and sleepy, but she wasn't sorry she'd come. It seemed Master Mimms was a man with political opinions—and he'd no qualms about sharing them.

"It's the regent's fault, these pirate raids," he grumbled to a cluster of men at the bar. "He shorts the navy the men they need, keeping stout sailors out of work so he can deck his woman in gewgaws and candies."

Arisa, who was hauling dirty mugs back to the kitchen at the time, stumbled and almost dropped her tray. Justice Holis had no woman at court or, to the best of her knowledge, anywhere else. And though she might not have known about it, Weasel certainly would, and he'd have told her.

"But the navy's the same size now as it was under the old regent," one of the men at the bar protested. "No one added, but none taken away."

"Then why isn't he adding more?" the tavern keeper demanded. "Why isn't he building up the ranks, with the pirates growing so much bolder?"

If any of the men had an answer to that, Arisa didn't hear it.

She worked until they locked the front door and Baylee's mother passed out whatever food they had left to the beggars who hovered around the back.

"You mind if I come in the evening again?" Arisa asked when the tavern mistress returned to the kitchen with her empty kettle and basket. "With all this mud, the laundry keeps—"

"Come whenever you can," Mistress Mimms told her. "You're a good worker. And we need your hands at night more than any other time."

Though it felt much later, it was only a few hours past midnight when Arisa finally made her way to her own bed. Most of the tavern's customers were working men, who had to rise in the morning themselves. She was exhausted, but her heart was light. The tavern staff had accepted her presence in the evening without suspicion. The next time the conspirators met, no one would think twice about Arisa's presence.

The persistent rain helped, giving her an excuse to nap the next few afternoons as well. Though "nap" might not be the right word— Arisa fell into bed after her etiquette lesson and slept till Katrin awakened her to eat dinner and dress for court.

She found herself growing accustomed to this schedule, and more important, her aching muscles began to toughen up. She was feeling almost cheerful about going to the tavern that evening, despite the drenching rain, and was just slipping on her coat when she heard a soft click from behind Katrin's closed door.

She froze for only a moment before leaping down behind her bed, then rolling beneath it. The wood floor was hard under her knees and elbows as she slithered to the other side to peer out.

Her heart skipped a beat. Her maid was already on the balcony, pressing her face against the glass with her hands sheltering her eyes. Arisa held her breath—if Katrin came in to check on her...

But the dummy in her bed must have been good enough. Katrin turned and climbed over the balcony railing. What would take her out on a night like this? There was nothing happening at the tavern tonight. At least, nothing they'd told Arisa about. And it wasn't that late, several hours earlier than the last time Arisa had followed Katrin to the tavern.

She snatched up her hat and hurried to the balcony door. Pressing her own face to the glass, she watched the maid cross the open lawn and enter the trees. The moment she did so, Arisa was out the door and scrambling down the wet vines. Even if Katrin looked back, the rain and darkness were enough to hide Arisa from view.

The grass squished under her boots as she crossed the lawn, though her coat and hat kept her relatively dry. Whatever Katrin was up to, it must be urgent to bring her out so early, on a night as miserable as this.

Arisa hesitated at the tree where her tavern clothes were hidden, but Katrin might not go to the tavern. And if she did Arisa couldn't risk being seen by her, even in disguise. Her maid knew what she looked like, dressed in any kind of clothes, better than her mother did.

The path to the wall was familiar now. Arisa climbed it and looked up the street toward the tavern. No Katrin. Startled, she looked the other way and saw the dark cloaked form walk down the street and turn the corner. She was still headed toward the sea, but going that way would add several blocks to her journey . . . if she was going to the tavern at all!

Could she be going to meet with her employer? The Falcon's enemy?

Arisa dropped off the wall and raced after her maid. In this residential neighborhood there weren't many people out. Arisa had to stay so far back that she lost sight of Katrin several times, when the rain came down harder, but she didn't dare draw nearer because Katrin kept looking back. Arisa had leaped to flatten herself against the nearest wall the first time Katrin stopped walking. In the darkness more than a block away, that was enough to render her invisible. By the time they'd reached the more crowded streets of the business district, the maid had become less wary.

It soon became clear that Katrin wasn't going to the tavern, for while she kept moving toward the sea, she also consistently turned north, and the tavern was south of the palace. They'd arrived at an area Arisa thought was mostly populated by fishmongers and grocers, and the crowd was thinning again. Katrin turned and went down a dark alley between a warehouse and a fenced area that smelled like a brewer's yard.

Remembering what she'd discovered the last time her maid had turned into an alley, Arisa's heart pounded with anticipation as she ran forward and peered in. She was just in time to see Katrin whisk around a corner. Arisa hesitated. The alley was darker than the street, where scattered gate lamps and candlelit windows produced some illumination. But if Arisa didn't follow, she'd lose her.

She crept into the alley, moving slowly. If she kicked something that clattered, or tripped, Katrin might hear her. Her boots were soaked now, her feet numb with cold. It was so dark she ran one hand along the brick wall to keep from missing the opening, but when she reached it she saw that she needn't have bothered. The alley opened into an empty lot behind the brewer's yard—empty except for several piles of broken barrels and casks. The brick wall was replaced by a cheaper wooden fence out of sight of the street, and several lanterns in the yard cast feeble stripes of light through its slats. The sprung wood of the shattered kegs looked like broken bones in the dim glow. But where was Katrin?

Arisa stared around. She couldn't see another exit from the lot. There was almost certainly a gate in the fence, but even more certainly the brewer kept it locked. Unless the brewer was a member of the tavern conspiracy? But why make Katrin come through the back gate on a night like this? For their meeting at the tavern, Stu had let the conspirators in through the front door. Could someone else be coming up behind Arisa right now?

She looked back down the alley and saw no one. Of course, the shadows in that alley could have concealed a full squadron of guards. She listened. No sound from either direction. She crept into the vacant lot. She had rounded the first woodpile and was looking for the gate, so she almost tripped when she stepped on something squashy that rolled a bit under her foot.

She looked down. A dainty woman's shoe, with a foot still in it. Her eyes swept up the skirted legs and stopped at the dagger lodged in Katrin's back. Blood seeped slowly into the fabric around it.

CHAPTER 10

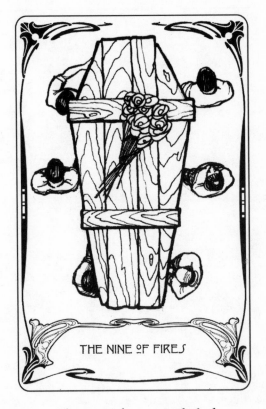

THE NINE OF FIRES

The Nine of Fires: untimely death.
A death before its time, whether through illness, accident, or murder.

10

Arisa made a choked sound and fell to her knees beside her maid. Once glance at the dagger told her she didn't dare try to pull it out— too near, far too near the heart. If Katrin wasn't dead already, she would be soon. Arisa touched the woman's neck, searching for a pulse. Her skin was still warm but there was no pulse she could feel.

Let her not be dead, not be dead . . .

She pressed her fingers harder into the yielding flesh and felt nothing. But she was still warm! Surely there was a chance . . .

She was still warm. And Arisa had seen no exit from the yard.

She shot to her feet and ran before she was aware of making the decision to move. Out of the lot, slipping on the wet cobbles as she rounded the corner. Sheer terror of what might happen if she fell kept her on her feet. Did she hear something behind her? It would have to be loud to make itself heard over the thundering beat of her own heart.

Arisa raced down the alley faster than she'd ever run in her life. When she reached the street, she started to scream.

There weren't many people around, not nearly the huge crowd she wanted. Of the scant handful on the street, two turned and walked away when she started screaming, but several others hurried toward her. Within moments a woman's plump arm was around her shoulders, and two men peered at her from under dripping hat brims.

Arisa didn't realize she was still screaming till the woman slapped her.

"... to tell us!" she snapped. "We can't help you if you don't tell us what's wrong."

"Sorry," Arisa choked, pressing her hands to her face. Sammel would be ashamed if he could see her now—he'd taught her better than to have hysterics in an emergency. "Katrin. A woman. In the lot behind the brewer's yard. She's been stabbed and I think she's dead and he may still be there!"

"Stabbed!" one of the men exclaimed. He looked at the other man, who shrugged.

"I suppose we'd better check it out." But his glance into the alley's dark mouth was reluctant.

"Don't leave me!" Arisa was embarrassed to hear her voice rise once more, and struggled for calm. "He might still be there."

All three citizens exchanged glances over Arisa's head, and her cold cheeks heated.

"I know how it sounds, but I'm not making this up! There's a woman, stabbed, in that lot. She may be dead. She might be dying right now!"

Another two men had come out of nearby buildings in time to hear this, and with five people around her Arisa's panic began to subside. She started to shake, and the woman's arm tightened around her shoulder.

"You could have been dreaming, couldn't you?" she asked gently.

I *wish* I *was.*

"No," said Arisa. "Check it out."

It took them several minutes' discussion, and another man had added himself to the group by the time they concluded that they should investigate.

Then there was further delay, while two of them went to fetch lanterns. Arisa stood and shivered. Katrin had been dead. She was almost sure of it. She didn't like the maid, but the thought of her dying, while these fools dithered, was intolerable.

On the other hand, wild horses couldn't have dragged her back into that alley alone. Wisdom or cowardice? Both? Arisa shivered.

By the time they finally went to determine the truth of her story, Arisa knew the killer would be gone. It seemed like so much time had passed that she half-expected Katrin's body to have vanished as well. But no, the woman's rain-soaked form still lay behind the woodpile, just as Arisa had left it. The bloodstain surrounding the knife hadn't spread much, she noted. And looking at the knife's position now, surrounded by lamplight and horrified citizens, she knew it had lodged in the maid's heart.

Arisa's stomach rolled and she looked away. She had seen her mother shoot Pettibone a few months ago, but it was different when you found the body. Different when it was someone you knew. She hadn't liked Katrin, but she hadn't wanted this.

At least Katrin would have died within moments of the blow. She'd almost certainly been dead when Arisa found her. All staying with her would have accomplished was to put Arisa in danger as well, for she'd been only a minute behind her maid. The killer must have been there. Watching her.

Her shudder was so convulsive that the plump woman gave her a worried look and held her tighter. One man went running for the city guard, and another went for a healer, though he didn't bother to run.

It wasn't easy to strike the heart on the first blow like that. When Sammel had taught Arisa knife work, he'd showed her the spot and the right angle, then draped an old straw-stuffed coat over a scarecrow and had her practice the blow over and over. Even when she could consistently strike the right place, he'd warned her that it was even odds that she'd hit a rib and the knife would be deflected.

This killer was either very well trained or very lucky. Either way, it shouldn't matter to her, Arisa told herself fiercely. He'd seen her, yes, but he knew she hadn't seen him. His job had been to kill Katrin, and he'd accomplished it. No need for him to come after anyone else. No need for her to fear . . .

Why had he wanted to kill Katrin?

One of the guardsmen asked her that, eventually. By the time the guardsmen had arrived, the brewer had been summoned to open his doors and rake up the fires, so they could wait warm and out of the rain.

On arrival the brewer had found his front door unlocked, and a back window unshuttered. Several men had gone to look at the fence and found bits of fresh mud. They'd cleverly concluded that the killer had escaped by climbing the fence, going through the brewery, and out the front door after they'd all gone into the alley.

He'd have watched them through the front windows, Arisa thought, timing his escape. Cool. Professional. Who could command a professional assassin and would want Katrin dead? Katrin had been working for her mother's enemy, and if his orders had been to make the Falcon's daughter look bad, then Katrin had succeeded. So he had no reason to want her dead. The members of the conspiracy might be willing to kill, though it was hard to believe it of Master Mimms. Master Darian, on the other hand, might well know how to hire an assassin—but Katrin had been on their side! The Falcon was Katrin's primary victim, but she could have fired the maid if she'd wanted to be rid of her. If the authorities had learned about the conspiracy, they would send the guard to arrest them, not assassins. Assuming, of course, that the conspiracy was against Justice Holis. Arisa had assumed that when she'd seen Master Darian, but she didn't really know what they were up to. Or that they were up to anything. Or why anyone at all would want to kill a ladies' maid.

It was far too nebulous to explain to the wet, unhappy-looking city guardsman who took her statement.

"They say you found the body, Mistress . . ."

"Benison," Arisa told him. "Arisa Benison."

His brows rose. "Any relation to lord commander Benison?"

"Her daughter. And the woman is . . . was my maid, Katrin. I don't know her last name."

She hadn't bothered to learn it. How could anyone expect to gain her servant's loyalty if she didn't take the trouble to learn the servant's name? Did Katrin have a family who'd grieve for her? Or who depended on her salary, as the Falcon had suggested? How strange to feel guilt, even something close to grief, for a woman she'd so disliked.

No one should die like that, whether Arisa had liked her or not.

"We'll find out her name," said the guardsman. "And a lot more, before we're done with this. What were the two of you doing here?"

He thought Katrin had accompanied her here, and for a moment Arisa was tempted to let him go on thinking that—but lying to the guard wouldn't help them find the killer.

"I saw her sneaking out of the palace, earlier this evening," Arisa said. "I wanted to see where she was going, so I followed her."

The guardsman's brows rose.

Arisa once more considered telling him about the tavern, but all she really knew was that she'd seen Master Darian go into the building. Once. It was a public tavern. He might just have gone in for a drink, or to get out of the rain. No, it hadn't been raining then. This long, dreary storm had started that night. And besides, Katrin had been working *with* the conspiracy. Telling the guard what she suspected would only confuse the issue. If they started their investigation without preconceptions, they might uncover something that Arisa didn't already know. How could she find out what they learned?

She'd been silent too long.

"Why did you follow her?" the guardsman asked. "If you wanted to get her in trouble, you could have told the master of household she was slipping out."

Arisa glanced away from the contempt in his eyes. "I did want to get her in trouble," she admitted. "But not like this! And you know nothing about it, so stop looking like that. She may be dead, but that didn't make her a nice person when she was alive. Not nice to me, anyway."

Why hadn't Katrin been nicer to her? It was foolish to antagonize your employer, and Arisa had been willing to cooperate with her maid in the beginning. Well, cooperate within reason.

"All right," said the guard. "You wanted to get her in trouble, so you followed her. Then what?"

Arisa related the rest of the night's events just as they'd occurred. And hours later, her brain numb with the need for sleep, she told her mother the exact same story.

"That was . . . small of you, Ris," said the Falcon coldly.

Given the incandescent fury that had greeted Arisa when the city guard brought her home in the middle of the night, cold was an improvement. Still, heat flooded Arisa's cheeks. Her motives tonight hadn't been petty, but she had planned to get Katrin into trouble the first time she'd followed her. It felt uglier, now that she was dead.

"You don't know what it was like," she told her mother. "And I only wanted to get her fired—or just away from me. It's not my fault she was killed!"

"It isn't?" the Falcon asked softly.

Arisa's jaw dropped. "You don't mean that! You couldn't possibly think I'd . . . I'd . . . Over a quarrel about corsets?"

"No," said the Falcon. "I know that you know how, but . . . No, of course not."

But she had thought it. She'd asked the question seriously, whatever she said now. Arisa's heart ached.

The Falcon looked away. "I'm sorry, Ris. That was uncalled for. But everyone knows you've been quarreling, and Master Giles told the whole court how good you are with a sword. I just hope no one else thinks you might have done it."

If anyone else thought she'd murdered her maid, they didn't show it the next day. Arisa slept late, and then went to her lessons. By the time she had to dress for court there was a new maid to attend her, a plump middle-aged woman who spoke in a murmur and hardly ever met her eyes.

She must have refused to take over Katrin's room, however, for no light appeared under the door that night. The guards would have searched it, Arisa knew, but having searched it herself, she also knew what they'd have found—nothing. If she wanted to learn more she'd have to return to the tavern. But not that night. She was tired, and her heart ached. Let Katrin's friends learn of her death in peace.

The next day Arisa followed her usual schedule, setting off for the tavern at the usual time. It was just nerves that made her think she heard an echo of footsteps behind her. The sound of the rain would have kept her from hearing it even if someone were following her, and as often as she spun around, she saw no one suspicious. *Nerves,* she told herself firmly.

The tavern was open for business, though the lines on Stu's face looked deeper when he opened the door. It was Baylee who told

Arisa that her cousin, Katrin, had been murdered two nights ago.

"I'm so sorry!" Arisa had no trouble sounding shocked. Katrin had been the Mimms' *niece*? Had her visit to the tavern been an innocent family visit after all? On the same night that Master Darian had been there? No, that was too great a coincidence. Wasn't it?

It would have been horribly rude, and out of character, to ask questions about a family member's murder, so Arisa resolved simply to listen and see what she could learn.

The Mimms were quieter than usual, and if they talked about Katrin's death, they did so when Arisa wasn't there. However, several nights later Master Mimms began complaining to his customers about the summary firing of the palace guard, who had served the realm so loyally and were now begging in the streets and sleeping on benches in the One God's church. Arisa didn't know for certain, but all the guardsmen she'd seen had been young fit men—she doubted many had been reduced to begging.

"Last week your pa was talking about the regent's woman, all dressed up in jewels and silk," she told Baylee when they found themselves working together over a tub of dirty dishes. "How'd he know such a thing? I mean, none of the customers here are going to the palace for tea, are they now?"

"He got news like that from my cousin Katrin, the one who was killed," Baylee told her sadly. "She was dresser to a fine court lady. Lived in the palace herself! She told us all manner of things."

Arisa could just imagine it. She winced.

"We'll miss her," Baylee went on. "We—my family—have been in service to the palace for generations. I might be working there myself, if Pa hadn't inherited the tavern. Now he's saying it's too dangerous for any daughter of his to go into the royal service, but that's nonsense. It wasn't in the palace she was killed."

"Who killed her?" Arisa asked. It was natural to ask that now.

"We've no idea," said Baylee. "The guard are guessing she went down a back alley and maybe surprised a gang of thieves, but no one knows why she'd go there in the first place."

"Could your father be right?" Arisa tried to keep her voice casual. "Could it have something to do with someone in the palace she worked for?"

Baylee snorted. "She was ladies' maid to a girl no older than me. A country bump—" She cast Arisa an apologetic look. "A country girl who'd no idea of proper dress or manners or anything, she said. How could that get her killed? But Pa wouldn't have let me work in the palace, anyway. He says he'd rather serve the people of Deorthas than their prince."

Regret mingled with the pride in Baylee's voice. She would have liked to be a palace servant—understandable, since even the lowest maid in the palace was several social ranks higher than a tavern maid. It was odd that a tavern keeper's family served in the palace at all, but from what Baylee said the connection went back several generations.

Serving "the people of Deorthas," or at least the new regent's failure to serve them, made up a fair portion of the tavern master's conversation. It wasn't obvious. Most would have taken it for the grumbling all people indulged in about their shareholder, or their employer, or their mother-in-law; anyone who had power was the subject of complaints.

But to Arisa's experienced ear, Master Mimms' comments sounded less like ordinary griping and more like a man arguing for a cause.

She knew all about causes, she thought, making her way home in the late-night chill. Causes were something that could get people killed. Had Master Mimms' cause been the motive for Katrin's death? How? And if that cause was Justice Holis' downfall, then maybe Arisa could find out why.

She cornered Edoran during their dance class the next morning, as they worked their way through an intricate set. They'd spent the first part of the lesson working on the different moves; only toward the end did they perform, or attempt to perform, the dance.

Both her dance and etiquette lessons had become easier since Weasel and Edoran joined them. Arisa's tutors had taken the firing of their fellows as a warning, and were now genuinely trying to teach—though they seemed a bit out of practice. Her music teacher was still simply despairing, but even he despaired more politely.

She was finally learning to dance, and Edoran was good at it. In the midst of the music, with the dancing master's orders and complaints, and the servants who'd been drafted to make up the numbers flowing around them, this was as close to privacy as she could manage.

"I want you to do some extra research for me," she told Edoran as the dance brought them together. "You, and Weasel."

Edoran bowed, right on the beat, curse him. Her own curtsy was half a beat behind.

"You should ask Weasel," Edoran murmured. Both of them were keeping their voices low. "He's the one who's good at it."

"Yes, but you're ..."

The movement of the dance turned him away.

"...you're the one who can talk and dance at the same time," Arisa finished, as the pattern brought them together. "Weasel can't." In truth, she wasn't sure she could talk and dance at the same time, but this was her best chance to talk to him. "Listen, we may not have a lot of time. Katrin's uncle, Master Mimms, owns ..."

This time she was whirled off, to dance with another partner for several turns.

"Katrin's uncle owns a tavern called the King's Folly. I want to know if he, or someone he cares about, had any trouble with Justice Holis. A judgment that went against them, or a kinsman ..."

The sequence of the dance pulled them apart again, but the grand rond was coming up and Edoran would be walking her around the circle. When they met for the beginning of that final promenade, however, he spoke first.

"You shouldn't worry so much about your maid's death. No one really thinks—"

"This isn't about Katrin's death," said Arisa. "Or not exactly. It's about the reason she died. And that reason probably still exists."

They both turned around. When they were face-to-face once more, Edoran was frowning. "How can the reason she died still exist if she's dead? Anyway, it's not the archives you want for that kind of thing. City records stay in the court files for fifty years, before they're passed into the archives."

He offered his elbow and Arisa laid her hand on it. "Yes, but you could get access to the city records, couldn't you? Without anyone finding out about it?"

"I can't do anything without everyone knowing about it," Edoran told her. "What do you expect me to do? Sneak out at midnight and break into the Justice Hall? Besides, I'm beginning to make progress with my own search." His voice, already low, dropped even further. "Did you know that my father had several accidents—near misses, which might have injured or killed him—in the year and a half before he died?"

"No," said Arisa. "But people have accidents, and near misses, all the time. If he wasn't injured—"

She stumbled as Edoran maneuvered her into the slow rotation that she'd forgotten occurred at each quarter of the circle. The couples on either side of them were staring. Arisa smiled, trying to make the low-voiced conversation look less intense than it was.

"The first time," Edoran told her, "something happened to the brakes on a wagon. It came rolling down the hill right at him, and would have crushed him if he hadn't gotten out of the way. Do you think that was coincidence?"

"It might be," said Arisa. "But even if it—"

"And the next time," Edoran went on, "he was hunting with a group of courtiers. He got separated from them, and—"

"We don't have time for hunting stories!" Arisa hissed. They were coming up on the second quarter pirouette, and the dance finished at the circle's end. "Even if you're right, even if they weren't accidents and Pettibone did kill your father, Pettibone is dead! You can't kill him again, can you?"

"No, but—"

This time he forgot the turn. She grabbed his arm and manhandled him through it.

"You can't punish him any further," she went on more gently. "I understand why you'd want to, and I see that you need to know for certain, though I don't quite understand why, but my research is urgent! Mine is important now!"

Edoran's face froze. "Your research is about a maidservant. Mine is about the death of a king."

The haughtiness of all his royal ancestors rang in his voice, and Arisa scowled.

"Are you going to help me, or not?"

"Not," Edoran snapped.

They finished the circle in angry silence, without missing a single step.

She thought about enlisting Weasel alone, but what could he do without Edoran's help? He might be able to break into the Hall of Justice, but he couldn't do all the research she needed without someone seeing the light of his lamp.

What she needed was for Edoran to invent some excuse to go there, like looking for more information about his father's so-called accidents.

Except, as they'd learned while looking at the investigation into the sword's disappearance, records from the palace guard went straight into the archives when an investigation was closed. And Edoran was using their search for the sword as an excuse to investigate his father's death.

Why would he bother to hide that, anyway? The man who had (or hadn't) killed the king could hardly become suspicious and flee. It made Edoran look paranoid and weird, but so what? Everyone who knew him thought he was paranoid and weird. The lucky ones who didn't know him thought he was a spoiled brat. And all of them were right!

But if he wouldn't help her, she'd have to find someone who would.

The next afternoon she postponed her nap and made her way to the stables. She told the head groom and half a dozen undergrooms that no, she didn't want to ride in this downpour, she just wanted a change of scene after all this time cooped up in the palace. Eventually they gave up, and she located Sammel in a small tack room.

"Do you want me to saddle Honey for you, Mistress Benison?" he asked in his "Henley" voice, laying down a broken bridle and rising to his feet.

"It's pouring rain," Arisa pointed out. "And I'm wearing a dress."

She looked around to make sure no one was paying any attention to her, and closed the tack room door.

Sammel grinned and sat down on the stool, taking up the bridle again. "I can't blame you for not wanting to ride out in this. No one does. The horses are restless, but when we turn them out to pasture they don't want to stay out in it, either. Downright unnatural, if you ask me."

"What, the rain? It always rains on the coast in winter."

"Not for eighteen days straight, it don't," Sammel told her. "They say this is the longest continual rain in anyone's memory. It should be flooding fields and cellars all around the city, but it isn't, and that's unnatural too, they say."

"They always say it's the longest rain, or the deepest snow, or the hottest whatever," said Arisa. She seated herself on a worn tack chest. "Sammel, I need your advice. Maybe your help, though I don't know what you could do."

His expression softened. "If this is about young Katrin's death, that wasn't your fault. It must have been a right shock finding her, and it was wrong t' try to get her in trouble, but—"

"I know it's not my fault!" Arisa snapped. "This is . . . This is a practical matter. I went to the prince first but he turned me down. Flat. Arrogant, spineless twit that he is."

"What else were you expecting?" Sammel asked. "He's the prince, after all. And it's not like you'll be putting up with him much longer, anyway."

"What do you mean? My mother wants me to *befriend* the royal runt. I'll have to put up with him forever!"

Sammel blinked rapidly. "Well, but he'll be growing out of it, surely. He'll have to. King's not a job that a spoiled brat can handle."

Arisa thought of Regalis. "I'm not so sure about that. But at least that isn't my problem."

"If your mother wants you to befriend him, it is your problem," Sammel said firmly. "Don't you go making trouble for your mother, young mistress. What with Holis against her and these pirates raiding ashore, she's got more than enough on her plate."

"I don't think Justice Holis is against her, exactly," said Arisa. "And there hasn't been a raid for weeks, so—"

Her heart sank at the sudden regret on Sammel's face.

"There's been another raid?"

"News came this morning," he said. "It's not known t' many, but the messenger babbled it out as he came off his horse. Rode the poor beast into a lather. Not that I blame the man. They hit Marsden."

Arisa frowned. "Marsden's one of the larger fishing villages. It's almost a town."

"The weather's better away from the city," Sammel told her. "So the men were out in their boats. Those left—the women, children, and old folks—they had no warning at all."

Arisa shook her head in shock and sorrow. Then she thought about what Master Mimms would say, and winced.

"Why doesn't mother hire more men into the navy? Send them after those . . . those killers."

Sammel sighed. "It's not just a matter of manpower, lass. The whole navy's searching the coast already, but the southern islands are a maze. You could send ten times the number of ships the navy's got, and still not find 'em."

"Then we need twenty times more ships!"

"Aye, but you can't build a naval sloop overnight—takes over a year start to finish t' make a ship like that. And even if we built 'em they'd need men to man 'em, and you can't train sailors overnight either."

Arisa rose and paced back and forth. "What about the army then? Have them patrol the coast. Stop them on land, since they're raiding the land."

And why were the pirates doing that now, for the first time in living memory?

"Your mother commands the army in name only," Sammel reminded her. "It's General Diccon they really obey, and he takes his orders from Holis, not your mother, whatever the rules might be. Nothing but a swindle, that lord commander flimflam."

His lips were tight with anger. He could never accept that the Falcon had taken second rank to Justice Holis, when it was her men who had defeated the palace guard and overthrown the old regent. None of the Falcon's men had accepted it—which was why Holis had dismissed the Falcon's men.

"But the navy's loyal to her," Arisa pointed out. "Some of the naval officers were hers even when Pettibone was in charge, and now those officers are in command. Besides, Holis wants those pirates stopped as badly as mother does—maybe more. There has to be something the army can do."

"They're trying," Sammel admitted. "They've put troops into every fishing village that might be a target. Small troops, for the most part, but they haven't got that many men to spare, either."

Arisa frowned. "Then why weren't there troops in Marsden?"

"They did have a troop there," Sammel told her. "But there were far more pirates than soldiers—and you're enough your mother's daughter to know how that ends."

Arisa thought of brave men bleeding out their lives on the wet sands, and wanted to weep. And she wanted to help, hang it! Somehow.

"But there's nothing either of us can do about that," Sammel told her, unknowingly answering her thought. "So what's this advice you want from me?"

Don't you go making trouble for your mother. If she told him about Master Mimms, in his present mood Sammel would probably stalk into the tavern one night and beat the man to a pulp. He would certainly stop Arisa from returning there.

"Nothing," she told him. "It doesn't seem important now."

It wasn't important, Arisa thought, wiping furiously at the mud the last dozen customers had tracked in on their shoes. She wasn't even sure what she was doing at the tavern that night.

Yes, Master Mimms was a blowhard with a grudge against the new regent. Who cared? The guard thought Katrin had surprised a bunch of thieves; they might be right. All she'd seen Katrin do was visit her own uncle's tavern. So what if she'd seen a man who looked like another man? Master Darian was probably three realms away by now, and still running.

Edoran's paranoia had rubbed off, that's what it was. Her maid hadn't liked her—that didn't mean there were enemies lurking everywhere. The court was so full of small minds, living small lives, that little things started looking bigger than they were.

Arisa rinsed her rag in the bucket, then moved to one side as a knock sounded and Stu went to open the door. It would be only another customer, bringing in more of this eternal mud. She was scrubbing floors, while pirates slaughtered villagers and undermined the government.

She glared at the muddy boots that had just crossed the threshold as if it were their fault, and then froze, the rag dripping in her hand.

Tall polished boots, that didn't belong under the hem of the ragged coat. The boots of a naval officer.

CHAPTER 11

THE FOUR OF FIRES

The Four of Fires: the liar.
Deliberate deception.

11

Arisa watched, surreptitiously, as Stu ushered the officer behind the bar and then through the door that led down to the cellar. Why down there?

Arisa frowned, despite the excitement racing through her veins. She understood wanting to meet somewhere besides the taproom, but she'd seen the cellar when the aunt who did the cooking had run out of onions. It was crammed with barrels and kegs and bins. There wasn't room for a meeting.

But whatever was happening, she wasn't just being paranoid. Something was going on! Soon Master Darian would arrive and . . . and he would see her, as clearly as she'd once seen him in the light that spilled through the tavern door.

The floor was still muddy, but Arisa gathered up her bucket and retreated to the kitchen.

Would he remember her? He'd seen her only once . . . but he'd been crouched in the corner, watching the entire drama of Pettibone's death. Arisa's part in it had been small, but he had seen her clearly, and under pretty memorable circumstances.

The part he'd played had been smaller than hers, and she'd recognized his ordinary face. And he didn't have—

"Finished the floor then?" Mistress Mimms inquired. "Good. We need someone to pick up mugs. We're almost out of clean ones."

—he didn't have red hair. Hair that would glow in the lamp- and firelight when Master Darian walked though the door. Unless . . .

"I'm not quite finished with the floor," said Arisa. "Though I don't mind going for mugs before I get back to it. But my hair keeps falling down into the muck."

She wrapped her long braid around her head as she spoke, then pulled a clean dishcloth from the cupboard and tied it tightly over her hair, tucking it in at the back so not a strand of red could be seen.

"Shame to cover it," said Baylee, who was washing mugs. "You've got beautiful hair."

"More shame to mop muddy floors with it," said Mistress Mimms, handing Arisa a tray. "Leave the other dishes till you've brought at least one tray of cups, and then you can help Baylee dry them. We're busy tonight, and . . ." Her lips pressed down over secrets. "Well, we're busy."

Arisa was on the other side of the room, clearing a table where a lively arcanara game had just broken up, when Master Darian arrived.

"Hello, Stu. You've got quite a crowd tonight." He glanced around the room as he spoke.

Arisa turned away, putting her back to the room. The nape of her neck crawled with tension, but she had little fear that he'd recognize her in a ragged dress, with her bright hair covered.

Weasel once told her that a servant doing servant things,

in a place where they were expected to be, was as invisible as the furniture.

She gathered up several empty mugs. No sudden cry of recognition. No hand gripping her shoulder to turn her around.

A cautious peek showed Arisa the back of Master Darian's coat as he descended the cellar stairs, the sixth man to do so. It must be getting crowded down there. Gradually her heartbeat slowed. Weasel was right—servants were invisible, the Lady be praised.

Arisa counted fourteen people going down to the cellar that night, four of them wearing officers' boots—fifteen if you included Master Mimms, who was the last man to go down.

After that Arisa was too busy to do anything but work. Mistress Mimms took over the bar, which left Baylee running the kitchen, and Arisa trying to do Baylee's job as well as her own.

She carried drinks and food to the tables for the first time that night, and a fan of mud spread slowly from the doorway, since there was no one free to clean it until Master Mimms came back and took over for his wife.

Arisa was mopping the floor as the conspirators departed, coming up the stairs one or two at a time, several minutes apart. Trying, she supposed, to make it less obvious that a meeting had taken place.

Master Darian was one of the last to leave, and his coat actually brushed against her, but Arisa didn't flinch. Just another piece of furniture. His companion's hard-soled shoes slipped on the wet floor.

"Curse this weather," the man grumbled. "You need deck shoes even on land these days. I've never seen anything like it."

"We'll all need deck shoes soon," Master Darian told him cheerfully. "For their proper purpose."

Arisa kept her gaze on the floor, wiping up mud, her ears straining to hear more. Deck shoes had braided-rope soles, to help sailors keep their footing on a sea-wet deck. Was Master Darian planning a voyage? When? Where? And why would they "all" need deck shoes?

"Well, if we need them," said the man cheerfully, "I trust your patron in the palace will—"

Master Darian's feet moved rapidly.

"Ow! All right, all right, I hope your unnamed patron from nowhere will provide deck shoes along with everything else. By the One God, you're cautious! There's no one listening, and even if there was . . ."

Stu opened the door, and they argued their way out into the soggy night. Arisa scrubbed the floor, her mind racing.

A patron in the palace. Katrin's employer? If the person who had hired Katrin to embarrass the Falcon through her daughter was Master Darian's patron, then she had linked Master Darian with both Katrin's death and her mother's enemy—but she still had no clue who that enemy was! And though she might be nearly invisible working in the crowded tavern, she would certainly be noticed if she carried in a tray of drinks during the conspirators' next meeting.

She couldn't spy on them while they met . . . so she had to find a way to do it afterward. Was there any chance they kept some sort of records?

Arisa was wiping the tables when Mistress Mimms did a final round of the taproom and latched the windows closed. It was the work of seconds to open a latch once the mistress had gone back to the kitchen.

Arisa might not have Weasel's skill at burglary, but she wasn't a total amateur.

After the tavern closed she walked down the street as usual, then made her way back from another direction, wiggling into her old hiding place among the barrels. She watched the lamps go out downstairs, bloom briefly in the upstairs windows, and then go out again.

She waited for the family to fall asleep. Allowing longer than usual, since Master Mimms would be excited about the meeting. Perhaps talk it over with his wife.

The street was empty now, and the light drizzle was soaking through her coat.

Still she waited, waited till her teeth began to chatter and she had to walk around the block to warm up enough to approach the window in silence.

Arisa swung it open slowly—there was no creak. Master Mimms said grease was cheap, and annoying your customers with squeaky hinges wasn't. The sill was low enough to reach, but high enough that she grunted as she pulled herself into the taproom.

It wasn't much darker than the street outside. Arisa went to the hearth, where the embers still glowed, and stood a moment, warming herself and listening for any sound from above. Nothing. All asleep.

She had worked here long enough that she felt like she was moving around in her own home. No, more than that. She wouldn't be half so comfortable sneaking around the palace in the middle of the night.

And if this was more home than the palace, did that make her a traitor? To friends, if not her family?

Rot, Arisa thought firmly, fetching the candle that Master Mimms kept behind the bar, and returning to the hearth to light it. The Falcon was her family, and home was where her mother was. These people were her mother's enemies! Even if they had been kind.

When the candle was burning steadily, she came back to the bar and crept down the stairs, closing the door behind her.

The cellar was much as she remembered, cluttered with kegs and bins near the door, and with all the discarded flotsam of the tavern's past crowding the back.

There wasn't room for fifteen people. No place to sit, and not enough light, either. Arisa kindled the lamp that hung beside the stairway.

There were no other lamps or candles, but in the brighter

light she could see that the crates beyond the area near the door were dusty. No one had sat on them, and in a meeting that had lasted several hours that was impossible.

Could there be another room down here? She didn't see any doors. Were there . . . She squinted. Yes! Tracks in the dust between some of the crates.

It took only a moment to lift the lamp from its bracket and follow the trail across the dusty floor. Excitement prickling down her spine, Arisa tracked the footprints to an old chest, in front of a tall panel that lay propped against the wall. Unlike everything around it, the chest was free of dust! Records?

It wasn't locked, so whatever was in it probably wasn't important, but Arisa lifted the lid anyway.

A jacket. Very rich brocade, cut in the old style. On top lay a pair of shoes, the leather cracked with age. There were dimples in the heels from where gems had been pried out.

Arisa remembered Weasel's tale of Regalis returning naked from a tavern, and grinned. Some ancient courtier had lost his shirt here—literally! But that long-ago man's losses had nothing to do with her present quest, and though she reached down to the bottom of the chest she felt nothing but old fabric.

No records. Nothing of importance. Then why was this chest so clean? Someone must have dusted it, and the only reason to dust it was because they'd handled it.

Arisa stood and studied the floor. Yes, the chest had been dragged aside, right there.

She hauled the chest to the left, till it lay in the rectangle that had already been etched in the dust. Behind where the chest had been was a long, weathered sign. Arisa tipped her head to one side and read, WAYFARER'S REST.

So the tavern hadn't always been the King's Folly, but she had no interest in some long-ago change of name. Marks to the right of the sign showed where it, too, had been dragged aside.

Grabbing the iron pin that still ran through the rings at its side, Arisa pulled the heavy sign across the floor. The door was behind it. An ordinary door, closed with an ordinary bolt.

Arisa pulled the bolt back, and the door swung open.

The scent of hot candles and human sweat gusted out to greet her. Even before she saw the long table and scattered chairs, she knew this was where the meeting had been held.

There were no maps, where X marked the spot. No incriminating notes—signed, of course. No papers, no lists, no hints of any kind as to what had been discussed in this room. Just a table, too small to accommodate the dozen mismatched chairs, and a straw pallet covered with blankets in one corner.

Arisa frowned. Had some of them sat on the bed? Their heads would have been lower than the table's surface, and they could easily have dragged in a crate or two instead.

Curious, she drifted over to the bed. Perhaps one of the conspirators stayed here sometimes? In all the days she'd worked at the tavern, she'd seen no sign that anyone lived down here. And why hadn't they pulled the pallet out into the cellar while the meeting took place? There wasn't much room, and it was certainly in the way.

Arisa grasped the blanket and whisked it off. She half-expected a flood of spiders, or even worse, rats, but only a faint clanking rewarded her efforts. Clanking from the shiny new chain, that a shiny new bolt secured to the wall, with a shiny shackle at the end.

This room had been outfitted as a prison.

CHAPTER 12

THE FIVE STONES

The Five of Stones: the weaver.
All of the arts. Beauty created by man.

12

She still had no proof. Arisa had spent most of the night wondering if she should tell her mother and Justice Holis what she'd learned, or if she needed some evidence beyond her word.

How could she get solid evidence? Wait till she saw Baylee carrying meals down to a prisoner? She shivered. They were planning on kidnapping someone. But Arisa still didn't know who or why! Or when. And that might have been the motive behind Katrin's death as well. Kidnapping wasn't as bad as murder, but she knew it could lead to deaths—Master Mimms' death, if no other. Kidnapping wasn't a certain death sentence, but you could hang for it.

And that was another argument against telling her mother— she didn't want to get Baylee's family in trouble. They might be conspirators, but they were kind, decent people. They gave food to beggars, when they could have sold it cheap the next morning, and they'd treated an assistant laundress like . . . like family. Baylee was her friend.

Not if you betray her father to the law, she won't be.

When her new maid awakened her from her uneasy doze, Arisa still didn't know what she should do. She ate only toast and tea, and absently allowed the woman to dress her in a pink gown that she despised, though it did lend her pale face a little color.

Yallin took one look at the dark circles under Arisa's eyes

and laid down her sewing. "What's wrong, lass? Can you tell me now?"

Solitude misleads you. Arisa knew that if she were going to tell anyone it should be her mother and Justice Holis, but perhaps . . .

"It's the same problem I had before," she said. "Though it's gotten worse. What should a person do . . . Yallin, if you had a friend, and you were afraid they were doing something wrong, something that might have serious consequences, should you tell on them?"

Put like that it sounded so childish that she blushed. But it would give too much away if she asked, *Should you turn them in to the authorities?*

"That's always a hard one," said Yallin, taking up her stitching again. "The first thing I'd do is ask why my friend is doing something bad. If they're acting out of ignorance or fear, if they're desperate, or have been misled by someone else, then maybe I could persuade them not to do it, or find some other way for them to escape, or get what they need. If they're acting from malice or revenge, I'd have to ask myself if I really want that person as my friend."

"What if they're acting on principle?" said Arisa. "What if they're like my mother, doing something bad for a greater good? For a cause?"

Yallin glanced up at her. "You'd know more about that than I do. But I do know that principles create a terrible lot of power. A cause isn't something to take lightly."

"But what if it's the wrong cause?" Arisa demanded. "What if they're not doing good, even if they think they are? You can't punish them for trying to do good!"

"All causes are good," Yallin told her calmly. "And those exact same causes are all bad, depending on which side a body's on. Regent Pettibone and his followers certainly thought your mother's cause was a bad one. To my mind, causes aren't about good or bad, in the end. They're about power. That's what makes them so dangerous."

Arisa opened her mouth to argue, and then closed it. Her head was spinning. Her mother's cause had been good! But weren't Baylee and her family also fighting against an evil regent, who they thought would corrupt the prince and harm the realm? They were doing exactly the same thing her mother had done! How could Arisa turn them in for that?

Her mother's cause had succeeded. What if they, too, won their fight? What if their cause had already resulted in Katrin's death? But Katrin had been working *with* them! So who had killed her?

"I don't know what to do," Arisa said numbly.

"With that, I can't help you," Yallin told her. "This is your test. But I do know there's something important going on. This unnatural rain tells me that, for it's surely a sign that the sword is becoming, just as the stars were the sign of the shield's becoming. In fact," she offered Arisa a wry smile, "I'd give a year of my life to know what's really going on. And I don't have many years left!"

Arisa was too distracted to smile back. Hadn't the Hidden

leader, who'd captured Weasel for a midnight meeting, talked about something becoming? Or had it all been about comets and portents? But their portent had been three shooting stars, streaking over the sky . . . and the shield of stars had been found. And how could Yallin know about that, anyway?

"You're not helping me make up my mind," Arisa told her. "In fact, you've made it harder."

"I'm sorry for that," said Yallin, "but if this is as important as it seems . . . Have you laid out the cards? They seemed to help you last time."

Arisa rubbed her temples, which had begun to ache. And she never had headaches. One of her mother's men had jested that headaches only plagued the indecisive.

"I'm afraid this decision may be too important to let the cards determine it."

"And I," Yallin dug into her sewing kit, "think this decision is too important to ignore them."

She held out the worn deck. Arisa reached for it, then pulled her hand back. "You're right. But I want to use my own deck."

And she wanted to be alone when she did it—sometimes Yallin was too perceptive.

"Then go do it," the seamstress told her. "I've a feeling that we're running out of time."

The new maid was gone when Arisa reached her room. No reason she should be there—ordinarily Arisa wouldn't have returned till after her dancing lesson.

Yallin was right. She needed to make up her mind and act, for better or worse. She pulled her deck from the bureau drawer, sat down at the small table, and shuffled the cards. She didn't have to concentrate on her dilemma—it would have been impossible to keep it out of her thoughts.

It was no surprise to see the storm fall into its accustomed place—she'd have been astonished if her withe wasn't working for this.

"This supports me," she said aloud, and laid the top card beneath the storm goddess' feet.

The traitor? Again? And in the same position. It must be an incredibly powerful influence, but Master Darian no longer seemed to fit. Had Katrin been a traitor, and been killed for it?

"This inspires me." The five of waters fell above the storm. Arisa frowned. Mistrust was a huge part of her life right now, but . . . No, it was inspiring her. Mistrust of the conspirators, of Baylee's family. And since her talk with Yallin . . . Could she really mistrust her mother's cause? She'd grown up in the rebellion, dedicated her life to it. When the battle was over, when they'd won, she'd all but lost herself. It wasn't the palace, the corsets, the courtiers, who'd left her so off balance. It was Arisa herself, drifting like a ship without a rudder. Her mother's cause had driven her whole life—no wonder she'd felt so out of step when it was gone. And now . . .

No, she might as well mistrust herself as doubt that the rebellion had been right.

"This misleads me," she said firmly, and laid the six of stones to the storm's far left. Yes, compassion for Baylee and her family *was* trying to mislead her.

"This guides me true." Reprisals. Arisa thought of prison, of the hangman's noose, and shivered. But if compassion misled her . . .

"This threatens me." She placed the three of stars to the storm's far right. The trial. A judgment she had to make wisely. "Fat lot of help that is," she grumbled. "I *knew* that."

And protecting her from the trial . . . Garbed in ragged motley, the fool grinned up at her. Her heart was full of misleading compassion, but her instincts screamed that the conspirators were dangerous, that they had to be stopped before something went terribly wrong. Something even worse than Katrin's murder.

Causes are about power, Yallin's voice echoed in her memory.

The Falcon's cause had been good—Yallin was wrong about that. But she was right about the power any cause could wield. Power for good or ill.

Arisa gathered up the deck. She had power now, and she had to use it wisely. She had to have proof, to know who was guilty of what before she acted. She had to know . . . and at least she knew where to look further.

Katrin was the key to all of it, Arisa thought as she set out for the tavern that night. She had donned her tavern clothes and was several blocks from the palace when she heard the swift boot steps on the street behind her.

Tonight the rain had lightened to a drizzle, and a lighter spot in the clouds revealed the location of the unseen moon. Between that and the gate lamps of the nearby manors, Arisa could just make out the tall form of the man behind her.

When he saw she was looking, he picked up his pace.

Arisa spun and ran, taking the fastest route to the city districts, to crowds, and more light, and a squadron of guards if she could find them.

At the end of the block she whipped a glance back and saw nothing—but that didn't reassure her. The fact that he might be somewhere else, ready to pounce on her with a knife, sent panic racing through her veins. Why hadn't she brought her own knife with her? She'd be helpless against an armed man. She didn't stop running till she reached Dock Street—crowded enough to make the most skilled assassin hesitate to take his victim.

She was gasping for breath, with a stitch in her side. She stood with her back to a building, watching people move up and down the street. No one lingered in a suspicious fashion. In fact, no one lingered at all. This relative break in the rain might have lured more people out, but they weren't standing around.

No one seemed to be passing her repeatedly, though bundled as people were, it was hard to tell.

Had it been only some footman, braving the milder weather to spend his free night in a tavern? He'd seemed to start moving faster when she'd looked at him, but at that distance she couldn't be certain.

Arisa kept close watch the rest of the way to the tavern—she'd have sworn that no one followed her.

More than one man was taking advantage of the light rain to spend an evening out, and quite a few women, too. The benches were packed, and Arisa was too busy to notice anyone who might be watching her.

It wasn't till near closing time, when she and Baylee were gathering up the crockery and wiping tables, that she had time to bring up the subject that had brought her there.

"I've been thinking about your cousin, Katrin," she said, as casually as if this weren't a total change of subject.

Baylee blinked in surprise.

"Maybe it's 'cause of the way my folks died," Arisa went on swiftly. "But I wondered if she'd children of her own. Or a husband who'd mourn her."

Or who she might have confided in.

"She'd not yet wed," said Baylee. "She spoke of this lad or that, but nothing ever came of it."

"So she'd no one but your family to care for her?" Arisa persisted.

"No, her own parents are still alive, and they're grieving something fierce," said Baylee. "She had two brothers as well, but she was the only girl in the family, and her folks . . . They kept her room, still, in their house, even though she lived in the palace and the One God knows they could have used the space. Her pa's a tailor," Baylee went on. "And my pa's sister worked in the palace herself before she married him. That's how they met—he clothed her mistress, and she was forever picking things up at his shop. More often than need be. He'd send a boy to deliver to those who didn't have pretty maids he could flirt with. And he says he never started forgetting things out of the orders he filled till my aunt started coming by to get them."

The sparkle in Baylee's eyes spoke of an old family joke. Her aunt and uncle clearly loved each other, and they'd loved their daughter, too. Arisa felt another pang of that odd grief for others that Katrin's death evoked.

But if they'd kept her room . . . "He must be fair prosperous," said Arisa, "to keep a room for someone who didn't live there." She could hardly demand the address outright.

"He does well enough," said Baylee. "But it's not that they don't need the room. They live over the shop, and they've got bolts of cloth stacked in the hallways, even going up the stairs. You want to watch your step, if you're going out to the privy after dark."

"Trip you up?" Arisa asked, to keep the conversation going.

"I skidded down half a flight on top of a bolt of fine kersey." Baylee grinned. "It wrecked the cloth, but it saved my shins."

"It sounds like a big place," said Arisa, though it didn't, really.

"No, it's one of those tall, narrow shops in the Weavers Row," Baylee told her. "It was only because they cared for Katrin so much that they kept her room for her."

Weavers Row! Arisa struggled to keep her expression indifferent. "I'm glad she'd someone to care about her. And glad she left no orphans hungry, though I'm sorry for her folks."

"The brothers, too," said Baylee. "She was the baby of the family, as well as the only girl, and they all spoi—" She broke off, looking uncomfortable.

"I understand," Arisa said, and she allowed Baylee to change the subject. She'd gotten a clearer picture of her maid from this conversation than she had from more than a month of knowing her. Was that Katrin's fault, or hers?

Whoever's fault it was, Katrin had a room on Weavers Row, and that would be a far more private place to keep incriminating papers than her room in the palace.

Arisa crept home from the tavern, watching with every step for someone following, but she saw no one suspicious—and as she neared the palace she saw no one at all. Had the man she'd seen been an innocent stranger? Either way, she was carrying her dagger next time, though it would be hard to explain to the Mimms.

The next day she hid out in the tack room where she'd spoken to Sammel, and when Weasel and Edoran came back from their ride she caught Weasel's arm as he passed the door and dragged him in.

Edoran, looking back to see what had happened to his companion, encountered her most ferocious scowl. His brows rose.

She made a shooing gesture, ordering him on his way.

He rolled his eyes in exasperation, but turned and walked off. A moment later she heard him ask a question, distracting the grooms. Spoiled maybe, stupid no.

"He's keeping them busy," she told Weasel, closing the door. "But we might not have much time."

"Time for what?" Weasel asked warily. "You're up to something, aren't you? You're going to get both of us in tons of trouble. Again."

"Again? Who dragged who into rescuing Justice Holis? Into dealing with criminals? Who got who arrested by the palace guard?"

"Who got whom," said Weasel. "And you got me into trouble more recently."

"Who got *whom*? You've been hanging around with too many lords—it's rotting your brain. Especially if you think that little fuss about teaching Edoran to fence was trouble."

He grinned. "All right. I got you into lots more trouble than you got me into. It's just that I'm afraid you're about to change that."

"You may be right," Arisa told him, sobering.

She started at the beginning, when she had first followed Katrin out of the palace, and told him everything.

Weasel listened, his frown of concern deepening. Alarm flashed into his eyes when she mentioned the man who might, or might not, have been following her.

"You could have been killed!"

"Assuming he's the one who killed Katrin, I could have. But he also might have been some assistant undergroom on his night off. And I never saw him again. It's like everything else—there's no proof! But I think I know where to look for some."

She told him what she'd learned from Baylee and then sat,

listening to the patter of rain on the roof. It had been raining for an awfully long time, even for a coastal winter.

"You want me to help you break into that tailor's shop," said Weasel slowly. "And search for something that might give you a clue to Katrin's mysterious employer. Or to the conspiracy's palace patron. Assuming, of course, that there really is a conspiracy going on, and that Katrin wasn't just trying to embarrass you because you annoyed her. Which isn't exactly impossible, all things considered."

"I saw two meetings in the tavern," said Arisa. "I found the cell. Can you think of innocent explanations for that?"

"A club of wine tasters," said Weasel promptly. "And a crazy relative who had to be locked up sometimes."

Sudden dread sent a chill over her skin. "You think I'm crazy, don't you? You think I'm imagining all this. That I'm making it up."

And now, with his new royal friend, he didn't need her or her problems.

"I might," said Weasel, "except for one thing."

"What?"

"Your maid was *murdered*, dummy! She had to be involved in something—something deadly serious."

"So?" Arisa's heart had begun to pound.

"So I think we'd better search her room."

Arisa had intended to go that very night, but Weasel insisted on taking a full day to scout their target. He wanted a week, but Arisa put her foot down at that.

She wouldn't have begrudged several days, except for the fact that Holis' and her mother's edict meant she couldn't go with him. He also insisted that she not go alone to the tavern, or anywhere outside the palace, until the stalker had been caught.

"But I'd have my dagger with me," Arisa had told him. "I'm not an amateur."

"Neither is he," said Weasel grimly. "Promise, on your word."

"But I can't just—"

"If you don't promise," he went on, "I'll tell Justice Holis and your mother the whole story. They may not believe there's anything to it, but I'll bet the Falcon can keep you here. She would, too."

"All right, all right," Arisa grumbled. "I won't go out alone until the stalker is caught."

Weasel looked skeptical.

"I promise," she had added. "I won't. Really."

He must have heard the sincerity in her voice, because he'd nodded and let the subject drop.

The next morning her dancing tutor told her that Weasel had been sent on an errand for the regent and would be gone all day.

Arisa wondered how he'd arranged that. He'd been Justice Holis' clerk, and still sometimes worked for him in that capacity, but how had he persuaded the regent to let him go?

He was good at that kind of thing, far better than she was. Her own talent was more along the lines of taking on an enemy with knife or pistol in hand . . . and it embarrassed her that she'd been relieved when Weasel had extracted that promise.

Being stalked by a professional assassin in the dark was different from fighting a man she could see, who would almost certainly underestimate her, and who probably wasn't as skilled as she was anyway. Her mother's men had not only taught her to fight—the best of them had taught her to reckon up the odds before she started a fight. Arisa had no desire to confront the man who'd put that dagger so skillfully into Katrin's heart.

The day dragged past. For the first time since she'd come to live at the palace, Arisa found herself looking forward to evening court. She stepped briskly into the overheated candlelit room and looked around. Through the swirl of dancers, she saw that Weasel was standing beside the prince, as usual. Arisa frowned. She'd have to get him away from Edoran before they could talk, and she wasn't sure how to do that without calling attention to herself. No one had forbidden her to speak with Weasel in public, but she knew her mother would prefer that she avoid anything that might make people gossip.

She drifted around the edge of the room toward the prince, keeping out of the dancers' way. She didn't even see Ronelle until the girl stepped into her path.

"Arisa, my dear, how lovely to see you here. We see you so seldom, since . . . anymore."

Since she'd been caught tussling in the hay with Edoran? Since something else? Danica stood to one side, smirking. Whatever Ronelle was getting at, it had been set up in advance.

"Nice to see you, too." Arisa moved to the side, but Ronelle blocked her path and Danica came to stand beside her. Definitely up to something.

"Considering what happened the last time we talked," said Arisa, "are you sure you want to have this little chat?"

Color flamed in Ronelle's face, and several people snickered. It wasn't just Ronelle and Danica; they had an audience. Arisa looked for her mother, but the Falcon wasn't there.

"I'm too well born to hold your unfortunate upbringing against you." Ronelle sounded as if she were strangling, but she got the words out. "I just wanted to say how lovely you look this evening."

Arisa's panicked gaze flashed to her dress, but nothing was falling apart or off of it. The dark green satin bore no stains that she could see. She grabbed the back of her skirt and pulled it around to examine as much of the fabric as she could, and Ronelle laughed.

"No, I mean it. You look very fine. Your new maid's doing a wonderful job. Surprising you could get such a talented woman . . . since you murdered the last one."

A murmur of delicious shock rose from the crowd around them. They'd known what she planned to say, Arisa realized, but she still felt chilled. This was what the Falcon had feared. Did they really think she might have killed Katrin? Did the servants? She struggled for something to say, something to prove her innocence, but she couldn't find it.

"You know perfectly well she didn't kill anyone," Weasel announced, suddenly appearing at Arisa's side. "If she was going to stick a knife in someone, it would be—"

"What's going on here?" The words were the same as last time, but it was Shareholder Ethgar who pushed through the crowd instead of the Falcon.

Ronelle lowered her eyes. "Nothing, Papa. I was just complimenting Arisa on her new maid."

"She called Arisa a killer," said Weasel bluntly. "But since she's a notorious liar, I suppose we shouldn't make too much fuss about it."

This time the crowd's gasp was unfeigned.

"That's enough," Ethgar snapped. "From all of you. Ronelle, come with me." He took her by the elbow and dragged her off. With a triumphant glance at Arisa, Danica followed.

Weasel glared at the staring circle of courtiers, until one by one they turned away.

"Don't let it bother you," he said. "Ronelle's nothing but a troublemaker, and everyone knows it."

"Do they?" Arisa murmured. "Do the servants know it too?"

Weasel's gaze slipped away. "If they don't, they will soon. Don't let it bother you."

He patted her shoulder, and then returned to the prince. Arisa found she had no more stomach for court and went back to her room. Her maid was waiting, despite the early hour. She didn't seem to be afraid of Arisa. Weasel was right. They'd find out who really murdered Katrin—then everyone would know. She could talk to Weasel tomorrow.

It wasn't till her maid undressed her, and the crumpled note tumbled out of her sash, that Arisa realized what he'd done. And the woman almost certainly got the wrong idea when Arisa snatched it up and thrust it into her dresser drawer. Was Weasel as bored with palace life as she was? He was certainly dusting off all his criminal skills.

When her maid left to fetch some hot water, Arisa read the note. At *the wall,* it said, in Weasel's neat hand. As *soon as you can.*

Of course, he hadn't known she'd leave the court so early. Arisa let the maid put her to bed. She picked up a book, but she couldn't concentrate on the story. She built the dummy in her bed, and waited till most of the court had retired before slipping out of her room and down the vines. The rain was heavy again tonight, but it had been raining for so long that she barely noticed it.

Weasel reached the climbable place in the wall soon after she did. He too wore a broad-brimmed hat, and his coat looked warmer than hers. When she started for the wall, he took her arm and drew her away. "If he's picking you up when you come over the wall, let's see if we can avoid him."

He led her down one of the bridle paths, stumbling on stones and ruts in the darkness, to a section of the wall that fronted a different street. When he climbed to the top, he looked up and down the street for some time before reaching down to give her a hand.

It was a harder place to climb, but Arisa managed—and Weasel had no need to signal for silence as they hurried down the street and turned onto another. They'd traveled several blocks before he spoke. "I don't hear anyone behind us. You?"

"Not a thing," said Arisa, light-headed with relief. Companionship, as well as the dagger in its sheath on her belt, made her feel much more comfortable. She was inclined to think that it had been some innocent stranger behind her the other night, and if it wasn't, they had lost him. "Did you learn what you wanted to about the tailor's shop?"

Weasel sighed. "Not nearly as much as I *want* to. But there are no dogs, the back door lock is one I can pick, and unless they noticed and refilled it, the lamp by their back gate should be running out of oil right about now. And I did find out the most important thing."

"What's that," Arisa asked obligingly.

"I found out which of the eleven tailors on Weavers Row recently had a daughter murdered."

"Eleven!" Arisa exclaimed.

"There are reasons," said Weasel, "why you should take a lot of time to study your target before you break into it."

When he led her straight to the correct back gate, Arisa began to agree with him. This area was prosperous enough that several gate lamps glowed in the narrow lane, but the lamp beside the gate Weasel stopped at was dark, just as he'd promised. Arisa drew her dagger and slid it through the crack between gate and post, lifting the latch. She pushed the gate open and stepped into the yard behind the shop.

Weasel didn't follow. She looked back. He was standing in front of the gate with a thin strip of wood in his hand and a scowl on his face.

"Well, excuse me for seeing the obvious," Arisa whispered. "Are you going to stand there till the guard comes by?"

"Not at all." Weasel came in and closed the gate quietly. "By all means, burgle the place yourself. The lock on the back door's all yours."

Despite his words, he was already pulling out his picks as he crossed the yard. If you had to work with a burglar, it was nice to have one who was too professional to hold a grudge. And he opened the lock almost as fast as Arisa could have done it with a key.

He pushed the door open slowly, but no squeal of hinges betrayed them.

"Even if they heard something," Arisa breathed, "they'd just think it was one of their workers going out to the privy."

"Assuming," Weasel breathed back, "that their workers live in. This is the city, remember? They might all lodge somewhere else. If I'd had more time . . ."

If he'd had more time he'd have known how many people slept in this house, where their rooms were, and probably a dozen other things that Arisa hadn't thought of. She resolved to let him lead the way from now on.

A resolve that was promptly tested, when the first thing he did after closing the door was to stand perfectly still while their eyes adjusted to the darkness.

There were bolts of cloth in the hallways, and even bolts stacked on the stairs. The boards creaked several times as she and Weasel climbed, sounding louder than a thunderclap to her sensitive ears, but no one came to investigate. The home and shop between them were three stories high, the second floor holding a dining room, a kitchen, and an office.

There were more bolts of cloth cluttering stairs to the third floor. Weasel stopped at the top and laid his head against the first door, the one that would look down on Weavers Row. There were small windows at each end of the hallway, but they didn't admit enough light for Arisa to make out his expression. She could barely see the gesture with which he motioned for her to listen too, but she stepped forward and pressed her ear to the door.

Snoring. Faint, but unmistakable. She grinned. It made sense that the tailor and his wife would have the best bedroom, but she wouldn't have known how to check it without opening the door.

The next two rooms were clearly used for storage. The one that opened onto the back of the house held shadowy bedroom furniture, and a bed with no one in it.

Weasel whisked her in and closed the door.

"We need the candles," Arisa whispered.

"I know, but not just yet." Weasel went to the bed and removed the pillows, which he laid against the bottom of the door so no light would show beneath. Then he drew the curtains across the windows. When he finished, he lit the candles they'd brought. The striker's rasp sounded loud in the stillness.

It was clearly a girl's room; the curtains, bed canopy, even pillowcases were trimmed with ruffles. The writing desk showed scratches and dents but it was clean. When Arisa stepped forward to search it, the faint, sweet scent of fresh wax reached her nose. It had been polished recently. After Katrin's death?

Arisa thought of a grieving mother, cleaning this room for the daughter who would never return, and tears rose in her eyes. She blinked them back and opened the desk drawer. She was on a trail that might lead to the man who'd killed that daughter, and perhaps other people's children too. And maybe it would be possible, when he was caught, to keep Katrin's criminal actions out of the public record—or at least away from public attention. Assuming, of course, that she had been a criminal.

The writing desk held a handful of old letters, which told Arisa nothing, and a diary that Katrin had evidently started keeping when she was nine and stopped keeping when she was twelve. Arisa wanted to believe the rest of the journals, including a current one, might be hidden somewhere—but the last book was half-empty, and the entries had become so sporadic that it was clear Katrin had simply abandoned it.

The small sounds Weasel had been making as he searched the rest of the room had stopped.

"Have you found anything?" Arisa asked, closing the drawer.

"Maybe," said Weasel. He sat on the bed, holding a jewelry box in his hands.

Arisa went to look at the trinkets he'd spilled onto the bedspread. "I never saw Katrin wear jewelry. I don't think maids are supposed to, or something. These are . . . maybe a little better than I'd have expected, but the gold's probably just a plating, and pearls aren't too expensive. Her parents are well-off, and they loved her. There's nothing out of the ordinary here."

"No." Weasel's hands were moving over the box. "But I think there might be . . . Ha! Got it!"

The bottom of the box fell open and a mass of sparkling jewelry tumbled onto the bed.

Arisa's eyes widened. Rubies, emeralds, and even a handful of diamonds weren't something a tailor's daughter would own.

"He paid her in jewels," she murmured.

"Someone did," Weasel agreed. He picked up a bracelet, gold studded with topaz, and examined it critically. "Not old enough to be remarkable, and not so new that the jeweler would remember who he made it for—if he's still alive. I'd guess these belonged to our villain's grandmother."

"So her employer is a nobleman," said Arisa. "Normal people don't pay their employees in jewelry."

"Or a noblewoman," said Weasel. "But it's still not proof of a crime. I've heard of servants being given jewelry to reward some extraordinary service—Or if their noble employer is short of cash, he might use old jewelry to pay eight or nine months' back wages."

Arisa held up a pendant, whose centerpiece was a ruby the size of her thumbnail. "It would take a lot of back pay to earn something like this."

Weasel eyed the glittering heap. "Agreed. It may not be proof, but it's certainly suggestive. Do you want to take this to Justice Holis and your mother now?"

Arisa frowned. "Would this jewelry be enough to identify the person who gave it to her?"

"Probably not," said Weasel. "It's the right age to have been locked in a strongbox for the last thirty years. Half the nobles in court probably have a collection like this. At least, those who haven't reset the gems in modern settings, or sold them because they needed the coin. Your villainous employer is one of the nobles who's really rich, not just faking it. That probably eliminates two thirds of the court right there."

"That still leaves a third," said Arisa. "It's not enough evidence. Let's keep looking."

The bureau, the wardrobe, and the bed yielded no clues at all. Weasel poked around the hearth, though in this modest a house he didn't expect to find a secret compartment—particularly in something that wasn't the main bedroom. Arisa saw the rim of a piece of paper among the ashes at the back of the fireplace and pulled it out.

It was almost entirely burned away. Only the bottom of the page and a bit of the left side remained. The side held bits of dates. The two lines on the bottom said, *5th Lordin, several ambassadors at court—perfect for incident. Horse show on 19th Lordin don't bother—only hawk lovers present.*

Arisa's heart began to pound.

Weasel had been reading over her shoulder. "It's some sort of instructions. Hawk lovers. Your mother's friends? But I don't—"

"The fifth of Lordin," said Arisa, "was the night my gown came apart. She was trying to make me look bad! To make my mother look bad. She was paid to do it."

"But there was no horse show on the nineteenth," Weasel objected.

"It's been raining too hard," said Arisa. "It would have been canceled."

"So we have a sample of his writing," said Weasel. "I don't suppose you recognize it?"

Arisa shook her head. "Not many courtiers send me notes. It's not signed." She turned it over to be sure.

"He wouldn't sign it," said Weasel. He took the paper from her, staring at the handful of words.

"Do you recognize it?" Arisa asked hopefully.

"No. But if I see it again, I will."

They sifted the rest of the ashes but found nothing more, and left the shop as silently and easily as they'd come.

"We didn't get much," said Arisa. "Nothing like proof." They were several blocks from Weavers Row and she spoke in normal tones, though it sounded loud in the quiet street. The rain had softened to a drizzle once more, but it was very late now and the street was empty.

Weasel snorted. "We found some pretty good evidence. What did you want, a signed confession?"

"Yes," said Arisa. "If more of that paper had survived . . ."

"That was probably the last page, judging by the dates," said Weasel. "He's too smart to sign something so incriminating."

"You don't know either of those things," Arisa argued. "He might have given her instructions for the next six months. He might—"

"Shh!" Weasel hissed.

"What do you mean, shh? He might have signed—"

Weasel was still walking forward, his eyes on the street ahead, but his body had stiffened. He reached out casually and grasped her arm above the elbow, his fingers pressing into her flesh.

"I meant for you to stop talking," he said. "But I suppose that's too much to hope for. I think someone's following us."

CHAPTER 13

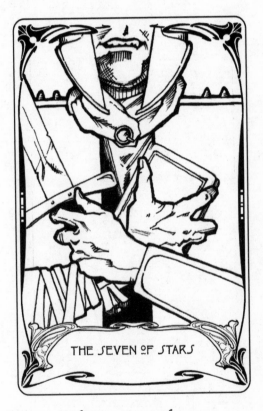

THE SEVEN OF STARS

The Seven of Stars: the reeve.
An enforcer of law, of order. Order imposed, possibly by force.

Arisa started to look back, but Weasel's grip tightened so hard she almost yelped. She listened instead. She could barely hear the soft footsteps.

"How far back is he?" Fear thundered through her, but this time she had a knife. And she wasn't alone.

"About half a block," said Weasel. "No, don't walk faster. Don't do anything till I tell you."

"How did he find us?" Arisa demanded. "I'd swear we weren't followed from the palace."

"Me too," said Weasel. "But if he knows we're sneaking out, he might guess we're investigating Katrin's death. And Katrin's home is a logical place for us to look."

Arisa's thwarted need to run made her skin tingle. She drew deep breaths of the cold wet air.

"But how did he know we were there? We closed the drapes."

"Enough light would have leaked out," said Weasel. "If someone was looking for it. Now!"

He dragged her into a side street, running at top speed. Aside from her startled stagger around the corner, Arisa ran every bit as fast.

"Why didn't you warn me?"

"I was afraid your body language would give us away before

we made the turn," Weasel gasped. "It usually does."

It usually did. Arisa had followed people for her mother, since no one ever suspected a child, and she always knew when they were going to turn before they did it. She was about to agree with Weasel when their pursuer came around the corner—now that he was running, his footsteps were loud. She risked a glance back. He was big, with broad shoulders. Not a man she'd want to tackle, but between the two of them they had a chance.

"Where do you want to try to capture him?" she panted.

"Capture him? *Capture him?* You're out of your mind!"

It sounded so familiar that Arisa smiled despite her fear. "I don't want to kill him . . . unless we have to. We need to find out . . . what he knows." Her breath was coming shorter. They'd have to do something soon.

Weasel said something from which only the word "lunatic" emerged clearly. Then he snapped "Follow me!" and shot into a side street.

Arisa looked back as she whipped around the corner. "I think we're gaining! Can we . . . outrun?"

This street would be a good place to try it. Short, and lined with crates and bins, it ended in cross streets that went in three different directions, none of them straight. If they could go down one, and turn off it before the stalker reached the intersection, they could escape! She started to put on a burst of speed, just as Weasel grabbed her arm and pulled her to a stop. He let go instantly to fling up the lid of a low wood bin. "In!"

It was his city, and she'd never gone wrong trusting him yet.

Or at least if she had, he'd rescued her from the consequences. Arisa climbed into the wood bin. The logs dug into her knees, then into her ribs as she lay down, curling up to make room for Weasel.

He spent a few precious seconds darting down the street half a dozen yards to throw open a gate—how had he known it would be unlocked? Then he raced back and rolled into the bin beside her, lowering the lid just as she heard the running footsteps grow loud again. Their stalker had rounded the corner.

Arisa, who'd been about to draw her knife, froze. She was breathing with her mouth open, deep silent breaths. The wood bin's sides were woven willow—she could see through the cracks but she didn't dare turn her head. She didn't need to; the killer was coming to them. If he thought to look in the bin, she was in no position to fight. Unless he grabbed for Weasel first. Boy and girl—he probably would go for Weasel, and then she'd have a chance.

Her fist clenched hard on her dagger's hilt, but the stalker ran past their hiding place to the gate, which still swung on its hinges. He stopped and peered into the yard. Then he looked at the three streets leading off the end of this one, and swore.

There was a lamp lit somewhere beyond the gate, and Arisa could see his face. He looked perfectly ordinary, except for the frustration that twisted his features. Neither old nor young, with his hair just beginning to recede. If she hadn't known better, Arisa would have taken him for a journeyman craftsman who'd just encountered some snag in his current project.

But she did know better, and she stopped breathing as his gaze swept back over the lane. He was listening. He looked through the gate once more, cursed again, and jogged to the crossing, looking first up one street and then the next. He hesitated, then set off to the right, but he was only moving at a fast walk now. He knew he'd lost them.

Still, it was several minutes before Weasel stirred, then lifted the lid and climbed out of the bin.

"I've used that one half a dozen times," he murmured. "It's never failed me yet. I'm glad those folks haven't gotten any smarter about locking their gate in the last few years. It's the moving gate that pulls them past the bin."

"I figured that out," Arisa told him, though he probably had a right to brag. She climbed out stiffly. Several of the logs had left what felt like permanent dents in her hide. "How are we going to get back into the palace?"

"Same way we came out," said Weasel. "If he wasn't watching the easy place, he'd have picked us up when we came out. And we'd probably both be dead."

Arisa waited for him to demand that now they go to Justice Holis and her mother. That hoard of jewelry was reasonable proof that Katrin had been up to something. Then the guards, or someone Holis appointed, would take over the investigation and her mother would lock her up for a year. Arisa sighed. Despite the discomfort, and even the terror, it had been wonderful adventuring with Weasel again. They worked well together, but she knew his limits.

So why hadn't he demanded they tell Holis and the Falcon? Unless . . .

"You have a new plan! Don't you? What is it?"

"I do have . . . well, the beginning of an idea," said Weasel. "I'll have to think about it for a while before I commit us to doing anything stupid. Like taking on an assassin, when we're armed with nothing but a knife."

Though he was willing to argue with her all the way back to the palace, he refused to say another word about his idea.

"You told the prince?" Arisa's voice rose incredulously, and Weasel shushed her. They were walking down the corridor after their etiquette lesson—the only lesson Weasel shared with her and Edoran didn't.

"We need him," said Weasel. "And he agreed to help, which is pretty brave, considering—"

"He isn't brave," said Arisa. "He's a—" The memory of a pin securing two panels of flapping cloth stopped her. "He's all right, some of the time, but you saw what he was like when my mother confronted Pettibone. He's got no physical courage at all. He'll mess things up!"

"You don't know that," Weasel protested. "You don't even know what the plan is."

"If it's got the royal runt in it, I don't want to know!" Arisa turned and stalked down another corridor, leaving Weasel standing alone. Why had he told Edoran? The prince was a total coward. He'd cave in at the first hint of danger, and probably get both Weasel and Arisa killed trying to protect— "Oof!"

She reeled back from the body that had just stepped into the corridor, and a stack of linen toppled to the floor.

"I'm sorry," said Arisa. "That was my fault. Let me help."

It wasn't a maid; it was Yallin.

"No harm done," said the seamstress. "I've mended this lot so well it wouldn't dare tear on me. But what's got you so fired up?"

Arisa knelt to gather up the scattered sheets and pillowcases. Her face was hot. But it was Weasel's fault! Everything had been going so well, and now . . .

"What would you do," she asked Yallin, "if a friend of yours told someone else something you'd told him in confidence?"

Yallin's brows rose. "First, I'd consider what his motives might have been. There's some things important enough to break a promise for."

"He didn't exactly promise," Arisa admitted. "But he knew I wanted it kept quiet. And now that he's included Ed— Now it's all wrong!" Tears of fury rose in her eyes, and she blinked hard.

Yallin sighed. "But young Weasel is the prince's friend too. And a thorny road he seems to have of it, between the two of you."

"How did you . . ." Some of the tumult in Arisa's heart subsided. "I suppose it is pretty obvious."

Yallin smiled. "Come in here, and we'll refold these." She led Arisa into the nearest parlor, conveniently empty, and closed the door behind them.

"Take the corners," she commanded, flipping one end of the

sheet to Arisa. "It's understandable that you're jealous of Prince Edoran, lass. But sooner or later you'll have to get over it."

Arisa felt her face flame. "I'm not jealous!"

Yallin folded her end of the sheet and stepped forward. When Arisa was little, the Falcon had lived in a house in a village, and Arisa had learned the soft, practical dance of folding sheets.

The older woman said nothing, and they walked through the steps for two more sheets before Arisa added, "Even if I was, it doesn't give Weasel the right to betray my secrets! This was something we were working on *together*."

"You said he hadn't promised," Yallin pointed out. "But that's between you and Weasel. It's you and Edoran I'm concerned about."

"There is no me and Edoran," Arisa said fiercely. "There never will be, no matter what my mother wants. He's too creepy. And he's . . . It's like he's two different people. Sometimes he's sort of decent, and then he turns into an arrogant twerp! He's crazy, that's what it is."

Yallin flipped out another sheet. "You might be right about that. At least, in part."

Arisa almost forgot to step forward and take the next fold. "*You* think the prince is crazy?"

"Most lads in his situation," said Yallin, "rich lads with no parents, or parents who don't care, they usually get raised by the servants."

"So he got raised by the servants," said Arisa. "So what? There are lots of worse things."

"There are," Yallin agreed. "And one is being raised by servants who were hired by your enemy, most of whom hated you."

Thinking suppressed some of her anger. "I've heard that," said Arisa. "That his servants hated him. I heard he did things that gave them reason to."

"Maybe he did," said Yallin. "Even I don't know the whole story behind that one. And it's a prob— Well, that's neither here nor there. But have you thought about what it would be like to be raised by strangers who hate you? Strangers who can make your life a misery in a thousand petty ways, yet you have the power to command them—even get them fired, if you're desperate enough. I'm amazed he turned out as sane as he is!"

Arisa scowled. "It's like . . . It's like he tries to be nice, but he doesn't know how. And when he gets confused, or can't figure it out, he falls back on being an arrogant twerp. So maybe it's the arrogant twerp that's real, and the nice Edoran that's fake!"

"Maybe they're both real," said Yallin. "People are hardly ever only one thing. Run along now, lass. That's all the sheets, and I can do the pillow slips myself."

Arisa still hadn't made up her mind when she met Edoran at the wall that night.

"I think this is a mistake," she told him.

"Well, it certainly wasn't my idea," he said. "If you don't want to go through with it, you should have told Weasel when he was taking us over all those maps."

Weasel had spent the morning away from the palace setting

things up, and the afternoon drilling his coconspirators. Arisa liked every part of the plan, except for the prince's presence.

Weasel's coat and broad-brimmed hat fit Edoran fairly well, but to her eyes he still looked . . . small. Small and weak and worthless. Was he as jealous of her friendship with Weasel as she was of his? Probably. But if she'd been misjudging him because of something as petty as that, then she owed him the benefit of the doubt. That was why she'd finally agreed to this. That, and because it was the best chance they'd ever have to learn the identity of the man who'd paid Katrin to try to harm her mother.

"Come on," Arisa sighed. "Let's get this over with."

She had to help him climb the wall, even in the easy place. Of course, she reminded herself, trying to be fair, he'd never done it before. Edoran dropped to the street neatly enough, and looked around nervously.

"Don't do that," Arisa whispered. She dropped down beside him and continued in an even lower voice, "We're supposed to lure him into following us. He might not, if he knows we're looking for him."

Edoran peered at her through the light rain. "After what happened to you and Weasel last night, I'd think he'd be suspicious if you didn't act wary. In fact, you'd have to be crazy to leave the palace again at all."

This was undeniably true. "Well, that's why we're going the other way tonight. This way."

Arisa set off down the street in the opposite direction from the tavern. It was Weasel's theory that the stalker would position himself to follow them in the same direction they usually went. If they went in the other direction, he'd be farther behind them and it would allow them more time—plenty of time to reach any of the five foolproof escapes Weasel had planted along their route.

It had seemed a much better plan going over the map with Weasel, in front of the fire in her own room. Now the back of her neck crawled with tension.

"We turn toward the city at the end of the next block, right?" Edoran asked, looking over his shoulder.

His constant turning would also force the stalker to keep his distance, Arisa realized. Until the man decided to strike.

"That's right," Arisa confirmed. "Then straight for two blocks, then—"

"Then turn right, go ten yards, and the ladder will be hanging down the stable wall," Edoran finished with her.

Weasel must have drilled him as relentlessly as he'd drilled Arisa. He'd wanted to show them the course he'd spent the morning setting up, but between the edict that Arisa not go out with either of them and Edoran's difficulty in escaping his escort, it just hadn't been possible.

Still, they both knew where they were going. In just a few blocks they'd reach the first of the places where Weasel had promised they could elude the stalker. Then Weasel would take over, and soon they'd know who was behind all of this.

"Weasel and I were talking about who it might be," said Edoran, almost as if he were reading her thoughts.

"It's one of my mother's and Justice Holis' enemies," said Arisa. "Someone who wants to take over the regency."

"I agree," said Edoran. "But Justice Holis appointed your mother as his successor. If they're both disqualified, with no one else named . . ."

Arisa frowned. "How would your regent be chosen then?"

"It should be my nearest kinsman, but he has to be confirmed by a two-thirds majority of the concordance of shareholders," said Edoran. "This is where we turn, right?"

"Right." Before she went around the corner, Arisa stopped to look back. She saw nothing in the dark street. She heard nothing but the soft patter of the rain, yet a chill moved over her skin.

Was he there? Or was it just her own tension that made her feel like she was being watched.

Edoran had stopped to wait for her, looking very much like Weasel in the dimness.

He has to see both of us, Weasel had said. *He has to lose both of us. Otherwise he'll start wondering where I am.*

"So who's your nearest kinsman?" Arisa asked, turning down the new street. This one was better lit than most—had Weasel chosen it because of that?

"Harald Wasserton," said Edoran promptly. "He's my father's only living cousin."

"He'd never be approved by the shareholders," said Arisa. "He's a drunk."

"I know. But after him the question gets murky," said Edoran. "Because if you're only looking at legitimate male lines, you have to go back six generations, and there are scores of descendants from that generation. If you're willing to go through the female line, which has happened three times in Deorthas' history, though technically—"

"I get the picture," said Arisa shortly. He was babbling because he was nervous, but she couldn't blame him for that. "You're related to, what? Half the court?"

"Only about a fifth," said Edoran. "If you count only the legitimate lines. If you start adding illegits, which the church claims is illegal, but which has happened at least once before, then it's probably closer to three quarters. Weasel's been reading more of those old diaries; he says if you believe all the gossip those women wrote down, I'm probably related to everyone."

"So we can't narrow it down by looking at kinship," said Arisa, caught up in the question despite herself. "Have you seen or noticed anyone trying to . . . to discredit or sabotage Justice Holis. Or maybe get closer to you?"

"Getting closer to me—we're back to everyone at court," said Edoran. "Sabotaging Justice Holis . . . If someone's doing that, they're being really careful. Is this our turn?"

"No, we don't turn for two blocks," said Arisa. They might have been careful, or Edoran might not have noticed what they were doing.

"But with kinship," Edoran continued, "it gets even worse if you start separating the pre-Regalis descendants from the post-Regalis ones. If someone could prove he wasn't the old king's son, they could—"

"If someone could have proved that, they'd have done it a long time ago," Arisa told him. "Do you hear something?"

Edoran stopped talking. Their own footsteps. Rain. But suddenly, Arisa knew.

"Run!" she commanded, and set the example. Edoran was half a dozen strides behind her.

Their sudden change of pace forced the stalker to run too. He was farther back than she'd thought, almost three blocks, and she and Edoran had only half a block to go before they reached the rope ladder. They'd have plenty of time to scramble up to the stable roof and pull it up after them. The stalker would run right by, and when he gave up looking for them, Weasel would follow him back to his employer, and all Edoran's blathering about kinship would mean nothing. They'd know who their enemy was.

Arisa kept an eye on Edoran as they ran—he wasn't catching up, but he wasn't falling behind. They were moving fast enough that the stalker wasn't gaining on them. Plenty of time to climb the ladder.

She whipped around the corner and ran ten paces, the ten yards Weasel had described. No ladder. She ran a few more feet, running her hands along the wall in case she was somehow missing it. She stopped to look back.

Edoran raced around the corner. "This isn't a stable," he gasped. "We're in the wrong place!"

"We can't be!" Arisa looked across the street to be sure the ladder wasn't there, either, though she knew it was supposed to be on this side.

HILARI BELL

"No stable there either," Edoran cried, already sprinting down the street ahead of her. "Come on!"

When she neared the cross street Arisa looked for the ladder again, in case Weasel had forgotten which end of the block he'd put it on, but there was nothing there. They were off course. Somehow, in the dark and the rain they'd missed a turn . . . and now they had no way to escape the killer who ran behind them.

Edoran turned left at the corner, still following Weasel's preset route, though he had to know that they were off the map.

Arisa put on a burst of speed and caught up with him. It took more effort than she'd expected—he was fast. But he was already breathing harder than she was.

"Where should we go?" she panted.

"City," gasped the prince. "More . . . hide."

They dodged left again at the next corner, down a smaller street, and Arisa looked back just in time to see the stalker charge around the corner. He saw her and put on his own burst of speed. Edoran was slowing. They didn't have much time before the stalker came in sight, but this was a shorter street—still mostly residential, though not so wealthy. The houses and yards were smaller, concealed by wooden fences instead of high stone walls. Arisa began to watch for a place, any place they could— There!

She grabbed Edoran's arm and dragged him into a narrow carriage drive that must have led back to someone's stable. It ran between two fences for half a dozen yards, cluttered with a brimming rain barrel and half a dozen crates . . . and it ended in a latched gate.

Arisa grabbed the latch and yanked it up—locked! And too high to climb.

Edoran slammed into her side, knocking her flat into the mud behind the crates, just as the running footsteps pounded up to the opening of the drive . . . and stopped.

Arisa lay unmoving, listening to Edoran trying to gasp quietly. He did pretty well. Evidently well enough, for the stalker hesitated, looking up the street and then back toward them.

She laid a hand on her knife, ready to pull it free.

Something clattered up the street. It sounded like a thrown stone on cobbles to Arisa, but the stalker spun toward the sound. He crossed the lane and moved up a bit farther, trying to see down the cross streets and still keep the end of the drive in view.

Edoran was moving beside her, writhing like a snake, but Arisa kept her eyes on their enemy. He wasn't going to fall for it—and this constricted space, with only Edoran to help her, was the worst possible place for a fight.

She felt a flash of pure despair, but that vanished as the stalker turned and came back toward the carriage drive. He was going to search for them. She drew her knife, silently. If she could spring before he was ready . . .

He was ready now. A knife flashed silver in his hand as he drew nearer.

Arisa almost jumped out of her skin when a cold, muddy hand clamped down on her ankle. She turned to the prince, but he had vanished! There was only an arm extending from beneath the fence, and a deep depression in the mud where he'd dug it away.

Arisa yanked her leg free and plunged her head and shoulders under the fence, wiggling through the rain-softened earth. Her buttocks stuck, briefly, but Edoran grabbed her shoulder and dragged her through.

He was coated with mud from the top of his head to the bottom of his boots—he'd evidently dragged both their hats through the hole before he'd signaled her. He bent to push the mud he'd piled on this side of the fence back into the hole, but Arisa caught his wrist and he froze.

The stalker entered the drive. It was dark behind the crates, but if he saw the hole Edoran had dug, he'd know where they'd gone. If he came under the fence, she could take him, thrust her knife into the back of his neck while the fence pinned him down. If he climbed over the top, her best chance would come when he jumped down and was still recovering his balance.

The fence posts were spaced closer than the wicker of the wood bin—Arisa could see only the man's shadow passing over the boards.

He tried the gate first. Then he looked behind the crates. He checked to see if any of the crates opened. He even plunged his hands into the brimming rain barrel, though no one could have held their breath that long.

Then he swore and stamped out of the drive and away, into the night.

Arisa released her breath in a silent sigh and slumped against the fence.

Edoran was shaking so hard his teeth would have chattered,

if he hadn't pulled down one sleeve and stuffed it into his mouth. He looked utterly absurd, but Arisa wasn't inclined to laugh.

They'd done what they'd set out to do. It was up to Weasel now.

They waited in her room, not even caring what would happen if they were caught together—though Arisa told Edoran that if she was forced to marry him it would be his own silly fault.

She understood why he couldn't go to his own room and wait for Weasel to show up there. She almost went out to wait for Weasel by the wall, but it was raining harder now, and far too cold to stand still for long.

Only a few hours later a dark figure rolled over her balcony.

Arisa flung the door open before he could knock. "Are you all right?"

"Of course." Weasel pulled off his dripping coat and dropped it onto the floor, heading straight for the fire. "Unlike some people, I know this city. And I know better than to walk three blocks when I'm supposed to turn at two."

"You should have warned us that first block was so short," Edoran told him. "It was less than half the length of most blocks. We both missed it."

"If you hadn't been so busy argu—"

"Never mind all that!" Arisa exclaimed. "Did you find out who he works for?"

"I did." The grin that spread over Weasel's face was intolerably smug, but she had to admit he'd earned it. "He went straight back to report to his employer. Who didn't seem to mind being waked up in the middle of the night, though he wasn't happy about what he heard."

Arisa glared at him.

Edoran glared at him.

Weasel grinned again and gave in. "It's Shareholder Ethgar."

CHAPTER 14

THE EIGHT OF STARS

The Eight of Stars: loyalty.

Being true to a person, or a cause.

14

They went together to find the Falcon the next morning, all three of them, only to be told that the lord commander was meeting with the regent. When they arrived at Justice Holis' office, his clerk, Kenton, was standing watch outside the door.

"I'm sorry, Your Highness, but the regent and the lord commander are discussing important matters. I'll let them know you were here."

"No, you won't," Arisa told him. "We need to see both of them. And this is important."

She feinted right, then ducked under his left arm and opened the door. Men always underestimated a woman's quickness, especially if she was wearing skirts.

Was that why her mother wore dresses so often?

The Falcon and Holis both turned when the door opened. The regent's office was bigger than her mother's, with a huge polished desk and padded chairs. Justice Holis looked tired and harassed, the lines in his face deeper than usual. Her mother's face was smooth and sharp, like it looked before a fight.

"I'm sorry to interrupt you," said Arisa, dodging Kenton's snatching hand, "but it's urgent."

The justice shot Kenton a look, and the clerk fell back a place. Then Holis turned the same gaze on Arisa, and she stiffened to attention. "Excuse us, Mistress Benison, but your mother and I really are—"

Edoran came in, with Weasel at his heels, and the regent's brows rose. "A delegation, I see. Is this urgent, or can it wait?"

The Falcon was frowning. "If Arisa thinks something is important enough to interrupt us, then it probably is."

Pride in her mother's trust welled up in her heart. She hoped she had enough hard evidence to justify it.

Most men, told that a fourteen-year-old girl had any judgment at all, would have denied it—or at best offered her indulgent, false acceptance.

Holis waved Kenton out of the room and resumed his seat, his weary gaze suddenly curious. "Very well. What is it?"

He looked at the prince when he spoke, but Edoran turned to Arisa. It was her story, after all. She decided not to begin with the fact that she'd quarreled with her maid—even if her maid had been murdered.

"Master Darian is in the city," she told them. "He's attending secret meetings in a tavern called the King's Folly. I don't know who's behind the meetings, but I think they're plotting to make some move against you, Justice Holis. Against your regency. I think Katrin's murder was part of it."

Though she still didn't know the motive for that murder. Was Ethgar Master Darian's "patron in the palace"? And did that patron command the conspiracy, or did he only supply money?

The number of things she didn't know became more and more evident as she told the whole tale. Justice Holis asked questions at every stage, extracting details Arisa hadn't even known she remembered. And what he didn't ask about, her mother did.

In the end . . . "I'm sorry," she said. "I know it's not much."

Justice Holis leaned back in his chair gazing at the three of them, his expression half-thoughtful, half-appalled—especially when he looked at the prince. A portrait of Edoran's father hung on the wall behind him. The last king had been bigger than Edoran, stocky instead of slight, but Edoran had his mousey hair and somber eyes.

Justice Holis shook his head. "No, you were right to be concerned, and right to bring this to our attention. But the way you went about it! You are all forbidden, absolutely forbidden, to pursue this matter further. I can't believe . . . No more chasing killers for any of you. Is that *perfectly* clear?"

"Yes, sir," said Edoran.

Weasel scowled. "But we learned a lot. We learned that Ethgar is behind some of it. And we learned that Arisa's maid was involved in something crooked too."

"Master Darian's mere presence," said Justice Holis, "indicates that something illegal is going on. The rest of it isn't conclusive, though it certainly points toward . . . Hmm."

"You're thinking about that comment about deck shoes?" the Falcon asked. "It's a bit of a jump from there to those cursed pirates. And I can't see how Ethgar would be involved in that."

"The pirates?" Arisa asked.

"Not conclusive, as I said," Holis told the Falcon. "Right now we're both so taken up with pirates that if the cook put too much

263

pepper in the soup, I'd see it as a pirate plot. Still, if Master Darian and Shareholder Ethgar are plotting against us . . . Arisa said there were naval officers at that meeting, and one of the conclusions we'd just reached is that someone is informing the pirates about the movements of navy ships."

"You reached that conclusion," said the Falcon. "I can't imagine any naval officer assisting pirates. I've known a lot of them over the years, and to *stop* pirates, to keep innocent lives and ships out of their hands, is what the navy does. None of them would betray that."

"It doesn't have to be an officer," Holis told her. "It might be some assistant clerk, who's never set foot on a deck, but who has access to the disposition of ships."

Arisa's mind was reeling with new information. "You think someone is telling the pirates where the navy's searching for them? Does Shareholder Ethgar have any connection with the navy?"

"No," said the Falcon. "He runs the palace, but that's all. And it might be someone, a series of people, in the villages and towns along the coast. Smugglers have created networks of informants like that. Why couldn't the pirates?"

"Because the pirates are preying on the same towns and villages those informants live in," Holis replied. "And even before that, the sailors on the ships they raided and sank came from the seaside towns. Your hypothetical informants would be setting killers on their own kinsmen and friends! But that," he added, as the Falcon opened her mouth to argue further, "is a problem for another time. Right now we need to investigate these conspirators of Mistress Arisa's."

"I could go back to the tavern," Arisa told them. "I could—"

"No!" The Falcon and Holis spoke together, in the same I'm-the-adult tone. The justice signaled for her mother to continue.

"Holis is right," said the Falcon. "I forbid you to go back there, ever again. I can't chew you out for it this time, since it never occurred to me that I needed to forbid you to spy on treasonous conspiracies." Her expression was a blend of horror and rueful humor—it looked astonishingly motherly, which her mother seldom did, and the corners of Arisa's mouth twitched in sympathy.

Then that expression vanished, and it was the commander of a successful rebellion who went on, "But I absolutely forbid it now. No more spying on conspirators—and that goes for all of you! If you see something suspicious in the future, you report it to me or Regent Holis. You *don't* follow up on it yourself. Clear?"

Arisa might have argued with her mother, but it was the Falcon who spoke now. Arisa had known this was going to happen. In truth, she was a little relieved.

"Clear. But if we hadn't followed up on it, you'd never have found the conspiracy at all. If I'd reported that Katrin was sneaking off at night, would you have done anything besides tell the master of household to keep better discipline over the maids?"

"Maybe not, but that's not the point!" A mother's exasperation crept back into the commander's voice. "You know better than—"

"I think that discussion is best reserved for a later time," Holis interrupted. "So long as all of you agree not to go chasing assassins in the future." He looked at Edoran once more, shaking his head in dazed astonishment. Edoran, evidently under the impression that this was a severe scolding, looked down at his hands, but Arisa drew a relieved breath—if it got postponed long enough, she might evade the rest of the "discussion" entirely.

"What we need to consider now," Justice Holis went on, "is how best to continue the investigation ourselves. The city guard—"

"The city guardsmen are probably known to most of the customers in that tavern," the Falcon told him. "If they're not customers themselves. It's a dockside tavern. A naval officer would blend right in."

"The navy is part of the problem," Holis said curtly. "Weren't you listening? We can't—"

"I'll send an officer who has my personal trust," the Falcon snapped.

Were meetings between Holis and her mother always so acrimonious?

"What about the army?" Weasel asked. "A lot of them come from the country, and they don't spend much time in the city, so they're not as likely to be recognized."

The Falcon frowned, but her expression was more thoughtful than disapproving. "Those boots Arisa saw could have belonged to an army officer, instead of navy."

"Their boots have a different cut," Arisa told her. "With a

higher heel. I was on my knees, scrubbing the floor. I got a good look at all their boots and shoes, and I know the difference."

Holis' expression had brightened. "Sending an army officer is a good notion. I'm sure Diccon has someone who's well suited to that kind of thing."

The Falcon was still frowning. "You've got a point. Would Diccon take that kind of order from me, or do you need to give it?"

Her voice rang with silken challenge, and Holis sighed.

"The army has never failed to obey any legitimate order you've given."

The stress on the word "legitimate" was almost too subtle to hear, but Arisa caught it. So the army wouldn't obey all their commander's orders, just the ones General Diccon considered *legitimate?*

Sammel was right. It was good that her mother had him close by, and officers loyal to her in the navy as well.

Still, it would be even better if she and Justice Holis could get along.

Arisa lay in her bed, staring up at the dark ceiling. They'd been forbidden to return to the tavern. They'd been forbidden to spy on the conspirators. At all. Arisa accepted that. She wasn't a fool. This was too big for a handful of kids to manage. It belonged in the hands of competent adult investigators, and that was where it was. Out of her hands. Not her problem. So why couldn't she sleep?

It wasn't that she wasn't sleepy—at least, she should be sleepy. She'd put on her coat and britches and ridden Honey around the park, despite the rain that still drizzled down. She'd returned to the stable soaked and exhilarated, and she'd spent the evening reading to avoid meeting Shareholder Ethgar at court. She'd expected to fall asleep immediately. She would have . . . except for a small voice in the back of her mind, wondering if Baylee needed help with the tables. If Master Mimms was telling the customers that this latest pirate raid was the new regent's fault.

Hang it, she was worrying about whether or not the floor was getting muddy!

It would take days, maybe weeks, for a new investigator to get himself accepted at the tavern, and anything might happen in that time. And what were they going to do about Ethgar? Weasel was a good enough actor to talk to the man without giving himself away, but was Edoran?

She rolled over in bed, pounding a fist into her pillow.

She'd promised her mother she wouldn't return to the tavern. Not in so many words, perhaps, but the Falcon had forbidden it and she'd acknowledged the order. "Clear" implied a promise, not only to her mother, but to her commander. She couldn't break it. She couldn't go back to the King's Folly. She couldn't spy on the conspirators in any way. She couldn't—

Arisa sat bolt upright.

She'd promised, and so had Edoran, but she didn't remember Weasel making any promises at all.

* * *

The streets were busier at this early hour—just after Weasel got out of evening court—but the stalker hadn't been arrested yet. They'd climbed over the wall at yet another difficult place, and the stalker had no reason to think they'd go to the tavern. On the other hand, who knew what the stalker thought?

Arisa jumped half a foot when Weasel grabbed her arm. "What is it? Do you see him? Hear him? Where?" She looked, but there was no one suspicious behind them and a crowd all around.

"Don't worry, it's not him." Weasel swung her into the next alley they passed, and pulled her down to crouch beneath a staircase.

"If it's not him, what are we hiding from?" Arisa whispered. Rain dripped off the stairs. Arisa was grateful that her promise to her mother left her no reason to wear her ragged tavern clothes. She couldn't return to the tavern—but she could stand in the street outside it, while Weasel burgled the place.

"Nothing," he whispered back. "At least, I hope they're not looking for us."

"Who are—"

Then she caught the sound that had already come to Weasel's sharper ears, the sound of boots, stepping in unison. A unit of troops marched past the alley without even glancing aside.

"Why are we hiding from them?" Arisa asked again, more loudly. "They could keep us safe from—"

"All right, maybe they weren't after us." Weasel rose from behind the barrel. "I just . . . It's better to be safe than sorry, when it comes to armed guards." Relief quivered in his voice, and Arisa realized that Weasel would never get over his fear of the guards. In his heart, they would always be coming for him.

"They're not after you," Arisa assured him.

"They may not be after us," said Weasel, "but aren't you curious who they are—"

"Baylee!" Arisa leaped for the street, but Weasel caught her collar and pulled her back.

"What are you going to do? Warn them?"

"I don't know!" said Arisa, twisting out of his grip. "I didn't dream they'd send the guards for them! Not so soon."

"Soon is good," said Weasel. "Isn't it? Soon means they're probably arresting Ethgar and his stalker right now. They're involved in your maid's murder. We're *trying* to get them all arrested, remember?"

"But Katrin was working with them! Those troops might be after someone else, right?"

She'd been walking as they argued, and now they turned down Dock Street, following the troop. She could just see them, passing in and out of patches of light several blocks ahead. Another patch of light revealed Weasel's skeptical expression.

"That was an army troop. Anything but treason, it would be the city guard. Even for treason it should be palace guardsmen, but since Holis sent the army to investigate your conspirators, I suppose—"

"They're not mine!" Arisa snapped. "And those soldiers might not be arresting anyone. They might be doing army things."

"At night, in the rain? After all we told them? It has to be an arrest."

But Weasel was following her down the street, and she was grateful for his company.

Despite her arguments, she wasn't surprised when the troop turned into the narrow lane that housed the King's Folly. By the time she and Weasel reached the corner, they'd gone into the tavern, and the uproar had begun.

Customers spurted through the open door, shouting, cursing, pulling on their coats. Some of them still carried their cups—one opportunist had picked up half a dozen mugs on his way out.

Most of them hustled away, looking for another place to drink and spread the news, but some lingered, shouting insults at the guard.

The soldiers brought out Mistress Mimms first. Her hands were tied behind her. The white apron in which she took such pride gleamed in the darkness. She stood straight, haughtier than any court lady would have been in similar circumstances.

It was the cook who wept when they hauled her out. Master Mimms was next, quiet now, but his rumpled clothes and a faint limp told Arisa he'd tried to defend his home, his family . . . his cause.

Some of the wetness on Arisa's face was tears.

Baylee was one of the last people removed from the tavern. She tried to emulate her mother's dignified calm, but her shoulders hunched with tension and her face was deathly white in the lamplight.

Arisa had taken two steps forward without realizing it,

when Weasel caught her arm and pulled her back.

"You can't do anything now," he said urgently. "Confronting them will only make it worse. For all of you! If you have to give them a chance to kick you, first give them time to settle themselves and face up to things. All right?"

"No," said Arisa. "It's not all right." She jerked her arm from his grasp and walked away, away from the tavern, from pain, and the destruction of lives.

She had told Weasel they weren't "her" conspirators, but that was a lie. They were hers, and she had betrayed them to this. To arrest and scandal, maybe even prison and hanging.

What else could she have done?

"They might even be in league with the pirates," Weasel said, trotting to catch up with her. "You had to turn them in. Those pirates are killing people."

"My mother killed people," said Arisa. "For a cause."

Weasel said nothing. The dark buildings and rain-slick cobbles rolled past them as Arisa walked on.

If the conspirators were in league with the pirates, if they were responsible for the deaths of innocent men, women and children, she *couldn't* have let it go on. Every death they caused after this night, all the blood they spilled, would have been on her hands if she hadn't stopped it. And yet . . . She remembered Baylee's terrified face in the lamplight and shuddered.

No wonder she had felt so at home among the Mimms—they were just like the people she'd grown up with.

Part of her wondered how such decent people could be

involved in something so horrible, but sacrifices had to be made for any cause. To lay down lives, your life and others, was the mark of a hero . . .

. . . or a villain, depending on which side you were on?

Was Yallin right? Was it only about power, not good or bad at all?

If they knew the side they were on was slaughtering villagers, surely that made them villains. If they knew . . .

Did they know? All of them? Master Mimms, perhaps, but Arisa would stake her life that Baylee wouldn't do such a thing! And Stu, who was so soft under his gruff exterior, and Mistress Mimms, who gave food to beggars. And Katrin had been killed by someone who was working *against* the conspiracy. Even Master Mimms might not know that his conspiracy was dealing with the pirates!

"I have to talk to my mother about this. I have to talk to her now. Tonight!" Arisa looked around the unfamiliar street and frowned. "Where are we?"

"This is Load Street," Weasel told her. "In the warehouse district, near the leatherworks. It's not the best neighborhood, but not the worst, either. You'd have been in the worst if I'd let you turn downhill, like you started to three blocks back. You'd have been—"

"I don't care where we are!" Arisa snapped. "Get me back to the palace. I have to talk to my mother and Justice Holis. Now!"

Weasel knew his city. He led her back to the palace in less time than Arisa would have believed possible, cutting through several work yards and over a rooftop.

She considered saving even more time by walking right up to the gate and demanding that the guard take them to her mother. But if she was going to ask a favor, it might not be wise to flaunt the fact that she'd . . . skirted her mother's orders. She'd probably have to confess that she'd taken Weasel to the tavern, even if she'd never intended to go in herself, and Holis would make him promise as well. But turning up in her wet coat and muddy boots would guarantee that result. So she and Weasel scaled the wall and climbed the vines back up to her room, where they stood, dripping on the expensive carpet.

"Do you want to go to bed and let me go to my mother and Holis alone?" Arisa whispered.

Weasel shook his head. "I'll stick with you. I can't let you face the consequences alone."

He sounded insufferably noble, and Arisa grinned. "You're just curious. I'd have to fight to keep you out of that room."

"I'd fight back," Weasel told her. "And I fight dirty. I'll meet you in the corridor, in dry clothes, in five minutes. And comb your hair. Justice Holis probably won't come down as hard on a girl."

He slipped out before Arisa could retort that she was a girl no matter what she wore. But he was right. Tonight she'd need all the help she could get.

She left her wet clothing in a heap on the floor, and wiggled hastily into petticoats and a simple blue gown. Then she yanked a comb through her hair and tied it back with a white ribbon. She wasn't pretty, but she looked young, innocent, and wholesome.

The Falcon would see through that in two seconds, but Justice Holis might not. It was worth a try.

Weasel was pacing up and down the corridor, waiting for her. Arisa led him swiftly to her mother's room, where the maid told them that the lord commander was in a late meeting with the regent. But when they reached Holis' office, it was dark and empty.

They finally found their quarry in the Falcon's office. Kenton stood guard in front of the door, but after one look at Arisa's face he stepped aside.

She had intended to ask a favor. She'd intended to be meek and ladylike. But now that the moment had arrived, all the grief and guilt and fear came flooding back. Arisa turned the knob and threw the door wide.

"How could you arrest them without telling me? I'm responsible for this!"

In this office Justice Holis sat in front of her mother's desk, leaving the position of power to the Falcon. And tonight, unlike her daughter, the Falcon wore the white britches and dark blue coat of the commander of the king's army. It gave her even more authority as she rose to her feet.

"Come in and sit down, Ris. Bring Weasel in with you."

"Good luck trying to keep him out," Holis muttered.

Weasel caught the words, and flashed his mentor a cheeky grin.

As soon as the door closed, the Falcon spoke. "I didn't tell you because I received the proof we needed in the middle of evening court. With a known traitor in the palace I didn't dare risk this kind of scene in public. I didn't tell you afterward . . ."

Her shoulders slumped, and she sank into her chair. "I didn't tell you afterward because I thought it would be harder for you to know about it in advance. Because I could see you were fond of these people, and if you knew . . ."

Her eyes narrowed suddenly. "How did you know they'd been arrested? The palace guard took Ethgar after you were in bed. Did that gossipmongering maid tell you?"

Arisa couldn't let them blame her innocent maid. She opened her mouth, but Weasel spoke first.

"Could you tell us what proof you found? Or is that still a secret?"

"It seems very little is secret from you," Justice Holis said mildly.

Weasel shrugged. "Arisa came to me."

Arisa paused to admire that masterful prevarication, then she added, "I'd like to know too. If it isn't secret, I think I have a right to know."

The Falcon and Holis looked at each other.

"It is confidential," said the Falcon slowly.

"But you've proved that you can keep secrets," said Justice Holis. "And you do have a right to know. We'd never have looked there if you hadn't put us on the right track."

"Looked where?" Weasel asked. "What track?"

Holis considered the matter a moment longer, then nodded. "We had the guard search Ethgar's palace quarters, then his house in town. There was nothing here, but in his house we found . . . Well, to make a long story short, the man who'd killed Mistress Katrin tried to flee. When the guards captured him, he confessed."

"Thus avoiding hanging?" Weasel asked bitterly. "Even though he murdered one woman, and would have killed us if he'd caught us?"

Justice Holis sighed. "We need his testimony against Ethgar. In fact, his testimony is the only evidence we have, though we may find more now that we know where to look. But according to your stalker—he was originally from Ethgar's country estate—Ethgar wanted to take the regency from me and my allies, and he paid Katrin to . . . ah . . ."

"To publicly embarrass me," said Arisa. "It's a lot safer than trying to publicly embarrass my mother. And Ronelle was helping him. I should have thought of that."

"From what we can determine," said Holis, "the lady Ronelle's actions were her own choice. Her father would have preferred for her to dislike you far less obviously. Of course, she may have been influenced by his dislike."

So Ronelle had hated her for her own sake. That was only fair, since Arisa hated her back. "But why kill Katrin?" Arisa demanded. "She was doing the job."

The Falcon snorted. "When he caught you and Edoran tumbling in the hay, he evidently decided the job was done. And when Holis fired all the tutors—Giles and the others were originally working for Pettibone, but when he died, they transferred their allegiance to Ethgar—it frightened him into taking the matter more slowly. According to his thug, when Ethgar stopped paying her, Katrin tried to blackmail him and he ordered her death. According to Ethgar, his bribe to Katrin was in response to Arisa's disrespect for his daughter, and when she tried to blackmail him, he ordered his henchman to only frighten her off. Nothing physical at all, according to Ethgar."

Weasel frowned. "Why did he think he could take the regency at all?"

"He's one of the prince's kinsmen," said Holis. "One of the closer ones, in fact. And he evidently worked closely with Pettibone as well. More closely than I'd realized. We're going to have quite a time, figuring out who his allies are."

"But why did you arrest the Mimms?" Arisa asked. "This has nothing to do with them."

"Not that we've found so far," Justice Holis admitted. "But since you spotted Master Darian there, we sent . . . a certain individual, who's been observing matters for us in and around the docks, to visit your tavern."

Weasel smiled. "Should I assume this individual has been trying to figure out who's working with the pirates?"

"You can assume anything you like," the justice replied. "But there we got our break—he recognized the door keeper, Stuart Collings, as a man he'd seen visiting the docks many times."

Stu. Arisa's heart throbbed once, and began to ache. *How could he? How could he do such a thing?*

"Our observer had already noticed the man, for whenever he

appeared he'd visit some small ship, which would then set sail with the next tide."

"You weren't watching him just for that?" Weasel asked.

Holis sighed. "It's not unusual to visit someone on a ship before it departs. But combined with Mistress Arisa's information, we felt we had sufficient cause to arrest them, search the tavern for evidence, and start extracting information from them."

"Extracting information." Arisa felt the blood drain from her face. "You don't mean . . ."

"Of course not," said Holis, shooting the Falcon a firm look. "Deorthas is a civilized realm. But we can and will bargain for information. And though I'm sorry if it troubles you, my dear, they must pay for any crimes they've committed."

"But you don't know that they did anything at all!" Arisa's heart was pounding.

"Don't look so frightened, love," said the Falcon. "We've already agreed that the Mimms will be allowed to give us information about the conspiracy in exchange for leniency in sentencing. If they tell us enough, they might avoid all punishment."

"Unless they knowingly assisted the pirates in raiding those villages," Holis put in. "If they had a hand in murder, they have to pay."

"Agreed, agreed." The Falcon made a casual gesture. "But the officer who arrested them tells me that Master Mimms seemed genuinely surprised and appalled when he was charged with abetting pirates. So whatever they're up to, I don't think you need to worry too much about your friends."

"The Lady be praised." Arisa blinked back tears.

Weasel, however, was still frowning. "That doesn't explain what Master Darian was doing there. Or how Katrin was involved with them."

"They were her family," said Arisa. "It might have been a coincidence that she went to visit them that night." But it didn't seem likely.

"We should find out soon," the Falcon told them both. "If they aren't involved with the pirates, it seems a pity to destroy the whole family. And the Mimms family has a long history of service to Deorthas, to the palace itself."

Katrin had gotten her job in the palace because of that connection, Arisa realized. That was how her maid had been hooked into the conspiracy, and she had brought Arisa into it. It was all . . . connected.

"But Pettibone's dead," Weasel pointed out. "Did everyone start working for Ethgar once Pettibone was gone? And whatever else he did, the pirates aren't Pettibone's fault."

"There are some," said the Falcon, "who say that the pirates are Justice Holis' fault. And I still want to know—"

"That's rot!" Weasel snapped. "The pirates are their own fault. You can't blame someone else because they suddenly got the bright idea of raiding ashore."

Arisa looked up at the portrait of Regalis, hanging to one side of her mother's desk. She wanted no part in this quarrel. How far back had Baylee said the Mimms' connection with the palace reached? Centuries? King's Folly. *Connections.*

"I'm afraid that's not true," Justice Holis told Weasel. "Raiding ashore is a change in their pattern. Something, some*one*, must have caused it. And if it was Ethgar, I'd very much like to know how he managed it."

"And I," said the Falcon, "would very much like to know how the two of you found out about this arrest. Which took place after you were in bed. Did you expect me not to notice that your hair is wet? Come on, Ris. Talk."

They'd be saying that to Baylee's family soon, and in much less loving tones.

Baylee's family, whose connection with the palace was centuries old. Who really weren't of the class that produced palace servants, and whose cellar held a chest . . .

She had thought that story about Regalis walking home naked was so ridiculous it couldn't possibly be true. It still might not be true, but if she wanted to divert her mother from what she'd been up to, this was a magnificent distraction.

Arisa lowered her gaze from the portrait and met the Falcon's eyes.

"I've found the sword of waters."

CHAPTER 15

THE FOUR OF STARS

The Four of Stars: the craftsman.
The good that comes not from nature but from men's work.

15

They went to get the sword first thing the next morning—Holis said if it had kept for several centuries, it would keep for one more night.

If he'd actually thought she'd found it he might have been in more of a hurry—Arisa knew her mother would have been. But her announcement did break up the meeting, distracting the Falcon from further inquiry.

As for Arisa herself . . . Nothing could be confirmed until Edoran examined it, but she was oddly certain that she was right. The connections were there.

And the connections between Ethgar and Master Darian and the pirates would probably be just as obvious, once they knew what they were.

The grooms wondered at having to saddle so many horses, so early, and in the rain, too. Sammel was doubly surprised when Arisa asked for an older, more placid mare instead of Honey. It could have been worse; only Holis, the Falcon, Weasel, Edoran, and Arisa herself made up the party, along with a couple of palace guardsmen for the prince's prestige, though they hardly seemed necessary.

Few people were on the streets, and they walked swiftly, bundled into coats and cloaks with their hats pulled low. They barely noticed the small troop of riders.

It would have been different, Arisa knew, if Holis had believed her. He'd have brought half the court as witnesses, and half the palace guard as well. This small audience was to spare her embarrassment when she failed, and Arisa was grateful. Even if she was right she didn't want an audience, and if she was wrong . . . She shuddered.

It took less time to cover the distance on horseback, and soon they pulled their mounts to a stop at the tavern door. A padlock with an army seal over the keyhole held it closed.

"I thought I'd forbidden you to go into this tavern again." The Falcon's voice was deceptively mild.

"I didn't go in," said Arisa. "I found the sword by remembering—well, several things I saw and heard over the last few weeks."

"I wish you'd let us know where we were going," said Holis. "I don't look forward to waiting in this weather while someone goes to fetch the key."

"We don't need to wait," Weasel told him. "I can—"

"I'm sure you could," said the justice. "But I'd prefer you didn't demonstrate it quite so publicly."

"Why not?" Weasel glanced at the guardsmen, who looked bored and miserable. Their uniform coats were neither waterproof nor winter weight. "They don't care. No one—"

"No one has to go inside," Arisa interrupted. "The sword is here."

All eyes turned to her, astonished, then turned away, searching the narrow, shabby street.

Edoran was the first to see it. "You're joking," he exclaimed.

"I don't think so," said Arisa.

"But . . . the sword of waters, holding up a *tavern sign*?"

"Yes. Just like any other hunk of metal, though it wasn't that way in the beginning," Arisa told them. "This was intended as a place of honor."

And it would have been good advertising, though it seemed foolish to say that to the prince who might soon be asked to issue pardons for Baylee's family.

Arisa guided the steady mare she'd chosen to a stop in front of the sign, and freed her feet from the stirrups. She had to stand on the saddle in order to reach the hilt. When she gave it a yank the sign swayed, and Arisa nearly lost her balance. The mare snorted.

"Hold on a minute." Edoran pulled his horse into position beside Arisa's, and the Falcon dismounted to hold both sets of reins as the prince stood on his own saddle to study the sword. "This has been painted. And the rings have worn notches in the blade."

Now that he'd pointed it out, Arisa saw that the iron links had worn grooves into the blade's thin edges, both top and bottom.

"Lift up the sign," Arisa told Edoran, and with a grunt of effort he did.

The sword felt looser now, but Arisa had to work the links out of their notches before the blade rasped free.

The sign crashed to the cobbles, cracking in two places, and both horses shied.

Arisa managed to fall more or less into her saddle as the mare leaped sideways. Edoran didn't, but the Falcon grabbed one of his shoulders on the way down, so his feet hit the ground first.

"It was heavy!" the prince panted.

"No harm done," Holis assured him. "Even in the best case, it will be some time before the King's Folly reopens."

"They have another tavern sign in the cellar," Arisa said. "With another name on it. That's one of the things that started me wondering."

Weasel, who'd kept his rump safely in his own saddle throughout, grinned. "Don't tell me you're thinking about that— what was the word you used, "Ridiculous"?—that ridiculous story about Regalis walking home from a tavern naked, because he gambled away all he had with him."

Arisa decided not to mention the trunk of clothing in front of the hidden room. Or the shoes, with the gems pried out of their heels. Regalis wasn't the only nobleman who'd worn jeweled shoes.

"There's only one way to know." She turned to Edoran. "Is this the sword, Your Highness?"

"How should I know?" said Edoran, exasperated. "It's been painted over. Several times, from the look of it. They were probably trying to keep it from rusting, but water got in where the links wore through. There's a layer of red paint under the black, and under that . . ." He was chipping it away with his fingernails. "Under that it looks like they painted it gold. Why put gold paint on a steel sword?"

"Because it didn't look rich enough, fancy enough, to suit commoners' notion of a legend," said Arisa, feeling oddly sure. "Those old Mimms could never have convinced their neighbors, their customers, that such a plain blade was the fabled sword of waters."

Holis was beginning to look intrigued. "But why didn't they turn it in for the reward?"

"They'd probably forgotten," Arisa told him. "I don't think Master Mimms and his family had any idea that this was the real sword."

"No, I mean the original owners. Why didn't they turn it in?" the justice persisted.

"I can think of three probable answers to that," Weasel said as he handed Edoran a penknife. The paint chips fell faster. He was working on the blade, Arisa noted, starting at the base and scraping toward the tip.

"What reasons?" the Falcon asked Weasel. She had mounted again, and was warming her hands on her horse's neck. "Why would anyone refrain from turning it in?"

"First, because they were the ones who stole it, and they were afraid they'd get caught," Weasel replied. "They might not have realized how much anger they'd stir up when they took it, and when they finally understood, they decided it was better to give up the money than risk hanging to claim it."

"That makes sense," said Holis slowly. "Though I have a hard time believing such bold thieves would suddenly become sensible."

Weasel shrugged. "The next possibility is that there was no theft. That Regalis knew exactly what had happened to the sword and never offered a reward because he thought he could win it back."

"That's nonsense," said the Falcon.

"Is it? Every gambler I've ever known is convinced he's going to win it all back. We already know that the investigation into the burglary was false, and that's where we first read about the reward. The diaries I've been reading say very little about the disappearance of the sword and shield, and those that do mention it say that the king 'wasn't much concerned with the matter.' It only damaged his popularity in the countryside, and Regalis never cared about that."

There was a thoughtful silence.

"And the third possibility," Weasel finished, "is that it's not the sword of waters after all."

"But it is." Excitement rang through Edoran's quiet voice. "This is the true sword, given to King Brend in recognition of his father's sacrifice."

The Falcon's mare snorted and tossed her head, as if a hand had suddenly tightened on the reins.

"Are you sure of that, lad?" Holis demanded. "I mean . . . I can't . . . Holding up a tavern sign?"

"The mark is there," said Edoran, "just as my father described it."

Dizzy relief swirled though Arisa's blood, but she wasn't surprised.

"Well," said Holis. "Well. I hardly know what to say. Congratulations, my dear. And to you, Your Highness. With both the sword and shield recovered in your reign, your popularity in the countryside will soar! This is an excellent thing!"

He looked so delighted. And it was all for Edoran, Arisa saw. He really wasn't thinking about what it signified for him.

A question she hadn't even realized she was considering resolved itself. She held out her hands to the prince, and after a moment's hesitation Edoran passed her the sword.

"You found it," he said. "It's your right to bestow it. It worked out well enough, last time."

Arisa smiled at Weasel. She had promised this, the day he had given her mother the shield. Now she could keep her word.

She turned to Justice Holis and held out the sword. "This is yours, sir. For as long as Deorthas needs your protection."

Holis took the blade automatically. "But I . . . Well . . . Thank you, my dear. And you, Prince Edoran. I am honored by your trust."

Edoran nodded gravely, which Arisa thought probably meant more to Holis than an antique sword. The prince had been given no choice of regent, neither the first time nor the second. His acceptance would matter.

The guardsmen were staring, openmouthed, eyes wide with wonder. The story would be all over the palace by noon, spread through the city within a day, and probably reach the borders of Deorthas before the week was out.

Weasel was grinning like a loon. And her mother . . . Arisa

turned abruptly to the Falcon, and was surprised to see an expression rigid with cold fury.

She gasped. "Mother? What is it? What's wrong?"

But even before she spoke, the Falcon's angry expression dissolved into neutrality. "Nothing's wrong. This is a great day for Deorthas, and I'm proud of you. I can't believe you actually found it!"

She was smiling now, with genuine warmth, and Arisa blinked. Had she imagined that sudden flash of anger? She must have.

"Which brings up the matter of announcing the good news," the Falcon went on. "Though before we worry about that, we should go back to the palace and have someone who knows what they're doing clean off that paint."

"What?" said Holis, coming out of an abstracted fog. "Yes, of course. It must certainly be announced. This is the best of good fortune! It will make a difference in the very parts of the realm most affected by the pirates. This might give us the political breathing room we need to bring them down!"

"So the sooner we make a formal announcement the better." The Falcon turned her horse toward the palace and set the party into motion. "You're the historian, Your Highness. Where were the sword and shield kept before they were lost?"

Edoran looked as if being described as a historian pleased him. Weird kid.

"In the old great hall," he said. "Which wasn't used much, even back then. It's only used now for very formal events. I think that big throne makes people nervous. The sword and shield used to hang on the wall behind the throne."

"Then I think they should be returned to their places," said the Falcon. "At least for the announcement party. And after, if we can guard them properly."

"I don't think they were stolen in the first place," Weasel told the Falcon. Why was he frowning? Because the Falcon had kept the shield in her office these last three months, and Holis wouldn't have the sword in his? That was nothing, compared to reuniting the sword and shield for the first time in centuries! And the Falcon was giving up the shield to do that.

"Party?" Holis asked. "That hardly seems—"

"'Party' may be the wrong word," the Falcon admitted. "I was thinking more along the lines of a grand ball, with every shareholder and minor noble in the realm invited to see what your regency has accomplished. If you serve free beer and sweet cakes in a couple of the major squares, you could earn some popularity in the city as well."

"Not a lot," Weasel warned her. "Oh, they'll drink the beer and eat the cakes, but it takes more than that to change the city's opinion. You'll have better luck if you can convince the One God's priests that this is a sign of His favor."

"I don't like to encourage these ancient superstitions," Holis told them all. "Besides, the sword and shield were gifted to King Brend by the priests of the old gods. I'd think the One God's clergy would object . . ."

The old gods, whose priests had been driven into hiding by those who claimed they'd sacrificed more people than just one long-ago king.

For a moment Arisa saw a whole web of connections stretching out from the plain sword, with its ugly peeling paint. Connections that reached beyond Regalis and the Mimms, back and back, between priests and people, between the people and their king, all the way back to Deor's blood, dripping slowly into the earth.

"Are you all right, Ris?" The Falcon had fallen back to ride beside her. "You're white as a ghost."

"It's nothing," said Arisa, shaking off the sudden chill. "Are you angry that I gave the sword to Justice Holis? Since Weasel gave you the shield, I thought—"

"I'm not angry," said the Falcon. "The symbols of power don't matter when you hold the reality. I'm lord commander of the army and navy of Deorthas—that's plenty for me. And I'm also the mother of the smart, courageous girl who found the sword of waters. I'm proud of you, love. Remember that."

The words warmed Arisa's heart, but she had been angry, no matter what she said now. Unless her mother was deliberately lying, Arisa usually read her very well. Usually.

This might be one of those exceptions, for the Falcon had volunteered to give up the shield. Perhaps the anger had swept over her before she'd had a chance to think things through. In any case, Arisa had accomplished an impossible task, and her mother was proud of her. That was what mattered.

As they rode toward the palace together, she realized that it had finally stopped raining.

CHAPTER 16

ASTRAY

Astray: the true path lost.
Mistakes, errors, bad choices.

16

In the three days before it could be held, the announcement ball turned into a costume ball.

"Which is worse than a regular ball," Arisa grumbled to Weasel and Edoran as they rode their horses down the still-muddy path. "You take a ball gown, which is bad enough anyway, and then add stuff to it."

The shepherdess costume had stood on a stand in her room for several days, growing ever more elaborate and uncomfortable. Surely no shepherdess had ever worn anything like it. Or trimmed her hooked staff with those ridiculous ribbons. Didn't any of these people know that sheep were dirty?

"You can go masked," said Weasel. "If it's a full mask, you could get up to all kinds of things and no one would recognize you." But even Weasel sounded as if his heart wasn't in it. Edoran looked almost as gloomy as Arisa felt.

On the other hand, the discovery of the sword of waters had created so much excitement in the court that the Falcon had loosened her edict enough to allow the three of them to ride together—as long as a groom accompanied them, for propriety's sake.

Today's sacrifice trotted behind them now, far enough back to keep from overhearing, but close enough to keep an eye on them. He looked thoroughly bored, and probably had some real work he was neglecting for this. And his presence wasn't necessary. The cessation of the rain had brought all the courtiers, who usually regarded exercise as a vulgar form of torture, out into the park to walk or ride. The place crawled with them, and Arisa almost wished for the rain back.

But the eternal storm had wrung all the water out of the sky—in the last three days, they'd seen only one brief shower.

Everyone's mood had brightened with the weather, except for Arisa's, because she still fretted about Baylee and her family.

"Just put on whatever your maid hands you," Edoran advised her. "Then take off any removable parts after the first hour. Unless your servants hate you, it shouldn't be too bad."

He would know. "My new maid doesn't hate me." Since the truth about Katrin's death had become common knowledge, the plump motherly woman was acting *too* nice. If she gave Arisa one more gentle pat she'd bite the woman's hand—that would do wonders for her reputation in the servants' hall.

Weasel laughed. "You two look like you're going to an execution! It's just a party. A boring party, I grant you, but there are lots of worse things. We could all be locked up in a cell somewhere, or . . ."

Arisa thought about Baylee, and shivered.

She went to see her mother after their ride. She'd been avoiding the Falcon for the last few days. She still had a feeling that her mother was angry about the sword—and if she wasn't, she might remember to ask Arisa how she and Weasel had known about the Mimms' arrest. Arisa no longer cared about being punished for breaking her word, which she hadn't, anyway, but she was less than eager to reveal her escape route. If her days became any more ladylike, she'd have to start running around the city at night to keep her sanity!

Since her errand wasn't urgent, she waited outside her mother's office until the current meeting broke up. Most of the men who emerged were naval officers, in full uniform, with their shiny familiar boots. Had they found the traitors in the navy yet? Were they tracking down the pirates? Arisa hoped so.

"Hello, Ris," the Falcon greeted her cheerfully as she came in. "I haven't seen you for a while. I'm sorry about that, but with one thing and another I've been cursed busy!"

She didn't sound angry. Had Arisa misread her mother's expression after all? "That's all right. But I have to ask . . . Has anything been decided about the Mimms family?"

The Falcon's gaze softened. "You care about them, don't you?"

"Not only them," said Arisa quickly. "I'm curious about all of it. Whether you found any connection between Ethgar and Master Darian, whether you've arrested the traitors in the navy, whether . . . All of it."

The Falcon drummed her fingers thoughtfully on her desk. "I can't tell you everything, but you can stop worrying about your friends. Master Mimms thought he was dealing with smugglers, and that the information he passed on was to help them avoid navy ships until they got their cargoes in. He's being charged as a smugglers' accomplice, but he's given us so much help that he'll probably get off lightly even for that. The rest of the family won't be charged at all."

"Lady be praised," Arisa whispered. But even as relief flooded her veins, suspicion pricked. Would Master Mimms have hosted such large meetings for a smuggling ring? Smugglers met in twos and threes, to avoid drawing attention—even Arisa knew that! Master Mimms had attended the meetings himself. He had to know what they'd discussed. But if she asked those questions, would Baylee's family get into more trouble?

"I'm afraid there's bad news to go with the good," the Falcon continued. "At least, bad for the investigation. There are plenty of connections between Ethgar and Master Darian. We think they must have been working together, but we may not be able to prove it. Ethgar hanged himself in his cell last night."

"He hanged himself?" Arisa repeated numbly. "*Shareholder Ethgar?*"

"I'm afraid so. And the Mimms say they don't know either one of them. We think that Master Darian might simply have gone to the tavern for a drink that night."

"I don't believe it!" Arisa exclaimed. "Shareholder Ethgar didn't have the dedication, the *spine* to kill himself—not just to protect his friends." Poor Ronelle. Arisa wouldn't have wished that grief even on her.

"I thought the same," the Falcon admitted. "But it appears we're wrong."

"Or that someone arranged his death." Arisa wrapped her

arms around herself, warding off the sudden chill. "But if Ethgar was the conspiracy's 'palace patron,' who ordered his murder?"

"It's almost certain that Ethgar was Master Darian's patron," the Falcon said. "There might be someone else involved, but I sent people I trust to investigate his death. If someone murdered him, they did a perfect job. There's no evidence of any hand in his death except his own. Knowing he couldn't get out of it, he might have chosen to cheat the hangman and finish it himself. In either case, it's a dead end," the Falcon concluded, with a wince for the gruesome pun.

"You don't cheat the hangman by killing yourself," Arisa objected. "You just give him the day off!"

"You may be right," the Falcon told her. "But if you are, there's no evidence. And you know what a stickler Holis is for evidence. He's throwing his weight around, these days."

"He's the regent," Arisa pointed out, troubled by her mother's grudging tone. "He's *supposed* to run things. It's not like you don't have enough weight to throw around."

"True," the Falcon sighed. "And I've been throwing it into this investigation with all my might, so I shouldn't complain about other people doing it too. I wish we agreed with each other more often, but that's not your problem."

Arisa's daughterly ear picked up the threat of incipient chores in that last sentence. "What is my problem?"

"Edoran asked me if it would be all right for you to be his partner at the ball tonight," the Falcon told her.

Arisa sat up straight in astonishment. "Why me? After that

stupid business in the old stable, I'd think I'd be the last girl he'd want as a partner."

"That's why he asked me first," the Falcon told her. "But a lot of the gossip has died down in the excitement about the sword, and since you were the one who found it, it makes sense for you to partner him tonight. It's not like you won't be chaperoned in a ballroom full of people, so I agreed."

"Why didn't he ask me about it?"

"He probably didn't want to get your hopes up, in case I said no," the Falcon replied. "Besides, he had a wicked gleam in his eyes. I think he's up to something, plotting some prank. That's allowed, almost expected, at a masked ball. Whatever it is, go along with it, Ris. We need his friendship."

"All right," said Arisa dubiously. Knowing Edoran, whatever he had in mind wouldn't be unkind. It wasn't like him to get involved in a prank, but he had been loosening up over the last few weeks. It just seemed strange that he hadn't brought her and Weasel into it—whatever it was.

The rest of the afternoon was taken up with a special etiquette lesson, covering the rules and restrictions of masked balls. Arisa had to suffer through it alone, for Justice Holis had finally found a tutor who met his exacting standards, and Weasel and Edoran had returned to their own lessons. To Arisa's dismay, a masked ball entailed a lot of etiquette.

At least her teacher confirmed that pranks were an old tradition. "Though at a royal ball, only jests in the best of good taste!"

If Edoran was up to something—tasteful or not—more power to him. Arisa began to look forward to the evening. It was supposed to be a celebration, after all, and she had plenty to celebrate. Baylee, and all her family except her father, would soon be free. Even Master Mimms wouldn't be treated harshly! They'd probably be celebrating themselves, in their cells . . . assuming someone had told them they were going to get off.

Arisa spent the rest of the afternoon trying to convince herself the matter was settled—and she failed. They'd probably been told—almost certainly been told! But the image of Baylee, cold and terrified in a noisome cell, still haunted her.

By evening Arisa was tired of it. She had more than an hour before she had to don the stiff and frilly shepherdess costume, but putting that off wasn't the main reason she lit a thick candle and took the long stairs down to the corner of the cellars where prisoners were lodged. She couldn't go to a party unless she knew that Baylee and her family were able to celebrate too—at least that they weren't still in terror of the noose!

When she and Weasel had first moved into the palace, one of the footmen had taken them on a tour that ranged from cellars to attics—or it was supposed to. The man had skipped a number of rooms near the servants' hall—the sewing rooms, the pantry, and several other work areas. The only part of the cellars they'd seen was the wine cellar, but their guide had mentioned that the cells were under the guardsmen's quarters, which was another part of the palace he hadn't shown them.

Arisa had a rough idea where the guardsmen slept. After

wasting some time wandering though a maze of wine racks and barrels, and a dead end trip down a corridor lined with gardening tools, Arisa finally found an arched gateway, blocked by a grid of steel bars. A heavy padlock hung from the latch. It was open.

And shouldn't there be a guard by this gate? She'd have posted several here, if she'd been in charge of holding prisoners.

The barred door swung back, without even a squeak from its well-oiled hinges. Its silence seemed more ominous than the traditional squeal.

Arisa crept down the corridor, with cells on either side, as quiet as an assassin—though the candle she held would warn whoever guarded the Mimms' cell of her approach.

There was no guard. Because there were no prisoners.

Frowning, Arisa traversed the corridor to its end and then returned, peering into the shadowy cells as if she might have missed them. Could there be another cell block under the guardsmen's quarters? There were certainly enough cells to hold all the people who might offend any reasonable king. Though last fall, when Regent Pettibone had arrested Justice Holis' conspiracy, the palace dungeons had been so full that Weasel and Arisa had been locked in a converted storeroom. A good thing too. They'd never have escaped from here. And if there were two cell blocks, surely they'd adjoin each other.

Baylee and her family weren't there.

Her mother's office was empty, but with the ball drawing near it wasn't hard to figure out where the Falcon would be.

Arisa burst into her mother's bedroom without knocking. "Where is Baylee's family? What's happened to them?"

The Falcon, clad in a plain robe, was seated in front of her dressing table, which held a collection of bottles and pots that would have put any court lady to shame. Until they'd moved into the palace, Arisa had never seen her mother use face paint except as a disguise, but the Falcon had started life as a courtesan. Had she missed silks, jewels, and perfume in the harsh years of banditry?

If she had, she'd never showed it. Now her eyes met Arisa's in the mirror, and a gesture sent her maid whisking out of the room.

"Why aren't you getting into your costume?" the Falcon asked. "It's almost time for the ball."

"The ball doesn't start for half an hour," said Arisa. "And my costume's not that fancy." She gestured to the stand, which held something that looked like a great red rose. The skirts formed its petals, and the bodice was the same dark brown and green as the narrow leaves that supported the blossom. The elaborate headdress was a nimbus of thorns.

"I suppose you're right," her mother admitted. "I wouldn't be dressing now, if I didn't have to put on so much paint."

Looking closer, Arisa saw a faint outline of leaves and rosebuds twining over her mother's face. Beautiful, and so much easier to wear than a stuffy mask. Arisa didn't care. "You haven't answered my question. Where are the Mimms?"

The Falcon sighed. "You went to the cells, I see. They were

released when the charges were dropped. All but Master Mimms, who was moved to the city jail since smuggling is handled by the city court. Only traitors, and prisoners of particular interest to the king, are held by the palace guards."

"Then where are the rest of them?" Arisa persisted.

The Falcon's white shoulders rose and fell. "I don't know. They were released."

She didn't even know. They were free. Free, and safe, and probably staying with Mistress Mimms' family. An explosive sigh burst from Arisa's lungs, and she sank into the nearest chair as relief weakened her knees.

The Falcon watched, her expression torn between amusement and exasperation. "Did you think I'd dropped them into an oubliette?"

"No, of course not. But I was so sure they were still in a cell. When they were gone, I didn't know what to think! Why didn't you tell me they'd been released?"

"I told you the charges were dropped." The Falcon dipped a brush into a pot of dark paint and traced the line of a rose stem down one cheek. "What else would we do but release them? Really, Ris."

"Sorry," said Arisa. "I wasn't thinking."

"You've got a habit of doing that." The Falcon's voice combined mother and commander in one. "You should work on breaking it."

"I know, I know." Her mother was always thinking. "It doesn't come as naturally to me as it does to you."

The Falcon laughed. "I have to stop talking now—I can't paint if my face moves."

"Then I'll talk to you," Arisa told her. "It's a rare thing for me to get both first and last word."

The Falcon grinned, then swore and picked up a cloth to wipe off a brush stroke that had gone awry. Arisa decided she'd better stop talking too, but she still felt restless. She rose and went to study the costume more closely.

The skirts were formed by layers of velvet and satin, scalloped and curled at the edges like real petals. The dark bodice was trimmed in dull bronze. It should have been drab, but against the deep crimson it looked richer than gold.

"You don't usually wear colors like this," said Arisa, looking at her mother in the mirror. "Your gowns are almost as demure as mine."

The Falcon, busy with her paintbrush, shrugged again. The robe slipped open, revealing a glint of gold at her mother's throat. A locket. The locket that Arisa had never expected to see again.

Her heart began to pound. Why was her mother wearing that tonight? She couldn't be making a move against her enemies. She had no enemies now! But Arisa had never seen her wear that locket for any other reason.

She opened her mouth to ask, *Why are you wearing that?* But the words that came out were, "Are you wearing brighter colors because this is a special occasion?"

Say "Yes." Say, "I'm wearing the locket, too because . . ."

"Mmm." The Falcon was painting small sharp thorns on the

307

rose stem. "I really can't talk now, Ris. You need to get into your costume too."

"You're right," said Arisa. "I'll see you later."

She escaped, before her stupid expressive face could give her away. Why shouldn't the Falcon wear that locket? Just because when Arisa had seen it before, her mother had usually been cleaning and loading pistols . . . Well, times changed. Changed for the better!

She went to her own room, where her maid pounced on her and hustled her into the shepherdess gown. Arisa offered so little resistance that the maid finally asked if her mistress was feeling all right. "If you've a headache, my dove, I've just the thing for it."

"No," said Arisa. "I'm fine." Which was a lie, for her temples were beginning to throb.

The Falcon hadn't *lied* about the Mimms being released, she'd just failed to mention it. Failed to mention it, when it would have been completely natural to say, *The charges were dropped against everyone but Master Mimms, so we released them and sent him to the city jail.*

The Falcon knew that Arisa cared about Baylee and her family. She *knew*. Why hadn't she wanted Arisa to know they'd been released? In case she told someone? Told whom?

Why was her mother so intent on celebrating the sword's return, when Arisa knew she'd been angry about the sword going to Justice Holis?

And why, come to think of it, hadn't she questioned Katrin's killer about who else Ethgar was working with? Maybe they had, and the Falcon couldn't tell Arisa because it was still secret. Perhaps she was wearing the locket because she and Holis planned to move against the others at the ball tonight! That made sense!

Arisa drew a relieved breath, and discovered that she'd been so preoccupied that her maid had slipped her into a set of corsets without her even noticing.

After a short, satisfying argument, Arisa was once more corset free. Her now-less-motherly maid set about dressing her for a second time, and brushed her hair into the mass of curls that went with the costume—though Arisa had never seen a shepherdess with hair like that either.

She resolved to check the stitching on every seam as soon as her maid left the room—though this maid hadn't had time to pull Katrin's trick, and it would get her fired as well.

Although Katrin hadn't been fired . . . at her mother's insistence. Her mother, who had hired Katrin to be Arisa's maid in the first place. But Katrin couldn't have been working for the Falcon and for Ethgar at the same time, could she? She'd certainly been working for Ethgar. Could Katrin have been working for the Mimms' conspiracy too? The Mimms . . . who had just been freed by her mother, even though Arisa *knew* they had been hosting a conspiracy in their tavern. A conspiracy that involved naval officers, officers Master Mimms could have identified! Her mother had always had strong connections with the navy.

Her mother, who had just donned the locket she wore only when she dedicated herself to the destruction of an enemy.

But Pettibone was dead! Ethgar was dead too, though he had been more Justice Holis' enemy than the Falcon's.

The Falcon regarded Justice Holis as her enemy.

Suddenly Arisa was sure of that, but she had to be imagining the rest of it. She had to! Katrin couldn't have been involved in two separate plots against Justice Holis! Could she? If all she did for Ethgar was to embarrass Arisa . . . If she knew that when she did so she wouldn't be fired, couldn't be fired because . . . No, that was ridiculous!

Then why hadn't the Falcon fired her? Why hadn't the Falcon questioned Master Mimms about the naval officers who'd met in his cellar?

When Arisa was dressed she dismissed her maid, but instead of tugging on all her gown's seams, she went to the bureau and pulled out her cards.

She shuffled carefully, longer than she needed to. When she cut the deck and turned the top card, the storm lay before her.

Good and bad in the same package.

Like daughter, like mother?

"This supports me," said Arisa, her voice too loud in the quiet room. The fool's bright motley appeared below the storm goddess' feet.

Which was a flat-out lie—far from supporting her, her heart and her instincts were screaming at each other. Her instincts usually worked better than her heart. No!

"This inspires me," she murmured, then closed her eyes in longing as safe harbor appeared above the goddess. She certainly wanted a safe harbor now, but that battered ship had to pass through a terrible storm before it reached the quiet bay the card displayed.

"This misleads me."

Loyalty. She knew full well where her loyalty lay.

"This guides me true."

Justice. Justice be hanged, if it meant turning against her mother! She had to be wrong.

"This threatens me." Her voice had dropped to a whisper.

The tower fell to the storm's far right. Arisa's breath caught. Never, not in the most desperate scrape, the most foolish escapade, had the burning tower appeared in her fortune. More terrifying than untimely death, the tower signified absolute loss, the destruction of everything good and decent and dear. Of all that made life worth living.

Exactly the kind of thing that would happen to her life if the Falcon really had turned traitor.

Arisa's hands were cold. Her face was cold. She offered up a prayer to any god who cared to listen as she turned the last card.

"This protects me."

The hanged man's blood spilled into the dust. But how could a sacrifice . . . No, not sacrifice. *Weasel!*

CHAPTER 17

THE STORM

The Storm: creation and destruction together.
Any force that brings both good and ill at the same time.

17

She found Weasel alone in his room, getting ready for the ball . . . after a fashion.

"What in the world are you dressed as?" she asked, momentarily distracted. "A beggar?"

"A burglar," said Weasel, tying a dark kerchief over his hair and forehead. "Nothing to make you stand out on the street when you've taken the kerchiefs off, but for disguise . . ." He held up another kerchief, covering his mouth and chin, leaving only a slit for his eyes. "There's nothing bright, and nothing that rattles or clanks. Soft-soled shoes."

"Isn't it awfully ragged for a ball?"

"For a ball," said Weasel, "it absolutely guarantees that no one will ask me to dance."

Arisa wished she'd thought of something like that.

"Forget about your costume," she said, rather unfairly, since she'd asked. "I need to talk to you about something important. When's your valet coming back?"

"Never," said Weasel. "Well, that's not true. He checks in twice a week and takes dirty clothes to the laundry. Justice Holis said that the prince's new valet could serve me, too, but he thinks I'm beneath his dignity so he mostly ignores me—the One God be thanked!"

"You're right about that," said Arisa, suppressing a flash of envy. "Why does Edoran have a new valet?"

"The old one was in Pettibone's pay," said Weasel. "At least my costume is authentic. I don't know much about shepherdesses, but that's ridiculous."

"My maid chose it. I think."

Had Katrin really been working for her mother, as well as for Ethgar?

Weasel saw the change in her expression. "What's wrong?"

"Weasel, I think . . . No, I'm not sure what I think, and I need to be sure. I need your help. But first you have to swear, on something you hold truly sacred, that you won't reveal what I tell you to anyone else unless I give you permission. Not Holis, not Edoran, not anyone. You have to swear."

Weasel snorted. "I don't hold anything sacred, so my oath won't do you much good. Oaths are silly, anyway. I don't know of anyone except priests who won't break one whenever they want to. Most priests will too!"

He was right about that, but . . . "Then I can't tell you," Arisa whispered. How could he help her, defend her from the tower's catastrophe, if she couldn't tell him anything?

Weasel frowned. "You're serious, aren't you? You really need me not to repeat this."

"Yes."

"Then I promise, for our friendship's sake, that I'll do everything I can to avoid it before I reveal what you tell me. If it's that important, I *can't* promise not to tell. I might have to break it, and you know you'd do the same. There's no such thing as an absolute promise. So you might as well go ahead and spill it."

He was right. And she had to tell someone. "Let me start at the beginning. My mother told me that Shareholder Ethgar hanged himself in his cell the night after he was arrested."

Weasel's brows drew down sharply. "Ethgar? That's rot! He'd keep trying to find some way to slither out of it till they put the noose around his neck. If he's dead, someone killed him."

Hearing it said aloud chilled Arisa to the bone.

"Yes," she whispered. "I'm afraid she did."

Her mother was capable of killing. Arisa had always known that, but killing for a cause was different. Wasn't it?

Weasel was still frowning. "She?"

Arisa told him everything—the Mimms' release, and her mother's failure to have Master Mimms identify the naval officers he'd met with. The flash of anger over Arisa's giving Holis the sword, followed by her pushing for a celebration. Her insistence on keeping Katrin as Arisa's maid, when anyone else would have fired the woman.

"Two different plots?" said Weasel dubiously. "It's not likely."

But he hadn't said it was all rot, that she was imagining things and should drink a soothing cup of tea, go to bed, and forget about it.

"I don't know what to do," said Arisa. "If Holis found out about this and she wasn't guilty . . . They have enough problems working together as it is. And my mother would never . . ."

No, she would forgive Arisa. She might even be flattered, and she'd certainly laugh. But some part of her would be hurt by her daughter's doubts. And she'd be very hurt if Arisa went to her enemy, instead of coming to her.

"You're right about that," said Weasel. "We can't go to Justice Holis, or anyone else till we're sure about this—one way or the other."

"We" was a wonderful word. The icy dread in Arisa's heart thawed a bit.

"How can we get evidence before something happens? If anything's going to happen—which we don't know. Not really."

"No," said Weasel thoughtfully. "But it's odd the Falcon suggested a celebration ball. A costume ball too, where everyone goes masked."

Her mother might have worn a lot of dresses lately, but she wasn't a ball kind of woman. She only wore dresses as a disguise. They *had* been a disguise, those demure gowns, Arisa suddenly realized. A way to keep the men she worked with from remembering who she was. But . . .

"But what could anyone do in a ballroom full of people?" Arisa asked. "Even if they're masked. It doesn't make sense!"

"We need more evidence," said Weasel. "And with your mother on her way to the ball, I know where to start the search!"

"I can't believe you're breaking into my mother's office," Arisa whispered, looking swiftly up and down the long corridor. "It's the middle of the evening! If we get caught . . ."

"If we get caught, it will be because you weren't keeping watch," said Weasel, twisting his pick in the lock. "All the clerks are gone for the day, and the servants are— We're in!"

The door swung open and he scrambled through, with Arisa on his heels. She closed the door behind them.

"I'll lock it again," said Weasel. "That will warn us if someone comes. You get those curtains and put something under the door."

Arisa moved to follow his orders, even as she asked, "You said drapes don't block all the light. Suppose someone sees it?"

"Then they'll think your mother had to finish up some work before she went to the party," said Weasel. The lock clicked once more.

By the time she lit the lamp, he was standing behind the Falcon's desk. As the light bloomed in her hands, Arisa glanced up at Regalis' arrogant painted face. *This is all your fault*, she told him silently.

She went to join Weasel, and regarded the piles of paper with dismay. Katrin's desk hadn't held enough to offer clues, but the Falcon's desk held far too much. "It would take *days* to read all this."

"So we take a shortcut," said Weasel. He pulled open the top drawer and examined not the clutter of pens, sand bottles, string, and sealing wax but its depth compared to the size of the desk.

"You're looking for a secret compartment?" Arisa asked.

"People don't leave evidence of criminal activity where clerks might see it," Weasel told her. "I've known enough criminals to be sure of that." He closed the top drawer and opened the one below it, running his hands to the back and bottom, around the papers stacked inside.

"This desk probably doesn't have secret compartments. It belonged to the old lord commander, who didn't have any secrets at all."

"You don't know that," said Weasel. "He might have had tons—"

The bottom drawer refused to open.

"Or," said Weasel, "he might have stored anything secret in a locked drawer."

Arisa felt almost numb now, but she had to argue. "Just because a drawer is locked, that doesn't mean what's inside is criminal."

"No." Weasel was already busy with his picks. "But it's either valuable or confidential, because constantly locking and unlocking a drawer is a big nuisance."

Arisa watched him work in silence. Was she betraying her mother? Could what they were doing be treason, if her mother had turned traitor first? She had to know. She had to know for certain before she saw her mother again; she could never conceal these doubts from the Falcon's keen gaze.

The bottom drawer was full of papers too. Arisa helped Weasel carry them to a small table so the papers on the Falcon's desk would remain undisturbed. He was a very good burglar. Justice Holis had done the world a considerable service when he'd converted Weasel into a law clerk.

She picked up a handful of loose papers while Weasel opened a big book that looked like a ledger. The first paper in Arisa's stack was a receipt for four bags of raw oats. The next was a letter describing weather patterns in the islands off the western shore.

"This is about hunting for the pirates," Arisa said, relieved. "Here's a set of tide tables. Maybe all this stuff is about the pirates, and that's why she locked it up. What are you reading?"

"A ledger," Weasel said, his eyes still scanning columns. "It doesn't have page titles, which is odd. Especially since it just lists people in her employ, and how much they're paid."

Arisa suddenly made another connection, and her heart sank. "Is one of them a groom named Henley?"

Weasel flipped a page. "Yes. Why?"

Betrayal, everywhere she turned. "His name isn't Henley; it's Sammel. He's one of my mother's men."

"From the bandit gang? But Justice Holis . . ." Weasel's startled confusion gave way to thought. "Do you know if she's infiltrated more of her men into the staff?"

"No one I've recognized," said Arisa. "But there are a lot of servants I never see. Cooks, gardeners. Even a footman, if he took care to avoid me."

Weasel turned another page. "Katrin is listed here too."

"She did employ Katrin! As my maid. Her name should be on a list of my mother's employees."

"The prince's household account pays the grooms' salaries," Weasel told her.

"Maybe Sammel needed a job, and they didn't need another groom, so she made some agreement to pay his salary herself," Arisa said fiercely. "It isn't proof!"

"What have you got there?" Weasel asked, ducking the argument.

"Nothing much. Some letters and a bunch of receipts. I think they all have to do with the search for the pirates, and that's why they're locked up."

"Could be," said Weasel. "Let's sort the receipts out of the pile, and concentrate on what's left."

When they'd been separated, the letters and other documents formed a far smaller pile.

"I'll take these," Weasel told her. "I can go back to the ledger when I finish."

Arisa eyed the huge stack of receipts with dismay. "These won't tell us anything. Why can't you finish the ledger while I read the letters?"

"The receipts have to be done," said Weasel firmly. "You can learn a lot from receipts. They're used as evidence in trials all the time. So unless you want to read the ledger . . ."

Evidence in trials. But she didn't want to read the ledger. She didn't really want to read the letters, either. She didn't even want to be here, prying into her mother's secrets. If the Falcon wasn't guilty, Arisa would gladly accept any punishment her mother set, even a lifetime of boring balls.

But if the Falcon had betrayed Justice Holis, then Arisa had to know. And then, somehow, she had to stop her.

She sighed and turned to the receipts. Hay, to go with the oats. Dried fruit, salt beef, and ink. Eight coils of rope, for some incomprehensible purpose. She was almost finished with the stack when she found it—a receipt from Prentice and Stubbs: Fine Tailoring and Costumers. Several parts of her shepherdess costume had come from them, but . . . Two hundred gold blessings? That couldn't be right. Two hundred blessings would keep most families for a year! Besides, this receipt was for a young gentleman's coat and britches, with a full-head mask in the shape of . . .

Arisa's heart began to pound. "What's Edoran's costume for the ball?"

Weasel grimaced. "A wolf in sheep's clothing. The clothes are all right, though anything that white is bound to get dirty before the night's out. But the mask is the most ridiculous thing you've ever seen. I think the idea was to hint that Edoran isn't as meek as people think he is, which you can't do with a costume anyway, and it looks . . ."

His voice trailed off as he saw her expression. "What?"

"I've got a receipt here for the prince's costume," Arisa told him. "But it costs too much, even for a costume for a prince. And I don't know why my mother would have paid for it. My mother . . ." Her throat ached. She had to swallow before she went on. "My mother told me that Edoran wanted to partner me at the ball tonight."

"Which is why you're dressed as a shepherdess," said Weasel. "But your mother didn't pay for the prince's costume. They had only three days, so his own tailor modified a coat he already had. The costumers just made the mask. And again, that would have been paid for out of the household budget."

"The costumers who made the mask had to see the rest of it, right? So the mask would match?"

"I guess so."

"Weasel, my mother told me that she thought Edoran was planning some prank tonight. That whatever he was up to, I should go along with it. I said I would."

Weasel reached out, plucked the receipt from her hand, and read it with a clerk's expert eye. "Your mother ordered a duplicate of the prince's costume. That's why it's so expensive. She's paying for secrecy and speed. It specifies a delivery date this afternoon."

"But it's almost on the bottom of the stack," Arisa protested. "If it came this afternoon it should be on top!"

"Hang me for a fool!" Weasel hissed. "When we sorted out the letters and receipts, we reversed the order. The top of the pile, the most recent receipts, ended up on the bottom. That receipt probably arrived this afternoon, along with the costume. An exact duplicate of Edoran's costume for this evening."

They stared at each other, stunned by the magnitude of it. Arisa finally found the courage to put it into words.

"She's going to kidnap the prince. That's why she told me to go along with whatever he did. So when someone who wasn't Edoran showed up in his costume, I'd think it was part of some prank. She's using me to shield her imposter, to give her, her men, time to escape with Edoran. Because no one would ever believe that she'd leave me behind."

She couldn't continue—her throat was too tight.

"She'd know you weren't in danger," Weasel said quietly. "Justice Holis would never harm you, and he'd know in a minute that you were innocent. If she'd told you, you'd never have been able to bring it off. You're not as bad a liar as some people think, but you're not *that* good."

"She didn't tell me," Arisa's voice grated, "because she knew I'd refuse to help. I do refuse! We have to stop this. We have to stop her before she commits herself, before she incriminates herself completely. We have to get to Edoran. Now!"

The prince's valet answered the door, looking down his nose at the prince's flushed, panting friends.

"His Highness is dressing," he informed them. "If you'd care to wait and . . . compose yourselves, he'll be out shortly."

Arisa's palms were damp. She wiped them on her fancy skirt, trying to think fast. The prince's old valet had been in his enemy's pay. Was this one?

How could her mother *do* this? And how dare she try to involve Arisa without telling her? Without *asking* her?

"We're going in," Weasel told the man firmly. "Now."

While the valet grappled with Weasel, Arisa slipped past them, dashed across the sitting room, and threw open the bedroom door—if Edoran was naked, tough. At least she'd be certain it *was* him.

He wasn't naked. He was sitting on his bed in his costume coat and britches, gazing gloomily at the full-head mask that sat on his dressing table. The wolf's muzzle emerging from the sheep's white wool was grotesque, and the one wolf ear sticking up though the fleece made it look silly as well.

Edoran gave Arisa a rueful smile. "I know my princely

authority won't stretch to canceling a costume ball on the spot, but there must be a way to get out of wearing *that*. Maybe a footman could walk behind me and carry it, or something."

No matter how ridiculous it looked, it would completely conceal the face of whoever wore it. And disguise his height, to a certain extent. It might even have been made to look like that deliberately, to distract anyone who spoke to the so-called prince if his muffled voice, or his manner, seemed a bit off.

Arisa suddenly realized that she was furious with her mother. A hard, slow anger that cleared her mind and steadied her nerve.

"You won't have to wear it," she promised. "I've got an ide—"

Weasel and the valet burst into the room, still grappling.

"Your Highness, he—"

"Edoran, get rid of this—"

Edoran raised his brows. His mild expression reminded Arisa of Justice Holis, and it had the same effect. Weasel and the valet stopped shouting and stepped away from each other.

Edoran turned to the valet. "I'll finish dressing myself, Jenks. You may go."

"But Your Highness, this is your first masked ball since I began dressing you," the valet pleaded. "I must assure that your appearance is perfect!"

Edoran grinned. "In that thing it can't be perfect. If I need assistance, my companions will provide it. You may go." He said it even more gently, but Jenks closed his mouth and went.

"You've got to get to Justice Holis," said Weasel, going straight to the point. "The Falcon plans to kidnap you tonight. Or maybe you should go to the guard, but I don't know which of them we can trust, so Holis it is."

"No," said Arisa tightly.

Edoran's eyes were wide, his mouth an O of astonishment. He looked like a fish.

"If Justice Holis learns about my mother's part in this, she'll hang," Arisa went on. "I can't allow that, and you promised to do everything you could before you told anyone what we discovered."

"But we can't—"

"You promised," Arisa snapped. "I'm holding you to it."

"But we can't let her kidnap Edoran!"

"No, and we won't. But the whole point of this monstrosity is that no one can tell who's wearing it," Arisa said. "If I put it on, they'll kidnap me instead of Edoran. Then I can talk with my mother. Talk her out of this."

Talk her into running for her life. The Falcon would never be able to hold any position of authority after this, not even be allowed to live in Deorthas. But she would live, and be free. Traveling in other lands, working as armed guards, even as soldiers, would be better than being a lady as far as Arisa was concerned.

If her mother forgave her enough to take Arisa with her when she ran. Even if she didn't, Arisa couldn't allow her to succeed at . . . treason. Treason against a just regent, and a prince who had in no way deserved it.

Weasel and Edoran were both staring at her critically.

"Do you really think you can wear this costume and pass for me?" Edoran asked. "It would be nice if someone explained what in Boraldis' cold hells you're talking about!"

"I'll explain," said Arisa, "while you strip. I'm only a little taller than the two of you, and my breasts aren't that big. In a coat, I'll be able to pass."

Weasel shrugged. "Let her try. It'll be faster than arguing."

Arisa went behind the privacy screen and twisted her gown around so she could unlace it and slip free. Thank the Lady she wasn't wearing corsets!

She and Weasel explained matters to Edoran in chorus. Weasel had reached the part of the story where they'd found the locked drawer, when Edoran's britches flew over the screen.

Arisa pulled them on. The waistband was three inches too small.

"Rot!"

There was a moment of silence.

"We did warn you they wouldn't fit." It was Edoran's voice, very polite.

"I don't think you could even have managed the coat," Weasel added. "But there was no way Edoran's britches were going over your hips."

"My hips aren't fat!" Arisa snapped, pulling the treacherous garment off of her feet.

"Of course not." There was a suspicious quiver in the prince's voice. "I'm the scrawny type."

"They aren't fat," Weasel added soothingly. "They're just girl hips."

Arisa growled and sent the britches sailing back. "We have to think of something else."

"Don't worry," said Weasel. "I've got an idea. You get dressed while I tell Edoran the rest of it. He can't help us if he doesn't know what's going on."

By the time Arisa had struggled back into her gown and petticoats, he'd almost finished.

"I understand why she's angry that Holis got the sword," Edoran said, as Arisa strode around the screen. "And I suppose a celebration ball would give her an opportunity to get hold of me. But why insist they be put together in the old throne room? She already had the shield in her possession. Why give it up?"

Arisa stopped in her tracks. Edoran was wearing Weasel's drab clothes, the dark kerchief concealing his hair. Weasel was half-dressed in Edoran's gleaming white.

"No," she said. She shouldn't have been surprised—she'd already seen that Edoran could fit into Weasel's clothes. "It's too dangerous. My mother's men won't hurt me, but most of them won't even recognize you!"

"All the better," said Weasel. "That means it will be longer before the switch is revealed, which gives you more time to get to your mother and put a stop to this. And they won't kill me, even when they discover the truth." His smile was strangely serene. "I'm not as valuable a hostage as Edoran, but at that point they'll need all the leverage on Justice Holis they can get. They'll need me alive."

The hanged man. Voluntary sacrifice, for the greater good. Arisa's heart ached.

"I won't let you do this." It was dangerous, whatever he said.

"You don't have a choice," Weasel pointed out. "There's no one else who can get into this costume, who wouldn't go straight to Justice Holis the moment you explained what's going on. We're out of time."

He was right. Her plan to find some footman's son of the right size, to try to pass it off as a prank, might have worked if they'd had several days. In the time they had, there was no chance. If she went to her mother, without telling Holis first, the Falcon would find some way to press ahead. Arisa knew what her mother was like when she committed herself—obstacles that would have stopped most people cold were simply challenges to her. It had made her a magnificent rebel leader. It made her dangerous.

"Maybe we should go to Justice Holis," said Edoran, worry plain on his thin face. "If there's a chance Weasel could get hurt . . . I could issue a royal pardon for your mother, in consideration of . . . of . . . Um."

There were no grounds for pardon, for forgiveness of this crime.

"Justice Holis would never pardon her," said Arisa. "And he's the one who's really in charge."

Edoran scowled.

"So this is the only way," said Weasel, wiggling into Edoran's coat. It fit him, Arisa noticed.

She couldn't let her mother kidnap Edoran. She couldn't turn her mother in to Justice Holis to be hanged. Sacrifice didn't always end in death—it usually didn't! Weasel was right. If she wanted to save her mother, from both the law and herself, this was the only way.

"All right. We go with this. Edoran can hide himself away, and when I get to the ballroom, I'll tell my mother that we've made our own switch. She'll have to abort the plan if she can't find Edoran. Then she'll have time to warn her men and we can run. They'll have an escape plan in place."

Weasel nodded, but Edoran was still frowning.

"You know, you're basing some big conclusions on very little evidence. I admit the costume receipt is suspicious, but to *kidnap* me? How could this Katrin have been working for Ethgar against the Falcon, and for her against Justice Holis? It's too far-fetched! And if she is making a play for the throne, then why did she give up the shield? It was the shield that made the army accept her command in the first place."

"I don't understand that myself," Arisa admitted.

"I do," said Weasel. "Katrin did it for the money, plain and simple. She probably adored being paid by both sides. And the Falcon's not letting go of the shield; she's making a grab for the sword as well. Justice Holis' office is on the same corridor as the palace guard commander's, and there are always guardsmen hanging around. It would be really risky to steal the sword from there. Now the sword and shield are both in a room in the old wing, where hardly anyone goes. Much easier to steal."

"They're on display in a public room," Edoran objected. "It's open tonight, so anyone who wants to see them can leave the ballroom and go there. People have been popping in to look at them all day."

"Which means there won't be as many there tonight," said Weasel. "Can you think of a better distraction for her imposter than the news that the sword and shield have disappeared? No one would pay any attention to your substitute after that."

"And if she gets the sword and shield," said Arisa, "after a few years have passed she might not even need you. It wouldn't take much to convince the country folk that Regalis wasn't Deor's descendant—even you believe that! If he wasn't the true king, then there is no true king, not anymore. Someone who had Deor's sword and shield in their possession would have a stronger claim than anyone else. Especially someone the country folk already consider a rebel hero."

She was cold to the marrow of her bones now, and even Weasel looked worried.

"Then we can't let her take the sword and shield either," said Edoran.

"So go get them," Weasel ordered crisply. "I'll play Edoran as long as I can. You two get the sword and shield out of that room and hide them. If she can't find them, she might give up on kidnapping the prince!"

That could work! Arisa's heart leaped. She grabbed Edoran's arm and hauled him toward the door. "Tie the other kerchief over your face," she told him. "We might be able to stop this before it starts, which will be much safer for everyone! You be careful," she added, turning to Weasel.

He had picked up the woolly mask from Edoran's dressing table, and his face held more laughter than fear. It made Arisa nervous.

"Don't take any chances you don't have to," she added, as Edoran concealed his face. "Not one!"

"I won't," Weasel assured her. "I won't leave this room until someone comes for Edoran, and I'll keep out of their hands entirely if I can. I never take unnecessary chances," he added, seeing her skeptical expression. "You're the crazy one!"

Hiding the shield and sword was more important than staying to argue with him. Arisa grabbed Edoran's arm again and pulled him through the sitting room into the corridor. She'd expected to find Jenks hovering there, but he wasn't. Reporting to her mother? Or simply gone to the servants' hall for a cup of tea, since his master had dismissed him? No way to know, but she was grateful for his absence as she and Edoran hurried down the halls toward the old wing.

"I still think we should go to Holis," Edoran fretted. "That way there's no danger at all."

"Except to my mother, who'd probably hang," Arisa snapped. "But you wouldn't care about that!"

It was hard to tell behind the mask, but she thought Edoran sighed. "She's your mother. At least I understand why you care. But if nothing happens, if it's only a plan that never came off, that we couldn't even prove she intended, she wouldn't need a pardon. Holis would probably fire her, but that's all he could do without proof."

Arisa's steps slowed. There was some logic there. Still . . .
"I think Weasel's right. The surest way to keep anything from
happening is to get the sword, the shield, and you, all hidden
away. Then nothing *can* happen."

Edoran was silent.

"What are you thinking? I can't tell through that mask."

"Why aren't you wearing your mask?" Edoran asked. "If I
have to wear mine—"

"I'm who I'm supposed to be," Arisa pointed out. "You're
Weasel, remember?"

He hadn't answered her question. But since her mother was
plotting to abduct him, Arisa decided she'd rather not know what
he was thinking.

The throne room was empty, guarded only by a dozen suits of
ancient armor propped on their stands around the tapestry-lined
walls. Not posting a guard in this room had seemed reasonable to
Arisa a few days ago. Now it struck her as lunacy.

She heard a click, and turned. Edoran had shot the bolt that
sealed the doors.

"If we're going to steal them we need privacy," the prince
pointed out.

"We're not stealing them," said Arisa. "We're . . . We're . . ."

They were stealing the sword and shield.

"We're out of our minds," she murmured.

"Steal them first," said Edoran practically. "Worry about it
later. How are we going to get them down without a ladder?"

The sword and shield hung on the wall behind the throne, roughly ten feet above the floor. "Could you stand on my shoulders?" she asked.

"I doubt it," said Edoran. "Let's see if there's something we can stand on in the staging room."

"Staging room?"

"Behind the throne," said Edoran, leading her across the long stone floor. "If they needed to bring out props for some kind of ceremony, they had a servant fetch them from in here."

"In here," once they'd drawn the bolt and opened the door, proved to be a small, windowless room, slightly larger than a closet. Except for a few rolls of tapestry, it was empty.

"Nothing we can stand on," said Arisa, turning back to the throne room. "Nothing out here, either. We can't do anything with the tapestries. The armor would fall apart as soon as we took it off the stands—and the stands are too flimsy to help us either!"

The swords clasped in the metal gloves were shinier than the sword that hung on the wall, even after its cleaning, and the shields were brighter and not so battered.

"There's nothing else in here," said Edoran. "Except..."

They turned together to stare at the tall throne. It rested on a low dais, about four inches above the floor, but it hardly needed the extra height. It was constructed of thick, dark wood. The elaborately carved back rose higher than Arisa's head, and the base looked as solid as a boulder, but...

"Do you think we could drag it?"

"I've never seen it moved," said Edoran. "It could be fastened to the floor, for all I know." He stepped onto the dais and examined the square base.

Arisa grabbed the back, braced her feet, and pulled.

Edoran yelped as the chair tilted, just missing his nose.

"It's not fastened," Arisa puffed.

It was too heavy to lift, but between them they were able to maneuver it off the stone platform. Once they got it to the floor, they dragged it over to the wall without much trouble.

Arisa started to climb up onto the seat, stepped on her skirt, and swore.

"Let me. I'm dressed for it." Edoran had pulled the mask off his face when they were wrestling with the throne, but he still looked appropriately burglarish as he scrambled up the chair's carved back while Arisa braced the bottom. He had to cling to one corner post as he reached up, but with his other hand he lifted the sword from its brackets and lowered it down to Arisa.

"Now the shield," she said. "Then we'll find a place to hide them."

"It's heavier," Edoran complained. It was also almost out of his reach. He pushed it up, bouncing it in its brackets several times before it fell—and he missed his grab. "Rot!"

The slab of iron and wood hurtled toward her, and Arisa leaped out of its path. The crash as it hit the floor made her wince, and the throne wobbled dangerously as Edoran hurried down.

"Why didn't you catch it?" he demanded. "It could have broken!"

"It could have broken me," said Arisa, dropping to her knees to examine it. "I think it's all—"

The bolt on the throne room doors rattled. "Is someone in there?" a man's voice called.

"The guards!" Edoran gasped.

"Or my mother's men," Arisa said grimly. "We'd better pray it's—"

The door rattled again. "Let us in," the man demanded. "We've come to . . . clean. To clean the floor. Who's in there?"

Not the guards. They were too late! Arisa's gaze darted to the narrow windows that divided the tapestries on the outer wall. They'd been arrow slots once, but then glass had been put in, and the lower panel, the only one that opened, was both narrow and short. The sword could be thrown out. The shield was too big.

"We have to hide them." Edoran looked frantically around the room. "But where? They'll look behind the tapestries first thing, and search the staging room right after that!"

"You hide them," said Arisa. "I'll go around and delay them as long as I can. Once the sword and shield are hidden, you can follow me out the window and hide yourself. When they go into the room, I'll go for help."

"Hey, in there!" It was a different, deeper voice. "We've come to prepare the room for the noble guests who've come to see the sword. Let us in."

"Hide them where?" Edoran whispered. "And you can't get out those windows—no one could!"

"Hiding them is your problem," said Arisa. She darted to the wall, unlatched the first window she saw, and pushed it open. Bushes below, bare of leaves in this soggy winter season. The window was shoulder height at the bottom, almost a foot wide and two feet high—no problem in britches, but it was going to be tricky in a gown. At least she wasn't wearing hoops!

She'd wiggled halfway through before her skirts jammed. The walls were thick enough in the old wing that lying on her side wasn't too uncomfortable, as she dragged yards of fabric through the gap between her hips and the top of the window. The cloth tumbled frothily over her head, obscuring her vision, but she could feel it when Edoran began pushing her petticoats through. Then two firm hands grasped her knees and shoved. Arisa smothered a shriek as she tumbled headfirst into the bushes.

She managed to get her hands up to protect her face, but that meant her arms took the brunt of the scratches as she floundered to her feet, then thrashed free of the brush and out onto the lawn.

"You withless runt!" she hissed at the open window. "I wasn't ready!"

Even from outside she heard the crash of a heavy body against the doors. The window closed.

Arisa turned and dashed for the low terrace, which opened onto the corridor that held the throne room doors. She shook dead leaves and twigs out of her skirts as she ran. A scratch on one wrist was bleeding, but there was nothing she could do about that—if there were marks on her face, the mask should conceal them.

She ran quick hands through her tumbled curls, then pulled the half mask from her pocket and tied it on. It was dark now, too dark to see her reflection in the glass of the terrace doors. It was also too cold for a fine lady to wander in the gardens without a cloak, but hopefully her mother's men would be too worried about their mission to think of that.

One final check to be sure her mask was secure. She took a deep breath and settled the act over her shoulders, like a cloak of calm, and then went through the door.

Four men stood before the throne room doors. They wore the crisp white and green of palace footmen, but their hard faces didn't suit the proper uniforms. She recognized one of them, vaguely. He'd been a liaison between her mother and a group of smugglers, but he wasn't one of the main troop, the men she'd grown up with. Men who would recognize her no matter where they saw her, or what she wore. If she met one of them . . .

She hadn't. *Concentrate on the battle you're in.*

"What are you doing there?" she demanded, in the best imitation of Lady Ronelle she could muster. It sounded pretty good. She'd been spending too much time with those people.

The men before the doors shuffled their feet, looking amazingly guilty. Their postures, their ungloved hands and ill-cut hair, everything about them proclaimed they weren't footmen. Clearly they were the second team. Was the first team kidnapping Weasel right now?

"We're supposed to inspect the room, Mistress," one of the men said. "Make sure it's clean, and fit for noble company. But someone's bolted the door and they won't let us in."

Arisa raised her brows. "Then why don't you get the master of household, and let him attend the matter? Whoever is in there, he can command them to open up. If they don't he can send for the guard. Surely that's more sensible than standing around beating on the door?"

"Yes, Mistress," said the man. "We'll do that."

They didn't move. She didn't dare move, for Edoran hadn't had nearly enough time.

"Then why don't you go? You'll not summon him by standing there."

The men exchanged glances, and one of them nodded. "You're right, Mistress."

He started down the corridor toward her, trying to look humble and downtrodden, as he no doubt imagined the footmen looked—though in Arisa's experience they were haughtier than most nobles.

"The master of household isn't on the terrace," she told him, getting ready to run.

The sudden flick of his eyes was her only warning, but it was enough. Arisa leaped for the terrace doors, yanked them open . . . and tripped over her own high-heeled shoes.

Strong arms caught her before she could fall, pulling her back inside, and a strong hand over her mouth muffled her scream.

She stamped one of those cursed heels down on his toes, and twisted half out of his grasp when he hopped. One more shove—

It felt as if her head exploded. Her vision darkened, and small lights bobbed in front of her eyes.

"Break it down," the man who held her ordered. "Now."

She was aware of the crash as he half-dragged, half-carried her forward. Her vision was clearing.

She saw the broken bolt, dangling from one door as it closed behind her. She saw Edoran standing by the throne, which was back up on its dais. How had he gotten it up there? And where were . . .

A sword and shield hung on the wall behind the throne. A fancy, shiny sword, and a gleaming silver shield. He had switched them. He was brilliant.

"Hey," said Edoran indignantly. "Unhand Lady Celeste, varlet!"

"Uh, she's a bit unsteady on her feet, Master. I daren't let her go. What are you doing in here?"

"We were going to meet here," said Edoran, coming toward her. He looked worried. "But she didn't knock . . . I mean, that's none of your business. You leave the lady to me, and . . . and take yourselves off."

Brilliant. By making it look like the men had interrupted a romantic assignation, Edoran had explained everything from the bolted door to her attempt to get them to leave.

Arisa let her gaze drift around the room, and spotted the real sword and shield in the clutch of a suit of armor so old it almost matched them. These men would take the fake sword and shield, and . . .

Edoran was an idiot! They'd think they had the real sword and shield! They'd report success, and her mother would have no reason to abort the plan! She'd kidnap Weasel, and then . . .

She drew another breath. She didn't know what she was going to say, but she never had the chance. The second blow almost knocked her out. She was vaguely aware of Edoran's indignant cry, of his furious protests as she was hauled, staggering, across infinite space.

Then she tumbled against someone, down and down. It was dark.

She lay still for a time, her mind drifting. She liked lying down, lying still. But eventually her nagging sense of worry gathered into thought, and she realized she was lying on her back, with her aching head resting in someone's lap.

"Where are we?"

"In the staging room," Edoran told her. The legs beneath her head shifted, so it was probably his lap.

"Are you all right?" he added.

"Yes. I think— No! They've got the sword and shield!"

She sat up. Pinwheels of light exploded behind her eyes. She lay down, quickly enough to be grateful for Edoran's skinny calves between her head and the stone floor.

"They don't have the real sword and shield," Edoran told her proudly. "They took fakes."

"I know that, you idiot! But if they think they have the real ones that's just as bad! They'll tell my mother they've got them, and she'll go ahead with the plan! I told you to hide them, not replace them!"

Her head was pounding.

"There was no place to hide them!" Edoran snapped. "They'd have been found within minutes, and you know it. I could have taken the sword and run," he added more calmly. "But then they'd have gotten the shield, and they'd still go on with the main plan. I'm not sure they'd abandon the kidnap plan even if they failed completely. Given the importance everyone seems to place on them, I thought it was better to let them take the fakes."

Was he right? Wrong? Either way, it was done. Arisa rubbed her temples. The headache was beginning to ease, but the skin around her left eye was puffy and tender.

"You don't think they're important?" she asked.

"What?"

"You said, 'Given the importance everyone else places on them.' Don't you think the shield and sword are important?"

Edoran hesitated. "Maybe I'd feel differently if I were Deor's descendant, but Regalis and all the kings who came after him, including my father, managed to rule without them. Pettibone murdered my father, and he ruled the realm just fine before the sword and shield turned up. So, no, I don't think they're that important."

She didn't have time to argue with the prince's obsession about Pettibone's killing his father.

"We've got to get out of here." She sat up, slowly. Her head throbbed, but it didn't knock her flat this time. She rose to her feet, despite her wobbling knees.

The staging room was nearly dark, but a dim line of light glowed beneath the door. She could make out the pale smear of Edoran's face, and lumpy rolls of tapestry.

"I already tried," Edoran told her. "Even if we had something to pry the pins out with, which we don't, the hinges are on the outside. The bolt's on the outside too, and the rods the tapestries are rolled on were too flimsy for battering rams even when they were new, and now they're rotten."

"You don't know that," said Arisa. "I'll bet you didn't check them all." She felt along the top of one roll till she found the pole in the center and tried to pull it over. The pole broke in her hand with a mushy snap.

"I told you," said Edoran.

"You haven't tried them all," she repeated.

Every one of them was rotten, just as Edoran had predicted. And the hinges were on the outside.

"There has to be a way," Arisa said stubbornly. "There has to."

"We won't be stuck here forever," Edoran pointed out. "Sooner or later someone will notice the sword and shield are gone and raise the alarm. They'll find us quicker if we make some noise."

He dragged one of the tapestries over to the door and sat on it. Stripping off one shoe, he banged the heel against the door three times. He waited a moment and did it again—bang, bang, bang. It made Arisa's headache worse.

"That's all you can think of?" she demanded. "Sit there and make noise till someone rescues us? There has to be a way—a way to fight!"

Edoran laughed. "You are the most . . . consistent person I've ever met. If you've got any other ideas, I'll be happy to assist you."

"We can try breaking down the door."

"Any sensible ideas," said Edoran. "There's no way we can break that door."

"You haven't tried."

She stood against the back wall to gain as much momentum as she could. Since the room was only six feet deep, that wasn't much, but she launched herself at the door anyway, ramming her shoulder into it with all her strength.

It felt as if she'd hit the stone wall instead.

"Ow!"

"If you're going to do it," said Edoran, "do it the smart way."

While she rubbed her bruises, he unrolled one of the tapestries and folded it against the door, high enough that their shoulders would hit the cushioning fabric. The tapestry blocked the light, but he shoved in the bottom with his foot till a narrow beam at each corner marked the location of the door.

Two of them together might make a difference! Arisa felt a quiver of hope.

"Start against the back wall," she told him. "And hit it with all your weight. On three. One. Two. Three!"

It felt like hitting a stone wall through a thick layer of fabric, but Arisa kept them trying till she was exhausted and Edoran insisted on clearing the door slit so they could get some fresh air.

He added the folded tapestry to the one he'd been sitting

on, picked up his shoe, and began pounding again. Three bangs, pause.

"There has to be a way," said Arisa.

"Not always," said Edoran. "Sometimes you can't fight. Sometimes, some things, you have to outlast."

"Is that what you did with Pettibone?" Arisa said nastily. "You *outlasted* him?"

"He's dead," said Edoran. "I'm not."

"If you really believe he killed your father, I'd think you'd be willing to take some risks, in order to take down your father's murderer."

"Fighting would only have gotten me killed too." She couldn't make out his expression in the darkness, but his voice held irritation. Verging on anger.

"Sounds like cowardice to me," said Arisa.

"Better a coward than a hotheaded fool!" Edoran replied. "Whose . . . Never mind."

"Whose mother is a traitor," Arisa snapped. "Say it! Say it, coward!" Tears burned down her cheeks.

"You just did." Edoran sounded tired. "It's not your fault."

"At least I can make more noise than that."

Arisa banged her fist against the door and shouted. Then she began to scream.

Edoran dropped his shoe and covered his ears.

She screamed till her voice was hoarse. She pounded till her fists were sore. Then she dropped to the floor and sobbed till she was exhausted.

Sometime during her weeping, Edoran picked up his shoe and started banging again.

"Things that other people do, or that happen to people you love, are some of the things you can't fight," he said quietly.

"I hate you." Arisa sniffed and wiped her wet face with her hands. She couldn't be sure in the dimness, but she thought he shrugged.

"Feel free."

She sat in silence for a time—well, silence with banging. Was this what it meant to be unable to fight something? This helpless despair? If this was what he'd lived with, all those years while Pettibone was regent . . .

"I don't hate you," she said.

"Do you always have this much trouble making up your mind?" There was laughter in his voice, and Arisa smiled.

She was smiling when the bolt clicked and the door swung open.

"What in the Lord's light are you doing in there?" Yallin asked.

CHAPTER 18

THE NINE OF WATERS

The Nine of Waters: safe harbor.

Only by passing through difficulty can safety be achieved.

18

"You weren't there," Yallin panted, as they ran toward the ballroom. "I knew you were supposed . . . to be with the prince. I helped work on your costumes. When he was there and you weren't . . . started worrying. Then I started looking. I went to your room, then that scamp Weasel's . . . then the stables. Must have been the Lady herself . . . put it into my head you might be looking . . . the sword and shield. By then I was fair frantic. No idea His Highness was with you."

Her voice had a country accent Arisa had never noticed before, and she was swearing by the country folk's Lady. And by the Bright Lord, a god most had forgotten even in the countryside. But if Yallin had secrets, right now Arisa didn't care. She was grateful, but Yallin wasn't running fast enough.

Thinking the apology she didn't have time to voice, Arisa poured more energy into her aching legs, racing down the corridor to the ballroom. Yallin fell behind, but to Arisa's surprise the gasping prince kept pace with her.

They burst into the ballroom together.

Edoran shot toward Justice Holis, darting through the crowded room like a fish through reeds. Arisa stopped in the doorway, her eyes sweeping over the crowd.

No tall woman in a crimson gown. No hawk-beautiful face with flowers painted on it. The Falcon was gone.

But someone sat in the big chair Edoran usually occupied, a ridiculous woolly helmet concealing his face. Someone.

Arisa followed Edoran toward the regent, bumping into people, almost knocking one man down because her vision was blurred with tears.

She heard Lady Danica exclaim "Well, really!" but she didn't look around.

Justice Holis was listening to Edoran, whom everyone had recognized by now. Arisa would never have believed the regent's mild face could wear such a hard expression. With a single gesture to summon the guardsmen, who stood near the wall, he started toward the sheep mask on the throne.

The boy stood as they approached and pulled off the mask. His face was flushed and sweaty. She had known it wasn't Weasel from the moment she'd seen that her mother had fled.

Fled, and left her behind.

"I have terms for you," the boy told Justice Holis. He tried to sound commanding, but his voice cracked.

"I'm sure you do," said Holis. "But not here."

He gestured again. The guards cleared a path and the justice led the boy toward a side door—the quickest route to his office.

The room was buzzing now, but since everyone could see Edoran, all but clinging to Justice Holis' coat, there was no panic.

Arisa was panicked enough for the whole crowd—and then some!

She fought her way forward and latched on to Edoran's arm,

just before a guard whisked him out of the room and shut the door firmly behind them.

"I have terms," the boy began again. "You—"

"Not yet," Holis repeated.

"But don't you want—"

"Not now." Justice Holis whisked down the hall to his office, leaving the rest of them behind. The guards pulled the boy along. His face was sullen, almost angry—the kind of anger that kept fear at bay?

Arisa wanted to feel sorry for him, but she couldn't.

Justice Holis spoke softly to one of the guardsmen, who hurried down the corridor when he'd finished. Then Holis opened his office door and ushered them in. There were plenty of chairs.

The boy sat in silence, radiating, *You'll have to ask if you want me to talk now.* He'd barely glanced around the room, his gaze only lingering on Arisa for a moment, and passing over Edoran as though he weren't there. He hadn't recognized the prince. He still thought the plan had worked. When he learned the truth, would he be sufficiently shaken to give something away? To reveal where they'd taken Weasel?

He wouldn't know anything. If he'd known anything that could help her enemies, the Falcon wouldn't have left him behind.

But judging by Holis' silence as he watched the boy, baiting his trap, the justice didn't know that.

Arisa was the only one in this room who knew her mother

well enough to predict what she would do. Though she certainly hadn't predicted this!

She fought back the creeping tears.

General Diccon came in without knocking. He must not have been at the ball; he wore his army uniform, and only part of that—his cravat was gone from his loosened collar, and he was still shrugging into the dark blue coat.

His gaze shot to Edoran. "Thank the One God, Your—"

"The God of Man will have enough to do tonight," said Justice Holis, "without you interrupting him. Now, young man. Your message."

The boy cast him a resentful glance. "I have terms from the Falcon, the true regent of Deorthas, ruler of the realm in Prince—"

Holis held up a hand to stop him. "What is her claim to regency? She wasn't appointed by the king, or the shareholder's concordance."

"The king didn't appoint you," the boy said. "And the shareholders had no other choice. The Falcon has been selected by the navy as Admiral Hastings' heir, to take up the rights and responsibilities that the old king laid upon him. She has the approval of Prince Edoran, who fled with her. And she has the sanction of the One God, as shown by the sword and shield, which were miraculously given into her hands. If you—"

"Miraculously, my ass," Arisa muttered.

Holis sent her an approving look. "Diccon, how many naval officers do you think she has? Not all of them, surely."

The commander of the army sighed. "Hard to say, since I clearly underestimated that number—badly!—before. A third? Half? Two thirds? If all the officers who lost someone to Pettibone's purge follow her, she'll have a majority at least. But they're not all idiots. Less than half, most likely."

"That's still enough that we can't rely on any naval officer," said Holis wearily. "Not till we've sorted out exactly who they are."

"She's always had contacts in the navy," Arisa told them. "My father's friends. Even when she was a rebel leader they'd send her news, sometimes transport her men."

"Traitor!" the boy snapped.

Arisa glared back at him. "You're calling *me* traitor? But even if I was," she added, "it's better than being a fool."

"She has a point," Holis told the boy. "Perhaps you should give us the rest of your message."

"It's simple enough," said the boy. "If you want to see the prince alive again, you have to give the regency to the Falcon. Formally, before the concordance of shareholders and the people of the city. Then you join the prince in exile. You'll be well treated," he added. "But you'll not go free."

He'd abandoned his memorized speech, and his low-class city accent reminded Arisa of the customers in the tavern. He reminded her of someone . . .

"And if I don't give up the regency and surrender myself?" Holis' voice was very mild. "Then what?"

"She has the navy," said the boy, triumphant. "She has the

sword and shield, and she has the prince! You work it out."

He sat back in his chair and folded his arms. Job done.

There was a short silence.

"I suppose," said Justice Holis, "that there's little to be gained by delaying the introductions any longer."

The boy scowled. "What do you mean, innerductions? I know who you are."

"And I don't much care who you are," Holis told him. "But I believe you might be interested to meet His Highness, Prince Edoran. He's sitting in the chair to your left."

"That's rot!" said the boy, glaring at Edoran. "You can't . . ."

He stared at Edoran, and the color drained from his face.

"You recognize him," said Holis. "Good. I was beginning to wonder if the Falcon had no one but idiots in her employ."

"But . . . But we . . . That can't . . . We took the prince! That can't be him."

"It is," said Justice Holis. "As for the rest, I believe I'll let His Highness explain how we thwarted your foolish plot."

If Arisa hadn't known better, she'd have sworn the justice had known everything from the start. The boy was gasping as if someone had punched him in the stomach.

"It's simple," said Edoran. "Justice Holis' clerk, Weasel, took my costume and my place. Your men captured him."

Staring at the prince, the boy missed the wave of pain that rippled through Holis' calm expression, but Arisa saw it, and fear clutched at her heart.

"And Mistress Arisa and I personally replaced the true sword and shield with substitutes," Edoran continued. "Which were also taken by the Falcon's men, so she doesn't have them, either!"

General Diccon whistled softly, and Holis blinked. The face Edoran turned toward his regent was bright with pride. The boy didn't understand the deep nod, almost a bow, that Holis offered the prince, but Arisa did.

"So you see," said Holis, returning his attention to the boy, "far from holding all the cards, your leader has nothing. No sword and shield. No prince. No acknowledgment of regency. Just a handful of treacherous officers, who will be forced to surrender when her plot—her failed plot—becomes public knowledge. And if she harms my clerk," his voice was very low, "she'll have a charge of murder against her. You'll be indicted with her, as an accomplice before the fact. For murder, that can be a hanging crime. Tell me where they are. Tell me where they are before someone gets hurt."

The boy's face was ghost white now, but he lifted his head and spoke clearly. "I'm not telling you anything. She got my uncle's family out of lockup, didn't she? She'll pull it off somehow. She always does!"

He must be one of the Mimms' cousins, Arisa realized. That was why he looked familiar. They were guilty, all of them—but even worse, this boy was in love with the Falcon. She'd seen it dozens of times over the years. Most of the Falcon's new recruits fell in love with her, and soon got over it—usually after they'd done something stupid, and she'd torn a strip off their egos. The younger they were, the harder they fell. And sometimes her mother had taken that love and used it.

He wouldn't tell them anything.

"One question," Arisa said, before Holis could start. "Why did my mother leave me behind? Why keep all of this secret from me?"

"You're to act as messenger," the boy told them. "You'll be the one who passes back and forth between Holis and the Falcon till the thing's agreed, 'cause she knows you'll tell her the truth. And she says you can slip any tail they send after you."

She could. Her mother had trained her well. Too well? Arisa's eyes closed in grief.

"I've already sent out troops," said General Diccon. "If they haven't left the city, we'll stop them. If they have, we'll be right on their heels. We'll catch them. We'll probably have them back by morning."

Pettibone had hunted her mother throughout the span of Arisa's life and never caught her. Amazing how a woman wearing a dress could cloud a man's perceptions. They wouldn't even catch the troop the Falcon had sent out to gallop over the countryside, while she—deck shoes and tide tables—took ship. They were already at sea.

Holis was talking to the boy, persuasive and terrifying in turn, and the boy had locked his stupid mouth shut.

"What do we do," Edoran asked, "if they aren't back by morning? What if she escapes, with Weasel as a hostage?"

Good question. Arisa opened her eyes, and even the boy looked interested.

Holis sighed. "As a hostage, I'm afraid Weasel only matters to me. If he's returned alive, unharmed, I might be able to commute her sentence to life imprisonment. But I can't even promise that, since I'm not the only one who'll be involved in that decision."

His face was grim. He was the only one in this whole accursed court who cared about Weasel at all.

"No," said Edoran. "I'm involved in that decision. In fact, I'm going to make it."

Not the only one who cared.

"Your Highness," said Holis, "the shareholders—"

"Can rot." Edoran rose to his feet. "General Diccon, you have till tomorrow's dawn to capture the Falcon and return her and her hostage to the palace. If they aren't here by sunrise, you will meet me in the courtyard with a troop of sufficient strength to guarantee my safety. Then we'll go after the Falcon, and when we find her, I will personally oversee the negotiations for her surrender. Is that clear?"

"Yes, Your Highness, but—"

"I command this," said Edoran. He turned and walked out of the room.

"Well, I'll be hanged," said the general. "The little runt sounded like a king!"

Arisa hadn't realized that other people called Edoran "runt." She winced.

"He did, didn't he?" Holis stared after Edoran, respect and regret warring in his expression. "I almost wish he could lead the—"

"Are you mad?" the general asked. "Someone just tried to

kidnap him, and they might try again! We can't even let him off the palace grounds once they realize they've got the wrong boy. He'll have to be guarded when he rides inside the walls as well. Security tightened all over, by posting ... Ah ..." He looked at the boy, then at Arisa. "Security tightened all over."

The heat of anger, of shame, flooded her face, but she couldn't blame him. Arisa stood and faced them. "I should go too. And leave you gentlemen to your work."

The boy looked nervous, which confirmed he was an idiot. Arisa was a lot more likely to beat information out of him than either Holis or the general.

"Go to Edoran," Holis told her. "He's going to need friends. Tomorrow, in particular."

Arisa nodded and turned away.

"My dear." The justice's voice stopped her with her hand on the doorknob. "Thank you."

Arisa's eyes filled. She nodded and left the room, without looking back. She didn't care whether she was crying or not as she walked down the corridors. Few people saw her, and no one tried to stop her as she made her way to the old throne room.

Edoran hadn't had time to tell them where the sword and shield were, and Holis hadn't had time to think about it—but the moment he did they'd be placed under lock and key, along with Edoran.

The sword and shield stood where she'd last seen them, propped against their ancient guardian.

"You did well," Arisa told the empty suit of armor. "Now it's my turn."

She took the shield first. Weasel had complained about its awkward weight, but the person who'd cleaned it had also restored the leather strap that allowed a knight to sling it over his back. Arisa did so. It was too big, and Weasel was right about the weight, but she could tighten the strap later. For now, it would do.

The sword came to her hand like the weapon it was. She hadn't noticed, when she'd pulled it from the sign, that its balance was so good. The slightly offset nicks worn by the iron links still marred its edge, but that edge was sharper than she'd expected. She could fight with this sword.

Arisa snorted at her own imagination. In the fight she was about to tackle, a sword would do her no good at all. Not as a weapon.

She found a sheath that fit it, and slung the sword over her shoulder as well. It was long enough that it would drag on the ground if she buckled it around her waist.

When she grasped the door above the broken bolt and looked out, the corridor was empty.

It took only moments to open the terrace doors and hurry down the steps into the shadows. She tucked the sword and shield into the first set of bushes thick enough to conceal them. It wouldn't hide them long. As soon as Holis remembered them the hunt would be on—of course, he had a few other things on his mind.

Arisa hurried back to her room, where she pulled her knife from the bureau and saved a minute by cutting off the torn and filthy costume.

Once she'd put on her old coat and britches, she slipped the knife's sheath onto her belt and filled a small pack. No food—she'd have to buy that later, and work for it when her money ran out.

She hesitated a moment over the deck of cards, but in the end she thrust it in. They'd tried to tell her the truth—it wasn't their fault she'd refused to see it. She needed all the guidance she could get, for this.

Finally, she grabbed a strip of leather and tied back her hair. She'd braid it when she got a chance. Her face, in the candlelit mirror, was as ordinary as it always was, but the eyes that stared back at her were as cold and focused as a hawk's. Her mother's eyes.

How could she have failed to see it? To guess? The Falcon had never given up on a fight in her life—why had Arisa thought she'd give up on this one?

She closed her eyes and turned away.

Her mother was going to give up on this one.

She would find her mother and make her listen. She would give her something to trade for her life and freedom—something of more value to the shareholders than one boy's life. She would make her mother see that Justice Holis wasn't another Pettibone, that Deorthas would be safe in his keeping, and in Edoran's after that. Once the Falcon understood that, she'd abandon this senseless war, and accept the exile they could buy with the sword and shield. She would. She had to. Because if she didn't, none of it had ever been real.

Climbing down the vines outside her balcony was almost as easy by now as going down the stairs, and it seemed that Holis was still focused on finding the Falcon; except for the throne room and the corridor leading to it, the windows of the old wing were dark.

That made it easy to retrieve the sword and shield from the bush where she'd hidden them. Easy to carry them across the lawn. Soon she would reach the trees, where no one would be able to see her. Treason was easy, when you didn't care.

But she did care. She hated knowing what Justice Holis and the others would think when they learned she'd taken the sword and shield. And Edoran . . . She wasn't sure what he'd think. He was a strange kid. Maybe strange enough to understand the truth.

But even if he thought her a traitor, she couldn't let it stop her. There was no law, no cause, no disgrace, nothing that mattered more to Arisa than saving Weasel from her mother, and her mother from herself.

She would fix this, whatever it took.

Arisa strode into the shadow of the woods, and vanished.